GUNFIGHT AT THE DUSTY ROSE SALOON

Sheriff Tibbetts cradled the shotgun close to his body as he casually thumbed back both hammers. His index finger rested on the trigger guard. Word of the showdown had preceded him. Main Street was empty. The lawman left the boardwalk and stepped into the dusty street. He came to a stop directly in front of The Rose.

"Perley Hall, this is Sheriff John Tibbetts." His voice was loud and strong. "Come out and face me."

The clamorous uproar inside the saloon gradually faded, then ceased altogether. Silence settled within the building.

"Perley Hall"—the lawman was relentless, not to be dissuaded—"come out, or I'll bust in there and drag you out."

"No problem, Sheriff," came the bold reply from within. "Come in and get me, Tibbetts. If you ain't scared to."

THE JACKLEG SHERIFF

Luke Short, Jr.

A DELL BOOK

Published by
Dell Publishing
a division of
Bantam Doubleday Dell Publishing Group, Inc.
666 Fifth Avenue
New York, New York 10103

ISBN: 0-440-20305-8

Printed in the United States of America

Published simultaneously in Canada

April 1989

10 9 8 7 6 5 4 3 2 1

KRI

To my better half, Sharon. Thanks for the help, inspiration, and TLC. Without it I could not have accomplished this.

Thanks to my tribe for their understanding. I love them dearly.

Special thanks to Ted Flanigan and Larry Ray Hyrup for their input regarding computers and horses.

CHAPTER
1

"Sheriff Tibbetts is showin' the white flag. He's yellow streaked."
Those words stirred up bile in John Tibbetts, but the fact that it
was Perley Hall who had uttered them truly galled him. Hall, a
two-bit gunslinger from Texas, was about as welcome here in
Jacob's Well as a "woman of easy virtue" in Sunday church.

John Tibbetts was a man of his word. His reputation had
been slandered. It was now a matter of honor to clear his name.
Perley Hall would publicly apologize, or Tibbetts would kill
him. Riffraff like him had drifted through Jacob's Well before,
and the sheriff still lived to tell it. Tibbetts wasn't a man taken
to braggin', but he had fared well. His deputy, Royal Ballou,
had been bushwacked and wounded. He had spent the last
month mending in Santa Fe. John wished he had him by his
side now.

Sheriff Tibbetts was poor framed. Thirty years of law work
had left him stiff backed and slightly stove up. His leathery,
craggy face complete with gray-streaked handlebar moustache
gave him a touch of distinction. His lynx eyes missed damned
little. "Whip-leather tough and mule stubborn" were descrip-
tions of himself that he took as compliments.

"Yellow streaked? Damn that man," Tibbetts swore quietly.
"I doubt not that he's up to no good. I don't know the man
from Adam, and suddenly he's slingin' mud. Those are uncon-
fused facts. Best set that fool straight," he said grimly. The
sheriff pulled mindlessly at his handlebar as he walked to the
gun rack.

Tibbetts lifted the ten-gauge muzzle-loader out of the rack
and fondled the shotgun with affection. He loved the feel of it,
solid and heavy; he showed a certain tenderness holding it,
almost like cradlin' a lady in his arms. The lawman reflected
for a minute on the day Jenny Longmont (before she became

Mrs. John Tibbetts) had given him that gun—a glorious day, and a night to remember. The missus had candidly offered to all who would listen that she had spent her wedding night with a wild man and a shotgun. Tibbetts smiled at the memory. A fine, fine woman.

Now, to load and check his guns. John took two percussion caps from a desk drawer. He put one on each nipple of the shotgun and fired them, clearing the vents of any oil. Next he poked a light squib charge down each barrel, capped, and fired both. The barrels were clean, with no oil or moisture to retard the powder ignition. He loaded a measured sixty grains of black powder into each barrel and tamped the wadding firmly over the charge. Then he counted eighteen 00 buck pellets and dropped nine into each barrel. The buckshot was held in place with shredded wadding. Finally, he capped both nipples and half cocked the hammers.

Sheriff Tibbetts examined the Colt Dragoon next. He took the heavy, long-barreled .44 pistol from the drawer, half cocked the hammer, and slowly rotated the cylinder. He checked each chamber carefully, loaded them and most important, sealed each with tallow. No chance of a chain fire—all six nipples were capped. He eased the hammer down and holstered the pistol. As a precaution, he stuck a Remington .41 derringer into his vest pocket. "Hope you're ready, Perley Hall," he reflected bitterly. "I am."

Jacob's Well was a small ranching and farming community in the high desert of the New Mexico Territory. The town skirted the banks of the Puerco River. To the south, the Little Colorado meandered through the rolling country. Raising cattle and hay were the means of a livelihood here, and both were profitable. The town core was compact, clustered along Main Street, and homesteads spread the length of the river valley. Main Street was either six inches deep in a fine powdery grit or ankle deep in quagmire. Merchant shops lined either side of the thoroughfare. The Dusty Rose Saloon, a principal waterin' hole in the town, also provided women of easy virtue and gaming tables, depending upon a gentleman's preference. The hotel, the town's eatery, was across the street from the Rose. Sheriff Tibbetts's office was at the end of the street, flanked on one side by a stable and corrals.

John Tibbetts pulled his office door closed behind him and

slowly sauntered up the street, little puffs of dust marking his every footstep. His pace wasn't hurried but deliberate, pensive. His mind raced, planning every move. He had to handle this showdown prudently. He did not want to be careless or overly anxious with Perley Hall. That man was a fool, although a dangerous fool. Tibbetts wanted to flush Perley out, force him into the alley away from busy Main Street. A blazin' gunfight in Jacob's Well wouldn't do. What if Perley wouldn't come out? Thrust, counterthrust. Move, parry.

Tibbetts crossed Main Street, stepped onto the covered boardwalk, and continued his measured walk toward the Rose. He nodded greetings to several townsfolk on the crowded boardwalk. Dr. Shubael Cates, the town medicine man, glanced out of the drugstore window and saw Tibbetts walking toward the saloon. He ceased his prescription work, threw off his white coat, and grabbed his bag of tools. He knew fixin' and healin' time was fast approachin'. Doc Shu had witnessed this scene before, and he knew that his services would soon be in demand, either as doctor or as coroner.

Sheriff Tibbetts cradled the shotgun close to his body and casually thumbed back both hammers. His index finger rested on the trigger guard. Word of the showdown had preceded him —Main Street was empty. The lawman left the boardwalk and stepped into the dusty street. He came to a stop directly in front of The Rose.

"Perley Hall, this is Sheriff John Tibbetts." His voice was loud and strong. His shotgun was aimed at the batwings. "Come out here and face me."

The clamorous uproar inside the saloon gradually faded, then ceased altogether. Silence settled within the building.

"Perley Hall"—the lawman was relentless, not to be dissuaded—"come out, or I'll bust in there and drag you out."

"Don't shoot, Sheriff" rang a shout from within the saloon. "We're comin' out." Tibbetts cautiously lowered the scattergun from the batwings. A baker's dozen rounders and ranch hands hustled from the saloon and out of the line of fire.

"He's awaitin' fer ya inside, Sheriff," one of the hands offered as he hurried past the lawman. John nodded.

"Is that where you want to die, Perley?" Tibbetts directed the ultimatum into the dimly lighted interior of the saloon.

"No problem, Sheriff," came the bold reply from within.

"I'm stayin' in here with my friends." An empty whiskey bottle sailed over the batwings. "Come in and get me, Tibbetts—if you ain't scared to."

Sheriff Tibbetts fudged to one side, keeping his eyes glued to the doors. He caught a faint glimpse of Perley Hall silhouetted against the bar. As quick as thought, Tibbetts raised the long-barreled scattergun and fired through the plate-glass window. The pane blew inward with a painful chiming of shattered glass. Tibbetts instantly dropped to one knee, paused a full second, and touched off the other barrel through the batwings. The right-hand door slammed back, knocked off its hinges, a fist-size hole blown through the slats. John leaped to his feet and sprinted for the boardwalk, running through the thick cloud of white smoke. He landed on the planks, set the shotgun beside the front door, and drew his Colt. He braced the big .44 at his chest as he played a deadly game of cat and mouse with Perley.

Perley Hall crouched behind the far end of the bar. He snapped off a quick shot at the fleeting figure of the sheriff—not even close. Peeking over the bar top, he waited for a sign of the lawman. The right side of his face was bleeding, cut by tiny shards of glass. His right thigh and calf were pincushioned with wood splinters from Tibbetts's second shot. Like a flash of lightning, the Colt Dragoon poked through the paneless front window. Perley ducked to save his life. The confined thunderous blast stung his ears. Several whiskey bottles on the bar top and on the shelf behind him exploded in a wet deluge of whiskey and broken glass. Perley crawled farther behind the bar, cutting his hands as he moved. He heard Sheriff Tibbetts walk into the room, glass from the front window crunching underfoot. The sheriff cocked his pistol again.

"How you doin', Perley?" Tibbetts baited the man. "Ready to talk yet?"

Perley panicked. He was trapped. Frantically, he searched for a way out—then he saw an escape route: the storage door secreted beneath the mirrored back wall of the bar. The barkeeps rolled beer kegs through this small door instead of carrying them from the back room. Perley crouched, touched off a quick, unpurposed shot at the sheriff with his Colt .36, then crashed headfirst through the thinly paneled door. Tibbetts heard the noise and raised his pistol over the bar top before pulling off another round. Pieces of oak flooring and sawdust followed Perley into the cool, dark room.

John scooted around the bar as Perley disappeared into the back room. John would not follow him. He heard Perley stumble in the storage room and took a gamble—the alley. As he retraced his way around the bar, John spotted a sawed-off shotgun behind the bar. It was loaded. He took it. The lawman crunched through the glass as he headed for the front window. He stepped over the windowsill and ran the length of the boardwalk, then ducked into the alley. Just as Tibbetts reached the rear of the saloon, the back door slammed open and Perley darted out. He hurled himself off the loading dock and landed in full stride.

"Stop, Perley, or I'll shoot!" The sound of both hammers being cocked got Perley's attention. Tibbetts had a chilling, professional look about him.

Perley took two faltering steps, then stopped dead in his tracks. He was shaken, more frightened than hurt. Tiny rivulets of blood and sweat streaked his face. His hands were deeply cut in several places. As a result of his diving exit through the storage-room door, there was a raw scrape on his left shoulder, and his pants were split from crotch to belt loop in the rear. He reeked of whiskey and stale beer. Tibbetts almost laughed at this "gunfighter," but experience tempered him.

Here stood a cornered, dangerous firebrand. Mind what you're about, John cautioned himself.

"Now, sir"—Tibbetts spoke deliberately—"you have two choices. A public apology, loud and clear; or death where you stand. Choose your lot." John's cold eyes never left Perley's uncertain ones.

Perley swayed slightly as he held his pistol beside his leg. He was cut, bloodied, shell-shocked, and relieved just to be alive. He weighed the options and decided to live awhile longer.

"You wouldn't shoot a man for a little overreckoned comment, would ya?" Perley taunted the sheriff as he searched for a means of escape. He was unaware of John's deadly posturing.

"For you, Perley, I'd make an exception," John flatly stated.

"I didn't mean no harm, Sheriff," he muttered quietly, beginning to realize that the sheriff was not to be underestimated.

"I can't hear you, Perley," the sheriff contested loudly.

"I didn't mea—"

"Shut up, Perley!" barked a new voice. Perley Hall went stone mute, his mouth agape.

Tibbetts jerked his head slightly to the right in the direction of the voice. A huge man stood at the edge of the alley, partially obscured in the shadows.

"Mister," Sheriff Tibbetts threatened, "this ain't none of your doin', so butt out."

"That's where you're wrong, lawman. Dead wrong," the man answered Tibbetts with unbred rudeness. "Us Halls stick together. You fight him, you fight me."

No slack out of him, John noticed. "Suit yourself," he shot back, still confident. "It's as easy to ask the cabinetmaker for two coffins as for one."

The man moved out of the shadows. He was tall, a full hand over six feet, burly and barrel chested. He weighed a good fifteen stone. His ruddy complexion was complemented by deep-set brown eyes. The eyes caught John's attention. They were hard and hostile, and they never left the sheriff as the man distanced himself from Perley. His catlike grace and economy of movement further hinted to Tibbetts that he had miscalculated the danger.

Tibbetts had a vagrant feeling that he was facing off with a professional gunfighter. Perley was visibly buoyed by the arrival of his older brother. Curly Hall positioned himself next to the loading dock. It was impossible for Tibbetts to cover both men. Curly would force the sheriff to make a choice. Anyone with a sound mind would measure Curly and know that Perley was the bait.

"You all right, little brother?" Curly inquired with misdirected concern.

"Ya," snapped Perley with a vengeful smirk, "but I want to learn this yellow-bellied lawman a lesson. You with me, Curly?"

"Right beside you," Curly bolstered. "Make your move anytime you're ready, Perley."

Curly was poised, his right hand hovering over his left hip, ready for a cross draw of the Colt .36. They must have bought them together, John thought. Perley had the same gun. Tibbetts took stock of the situation. Perley was the immediate threat. His pistol was drawn. Hit him first, and pray to beat the big fella. Besides, Perley was unfinished business. He would pay for his runaway mouth.

"Perley"—Tibbetts spoke with fatal foresight—"you're the first to die. Make no mistake about it!"

Perley glanced at Curly and received a barely detectable nod. The cowboy snapped up his Colt and aimed at the lawman. Sheriff Tibbetts squeezed the trigger when he saw Perley's hand jerk. Nine 00 buck pellets nearly cut Perley in half. He was spun wildly yet almost gracefully around while still on his feet. His own Colt discharged skyward. Through the light haze of shotgun smoke, Tibbetts switched his attention to Curly.

He stared as Curly drew his pistol. The gun cleared leather and came up lazily toward him. The scene was played out at a snail's pace. The sheriff could vividly see the muscles and tendons in Curly's forearm contract as he pulled the trigger. John struggled to sweep the scattergun around, but his motions were not punctual. A smoke ring puffed leisurely from Curly's pistol barrel. John's life raced before his eyes. An electrifying jolt of pain exploded in his chest. He instinctively tensed, inadvertently pulling the second trigger of the shotgun. That blast hammered the still-pirouetting Perley Hall and drove him crashing through the small shed of The Rose. The last blurred image John Tibbetts saw was Curly steadying his pistol for another shot. Daylight began to fade for Sheriff Tibbetts—he staggered backwards and landed heavily in the dust.

The exchange of gunfire had lasted a mere three seconds. Two men had died within that brief time span. Curly casually approached the downed lawman. He quickly noted with satisfaction that both shots had hit Tibbetts in the chest. "Not bad shootin'," he said with a feeling of accomplishment. He walked to the shed and looked at his younger brother's badly mutilated body. "Blunderhead," he gibed, "always poppin' off at the mouth. And he never could shoot straight." He shook his head in disgust and turned away.

Doc Shu hustled toward the alley. For a man of sixty-three, he still had some kick left. He rounded the corner, then stopped in his tracks. Forty years of doctoring told him there was no need to rush. With reluctance, he walked down the alley to Sheriff Tibbetts and knelt beside him. Hoping against hope, he pressed his fingers against Tibbetts's neck. No pulse. John's .41 derringer was jutting out of his vest pocket. Doc Shu pocketed it before it fell completely out. Then he stood and headed toward Perley Hall.

"Don't touch him!" Curly barked at the doctor. "He's kin. I'll handle it."

Doc Shu cast a glance toward the mouth of the alley and beckoned his two assistants to come. They carried a stretcher and hurriedly crossed over to the doc. Doc Shu moved in a daze, not wanting to believe that his old friend Tibbetts was dead. The sheriff was gingerly laid on the canvas and covered with a blanket. Doc Shu motioned with his head toward his office. The two men crouched over the stretcher, tested the weight, and in unison picked up the dead man. After they left, Doc Shu solemnly kicked dirt to cover the bloodstained earth that marked the spot of John Tibbetts's death.

In the meantime, Curly had found a tarp. He loaded Perley's body into a buckboard and covered the body with the wrap. Then Curly headed out of town toward the cemetery.

"God takes soonest those he loveth best. . . . Lord . . . Amen." The words were lost to the wind. A small group of personal friends buffeted by the afternoon winds clustered around the grave. The tall prairie grass swayed with the breeze. It swished gently as if to drown out the muffled sobs of the ladies present. The women, stressed by the pesky gusts, held their hats in place while trying unsuccessfully to keep their long skirts from being blown about. Preacher Smith, the new reverend, attempted to drop a poke of good earth onto the pine box. It came back in his face. The group dispersed to respective surreys and buckboards and drove down the grassy knoll into town.

Doc Shu comforted the young woman who clutched his arm tightly to her body. She wept openly and appeared to be on the verge of losing control. Although she stood taller than the doc, she looked frail—almost fragile. An impertinent gust of wind sent her hat flying. Long, dark brown hair that had been neatly bunned was now free. It swirled about her broad face and covered her wide shoulders. Dark green eyes set under gracefully thin eyebrows were red and puffy from grieving. The lady captured a tear with a handkerchief and softly daubed under her pert, slightly upturned nose. Her full-lipped mouth was a slash of bitterness, downturned at the corners.

"Remember your faith, child." Doc Shu spoke lovingly in a low voice as he supported her. "We'll get through this, no matter how long it takes."

"But why, Doc?" She begged for an answer and clutched his arm even tighter. "Why?"

"I'm at a loss, Abbie." He sadly shook his head. Then as a flare of temper and stubbornness flashed, the doc firmly grasped Abbie's hand. "It makes no sense. But I promise you I'll get some answers. Let's go home. We've done all we can here." They walked slowly to the doc's surrey. "Now, remember what we discussed. You are off to Sedalia tomorrow."

"But, Doc, I don't want—"

"Say no more. It's settled." He was firm. Abbie knew it too.

Doc Shu, a feisty Missourian, ran his gnarled fingers absent-mindedly over his baby-bottom-smooth head. "Worn to a shadow and not overtall" was how the late Mrs. Maude Cates had referred to him. Doc Shu thought about her and smiled deep creases on his round cherublike face. Crow's-feet marked the corners of his slate gray eyes, eyes that had seen too much dying for one lifetime. The doc had honed his medical skills with Old Hickory at New Orleans. He thought he was callous to death. After the burial of his old friend John Tibbetts, memories and horrors crept back into his head.

"Hellfire, Royal! Where in the dickens are you when you're needed the most?" the doc called out in frustration. He knew full well the deputy was recovering in Santa Fe. Nevertheless, he vented his pent-up fury at the absent lawman. The doc put his optical devices onto the bridge of his nose and read the headlines of the month-old paper for an unnumbered time.

DEPUTY WOUNDED, GUNMAN KILLED

The proprietor of Jacob's Well's weekly *Gazette*, Elliot Lightshield, was a transplanted native of St. Louis. He scanned his evening's work with satisfaction. The *Gazette* had earned the respect of the citizenry. It was folksy yet newsworthy. Elliot, portly yet rather proper, was a neighborly gentleman. His manner was warm and sincere, which put his guests at ease in an interview. His soothfast reputation was based on honesty and a strong belief in the First Amendment. He had expressed his feeling strongly and forthwith in a recent edition.

He was typesetting late one night in his print shop when a loud and persistent knocking pulled him away from the back room. Two men were standing out front. He set the lantern on the desk and finished wiping the ink from his hands. The men turned their faces away from the light as the proprietor unlocked the front door.

"Evening, gentlemen. How may I help you?" Elliot stepped aside to give them passage. The mutton chops outlining his rounded features framed a hesitant smile on his jowly face.

A gloved fist hit Elliot's rotund belly just above the belt buckle. He doubled over. A second fist smacked him flush on the cheek as he staggered on wobbly knees. That blow knocked him out and sent him crashing backward into the interior of the shop. The intruders hustled inside. One man locked the front door; the other turned down the lantern. Straddling Elliot's limp body, the men grabbed an arm each and dragged him into the print shop. Lightshield was unceremoniously dumped into the middle of the floor.

Then the interlopers proceeded to destroy the shop. Trays of type were hurled against the walls, and bins of letters and numbers were strewn across the floor. Shoulder to shoulder, the men overturned Lightshield's prize printing press. It crashed to the floor with a twenty-hundredweight shudder. To top off the destruction, a full fifty-gallon barrel of ink was spilled onto the floor. By good fortune, Elliot was lying on his back; otherwise he could have drowned in the ink. Pleased with their efforts, the men exited the shop through the back door.

Doc Shu looked as if he had just come from the graveyard shift in a coal mine. His clothes were filthy black, hands and forearms ink stained. He and Elliot were sitting in the front office. It had taken two extra tubs of hot water to wash the ink from Elliot. An ugly purple bruise discolored his right cheek. It had taken four men a full hour to upright the printing press, but it was back in place. The pool of ink had been mucked out of the shop's back door. The alley drainage ditch was now several inches deep in jet black ooze.

"Shubael, I would offer you a drink, but my bottle of spirits was also destroyed last night," Elliot humbly excused.

"Thick-ey'd musing and curs'd melancholy! Aha!" Doc Shu slapped his thigh with glee and laughed heartily. "I remember that from the classics."

"*Henry IV,* I believe." Elliot tried to keep a straight face as he knocked the wind out of Shubael's sails. But he failed. Doc Shu joined him in a moment of mutual laughter.

"Stifle your grief, Elliot. I've got some cure-all in my kit." The doc stood and fetched his medical grip. He rummaged inside and produced a flask of "medicine," then filled the flask cap for Elliot. With flask and cap in hand, they toasted the better days ahead.

"About whom have you been writing nasty things, Elliot?" Doc Shu bluntly inquired. "Someone is blustered over the news."

"Shubael"—Elliot shook his head—"I don't have the slightest indication. I don't write slanderous news. At least, not intentionally." He was naïvely innocent of his paper's power in a small town.

"Well, sir, you sure as hell prodded someone." Doc Shu pointed his finger accusingly at Elliot. "What news have you been reporting in the last few issues?" Together they went over to an untouched stack of past *Gazette* issues and began thumbing through them.

"Our lead story a few weeks ago was to explain how the late Preacher Dobbins met his maker in Miss Clarity Clemmon's parlor." Elliot reread the headline and smiled. "I handled that untimely death with considerable discretion." A smug look settled upon his features.

"That you did, sir." Doc Shu smiled with Elliot. "Think hard. Did you offend or insult someone? There has to be a reason for the print shop mess." He searched Elliot's face for an answer.

Elliot stroked his double chin and reflected out loud. "Mr. Hamson was slightly agitated when I ran that article about his gamin' losses at The Rose. Apparently the missus had thought he was at work." They both chuckled over that nasty episode.

"Concentrate, Elliot." Doc Shu urged the man into action. "Let's examine these week by week. Headlines and cover stories only."

The men searched through the stack of outdated papers. Nothing. Then they saw it:

SHERIFF TIBBETTS'S DEATH QUESTIONED— MURDER SUSPECTED!

The headline flashed at both men from the previous week's issue. They knew it was the answer. John Tibbetts's funeral was too fresh in their minds.

"That's the one, Elliot," Doc Shu stated with conviction. "I'll bet money on it."

"You know I'm not a betting man"—Elliot graciously refused the wager—"but I think you're correct."

"Something else, Elliot." The doc's manner was set. "I've a nagging suspicion that the bushwacking of Royal awhile back and this breakin' of your shop are connected. I'm not sure how, but they are connected."

"It warrants further consideration," Elliot agreed. "Did you receive an answer from Santa Fe? And what about that gunfighter Hall, or whatever his real name is?"

"Nothing yet" was the doc's dejected reply. "I'm waiting to hear from Royal any day now. As for Curly Hall, no one seems to know who he is."

"Or maybe they do but they aren't talking," Elliot suggested. "Ever think of that?"

"A point well taken. I'm on my way." Doc Shu packed his medical bag, then turned and addressed Elliot, looking him in the eye. "Do me a favor. Don't answer your door if unknown men are standing outside. Especially at eleven o'clock at night."

Doc Shu and Elliot shook hands as they parted. "Thanks, Shubael, for your help. Get me some news, and I'll print it. The risks be damned!" he shouted to Doc Shu's backside as the old man beelined across the street. He got a half-mast wave of acknowledgment.

Doc Shu pushed through the front door of the telegraph office. The day telegrapher, Paul Plummer, was busy sending and receiving messages.

"Hello, Paul." The doc was impatient. "Any messages for me?"

The clerk was concentrating on his key and held up a hand to silence the doc. The next several minutes were a constant clatter of dots and dashes. Finally came a respite.

"Doc Shu," the young man addressed him, "what can I do you for?"

"Anything for me?" A look of expectation raised his eyebrows. "I'm waitin' on several replies."

Paul thumbed through the day's log. "Not a thing today. Or yesterday, for that matter."

The doc was soundly disheartened. "How long should something take from Santa Fe? It's been three—no, four days."

"You should have heard by now." Paul rolled his chair across the floor to the filing cabinet. He searched the files and pulled out copies of the last week's messages that the doc had sent. "Elihu sent them out on Thursday. He initialed the copies and noted the times and dates."

"Would you please send them all again?" the doc asked politely. He rapped his knuckles firmly on the countertop. "To hell with the cost."

The young telegrapher grinned. "Don't you worry about a thing, Doc. I'll send them today."

"I appreciate it, Paul. I want some quick answers." Doc Shu was halfway out the door before Paul had chance to say goodbye.

As Doc Shu dashed off toward his store, he watched the Santa Fe Express stage thunder into town and skid to a stop in front of the freight office. He perked up. "I'll send the letters through the mail, by damn. They'll get there sure. With Big Red drivin' the mail, my correspondence will be hand delivered."

Doc Shu knew he had a half hour to write his letters. The stage would change teams here. Big Red, the driver, and the paying customers would take lunch at the hotel. When the driver walked out of the dining room, the goin' passengers had best be right on his heels.

CHAPTER
2

Four men were encamped around a green-felt-covered poker table. A coffee cup was carefully placed on a dolly in front of each. The chitchat was sparse. No news was exchanged. These men constituted the duly elected government of Jacob's Well. The rotund mayor, Ellery Albee, was a small-time rancher and businessman who owned the dry goods store. He was not only the power behind the town government, but he was a scheming, plotting opportunist. The consummate Machiavellian, he sought constantly to improve and protect his position. His obedient councilmen—Lemuel Tilden, of the General Mercantile Store; Hervey Brown, of Herv's Groceries; and Asa Hemmingway, of Prime Meats—were known as the Three Evils. They voted in favor of mayor Albee's every whim and fancy.

The sound of heavy footsteps stilled their sparse talk. Seconds later, a pugilist-bouncer named Willis Clampett strode into the back room. The surly gunfighter scanned the room and found it safe. He relaxed visibly and stationed himself by the door, calling over his shoulder, "All clear, Mr. Colburn." He breathed with difficulty through his flattened, broken nose.

A tall, slightly stooped man in the meridian of life entered the room. The mayor and councilmen stood. His presence evoked a "city dude" response. A dapper dresser, the man reeked of power and wealth. Hand-stitched custom leather boots, dress trousers, a silk shirt, and a top-grade calf-leather vest and jacket completed the image of success. His temples were graying. A close-cropped salt-and-pepper moustache outlined a narrow, sinister face. His heavy, bushy brows and sunken eyes gave credence to the appearance of evil. The man was spindle-shanked and bobbed slightly as he walked across the room. He toed up a chair and slacked into it. A busted hip on a roundup many years before reminded the man that he was mortal. The very thought chafed his ass.

Hammond W. Colburn was the largest landowner in the northern New Mexico Territory. A cattle baron, he supplied the United States government and its military establishments in the Southwest. His land office was in the Main Street building beside the hotel. He spent two days a week in Jacob's Well. A confirmed bachelor, he gambled and played poker on his nights in town. The remainder of the week he spent on his H bar C spread. Colburn had come from landed aristocracy in Georgia and was well schooled in land management. Through shrewd land transactions, he had obtained legal title to the several hundred thousand acres that made up the H bar C. A smooth, convincing salesman, he was ruthless and unforgiving.

The governing body resumed their respective seats. "Morning, gentlemen," Colburn spoke. His gravely voice dominated the room, and a hardened smile slashed his face. "Nice of you to come." As if we had a choice, Ellery reflected sourly as he shifted his corpulent bulk to a more comfortable position. That head-knocker Clampett had said to be here at nine o'clock sharp, or he'd come looking for me.

The four men mumbled a greeting. Colburn got straight to the point. He glanced around the table. "We have a pressing matter to address. I want your honest opinion on the merits of this proposal." My opinion had better coincide with his, Ellery cautioned himself. "Mr. Mayor, I propose that you call a special election as soon as possible."

"A fine idea, Ham," Ellery gushed with shabbily disguised resignation. "Who are we electing, and why are we electing him?"

"A new sheriff for Jacob's Well," Colburn retorted with pride. "And as expeditiously as possible."

The mayor and councilmen sat in silence, struggling to absorb the proposal. John Tibbetts was freshly buried, and Colburn was ready to exploit the situation. Ellery weighed the pros and cons and quickly saw the worth of the plan. He straightened his coat around his wide girth.

"I like the idea, Ham. Of course, this will take some time. We'll have to schedule dates, print ballots—"

"Damn it, Ellery," Colburn rudely cut him off. "Don't vex me with the chickenshit details! I said as soon as possible." The old man was getting testy. He sensed the council's reluctance to participate. "Gentlemen, think of it. A Sheriff who thinks as we do. Our own man. Lots of possibilities there."

"Well, sir," Ellery thought out loud, "I suppose if we got right on it, a week. What do you think, Lem?" He had neatly passed the buck to his cohort.

"Don't know, Ellery," Lem Tilden vacillated. "Damned short notice." His ever-present tic distorted his mouth.

"Can you do it, man?" Colburn prodded. The lack of an affirmative answer needled him.

"We'll need to approach the printer" was Lem's noncommittal reply. Again the tic twisted his face.

"I think Mr. Lightshield will be delighted to print ballots as a personal favor to me," Colburn stated with confidence, and smiled at Willis. This veiled threat was fully appreciated by Asa Hemmingway, who had made the mistake of purchasing twenty-four head of breeding cattle two months before from an outside buyer. All had been poisoned at Asa's stock pond within the week. The only beef bought or sold in this territory had the H bar C brand on them. Asa perspired, remembering the humiliation he had endured. A strong meaty aroma came off his body.

"It should take three days at most," Colburn declared. "Tomorrow's paper will be the election edition. We'll get the news out to all the businesses. Asa, you'll handle that," Colburn pigeonholed him. "Lem, I want you to write a story—vandalism is rampant, crime is on the rise, that sort of thing. Hit on the destruction at the print shop and the unfortunate incident with Asa's cattle. Also mention the gunfight of several weeks past. Stress that we need a return to law and order immediately. You got all that?" Colburn asked. Lem merely nodded his head.

"Who do you have in mind for sheriff, Ham?" Hervey Brown inquired around his ever-present cigar. "We had a good one till recently. Royal Ballou should return within a fortnight."

Colburn tactfully dodged the question. "My point exactly, Hervey. We need one of our very own in the office. Mr. Ballou doesn't fit our mold. He isn't one of us. Our sheriff must be elected before Mr. Ballou returns."

"Excellent idea, Ham. My compliments," Ellery chimed in with genuine conspiracy, his double chin bulging over his collar. "With a sympathetic lawman and an already cooperative judge, we'll be in fine fettle. A most advantageous arrangement. Don't you agree, Hervey, Lem, Asa?"

Their consent was unanimous. The three council members nodded in unison, a simple, three-headed marionette.

"Ham, any legal problems that Judge Williams can't handle concerning this shotgun election? We don't want to step outside the law." Lem smiled slyly, only to have the tic twitch his mouth.

"Lem, we both know that Judge Williams will provide the best legal advice that money can buy. That's what he's paid for, right?" Colburn smiled wickedly—that aspect was covered.

Lem concurred. A friendly loan several years back had put the judge in Colburn's pocket. He had readily accepted Colburn's treacherous offer. With honeyed words, Ham had trapped him.

"If there is no further discussion, let's get on with it. There's a lot to be done. We are adjourned." The men stood as Colburn exited, his faithful friend leading the way.

"Oh, Ham," Ellery asked as an afterthought. "Who are we running for sheriff?"

"Thanks, Ellery," Colburn bruskly apologized. "In all the excitement, I nearly forgot. I have two candidates in mind. The first is Hayes Jacobson." Colburn's face was deadpan as he dropped the name.

The men laughed together. Hayes Jacobson was a stablehand in the H bar C stockyards, a witless dunderpate of a man.

"Fine choice, Ham," Ellery volunteered. "He's of the same caliber as the late Sheriff Tibbetts." The men chortled at Ellery's bad taste. The mayor's stomach jiggled as he laughed. They all knew better.

"Who's the other candidate, Ham?" Hervey anxiously asked, his words slurred by the cigar. He wanted to see if Colburn could top Hayes Jacobson. Colburn, already on his way out the door, turned his head and said over his shoulder, "Rutherford Hall."

Asa looked around at the other members of the council. "Who in the hell is Rutherford Hall? Never heard of the man."

An instant before the door closed behind him, Colburn called out, "Curly."

Caught off guard, the council and mayor sat wordless. Then

Ellery forced a weak laugh. "Well, I'll hand him one thing—
he's got a talent for getting to people."

"He's got stones, I'm telling you," Asa answered. "I hope we
pull it off, gentlemen. If we don't, we're out of this town on a
rail. The town might have to import one, but by damn, they'll
do it if this ploy fails."

Election day was dry and dusty. The mid-afternoon tempera-
ture in the shade was a blistering ninety-five degrees. The official polling station was Lem Tilden's General Mercantile Store.
Millicent Tilden and Eulalia Albee were the election aides. The
election judge, Mr. Goodwin, was sitting unobtrusively off to
one side in the corner. Eulalia had rendered him a token par-
ticipant. The driving force behind Mayor Albee was his wife
Eulalia—Lay to close friends. Beneath her plump, buxom
grandmotherly exterior was a calculating, ruthless power bro-
ker. Seldom if ever did she miss an opportunity to further her
influence or control. She weighed and judged every situation,
then delivered her iron-fisted decision with a silk glove.

Millicent Tilden was an unwitting accomplice. She was honest, forthright, and bird-witted. Eulalia easily manipulated her.
Millie's frail, bony figure contrasted sharply to Lay's. Millie
had a freshly ironed handkerchief in her hand, and she nervously daubed at her nose with it.

Rutherford "Curly" Hall was standing outside the front door
of the General Mercantile Store. His coat and tie were out of
character. He was in full feather, smooth and gracious. His
other calling in life was as a "drummer." Silver tongued, he
would sell you a pig in a poke, smilin' all the while.

"Mornin', ladies," he offered as he strode into the cool interior of the store. "And how are you this fine but hot day?"
Curly was *the* gentleman, courteous as he chatted with the
women. "With your help, I'll return law and order to this
peace-loving town." He flashed his winning smile. He had pre-
viously discussed the voting procedure with Ellery. Lay had
been enlightened concerning the advantages of having Curly
Hall as sheriff. She would take care of the ballots.

Curly excused himself, went outside, and ducked into The
Rose. His bullies were holding down the bar.

"How we doin', Curly?" George Petts inquired, his tanned

face aglow with a whiskey shine. Curly faked a left jab at Willis.

"Fine, Georgie Boy. At this rate, I'll be elected by a landslide." He grinned confidently. "Things quiet here?" he asked as he surveyed the bar. George Petts nodded with a mellow ease. The bar was under his strong arm. Curly flashed his smooth grin. He wanted to keep a tight lid on the drinking and partying until after the "election."

As Curly started to leave, George's sidekick Dolph Stickney joined them. "Allow me to buy you boys another round. Let's go in the corner and talk." Curly invited George Petts, Dolph Stickney, and Clampett to join him.

The close-knit trio followed Curly and sat down at a table. Curly had met them while serving time in the territorial prison. When he had hired on with Hammond Colburn, he had offered their services. Colburn had quickly agreed.

Curly reaffirmed his intentions for the evening. "Mr. Colburn doesn't want any hell-raisin' tonight. Keep a handle on the saloon. George, you and Dolph watch the bar. Got it? Have a few but stay sober." He looked at them. They nodded acknowledgment. Then he turned to the silent Willis. "On the off chance we have a troublemaker, I want you to end it fast. No fuss. No muss." The boxer smiled and breathed through his mouth. His nose, flattened from many fights, was more ornamental than functional. He looked forward to the opportunity with anticipation. "Well, boys, back to buying votes," Curly fessed up with frank bluntness.

"We'll be here in case you need us, boss," Dolph offered. A gapped, no-front-teeth smile flashed on his rawhide face.

"Right, Dolph. Stay within earshot. I may need some help." Curly winked at him. Then he spotted two men walking toward the polling place and excused himself. "More votes coming my way," he said with disdain.

Curly quickly stepped out of the saloon and slipped into the shade of the Mercantile Store. He plucked two bottles of whiskey from the case stashed inside the entryway and deftly tucked them behind his back. The men had just topped the stairs when Curly approached and handed them the bottles. "Gentlemen, a small gift to show my appreciation for voting on this special election day." That winning grin creased his face again. "Cast your votes wisely, as I'm sure you will." The men were startled, then smiled reluctantly as Curly left them.

Later that day, Lucas Boothe, owner of Boothe's Saddlery and Gun Shop, hustled into the polling place. He was neither big nor solid but was of clear grit, plucky. Although he was only thirty-two, he had done well with his shop and the small farm he owned. He lived modestly with his wife, Sarah, who was heavy with child and due any day. A man of few words, he nonetheless seldom left any doubt as to his opinion.

"Ladies," he nodded formally, "I'm here to vote." He was impatient as he waited for his ballot and voting instructions.

"Mr. Boothe, we're terribly pleased that you came—" Lay had just started her well-rehearsed spiel when Lucas cut her short.

"Ma'am," Lucas told her bluntly, "I'm a working man, and time is money to me. I'm wasting my time right now. My ballot, please." He settled his darting eye on Lay. He wanted to vote and be done with it.

Lay was furious, seething at the short treatment she had just received.

Millie, oblivious to Lay's open hostility, plunged right into the brewing fracas. "Mr. Boothe, here is your ballot. The quill and ink are on that table yonder." She waved her handkerchief toward the small foyer at the rear of the store. "When you are finished with your ballot, we'll take it." She flashed her practiced, void-of-emotion smile. Her calm manner tempered Lucas for the moment. He turned his back on the still-fuming Lay and walked to the foyer. Within a minute, he returned to the table. Millie was alone, since Lay had stepped away.

"Ma'am, I believe I need another page. There are only two names on this ballot." He held up his ballot as he spoke.

"That's all there are, Mr. Boothe." Millie apologized and dabbed at her nose with the handkerchief. Lay returned to the table as if to support Millie.

Lucas backed off and scoffed. "This is the damnedest farce I've ever laid witness to. Hayes Jacobson?" He laughed with contempt. "He's dumber than a post. Curly Hall? I could run my team for sheriff and have more smarts than him." He completed his tirade, crumpled the ballot into a tight wad, and winged it toward the corner trash basket. The wadded ballot was well on its way when a big fist slammed it back to Lucas's feet. Lucas glanced up and saw the bulk of a huge man emerge from the shadows.

"A problem here, ladies?" Curly's deep voice cut the air.

Lucas was startled. Curly was a brute of a man, yet he had battled down the wadded ballot with ease and grace.

"No, no problem at all, Mr. Hall," Lay volunteered with a sinister look to Lucas. "This gentleman was merely commenting on the combined intelligence of the two candidates."

Curly stepped cockily to Lucas. He towered over him by a good six inches. Curly said condescendingly, "Would you care to address one of the candidates personally?"

"You're damned right I would" was Lucas's feisty reply. He was running a close second to Hayes Jacobson in exercising good judgment. Then he jabbed toward Curly's chest with his index finger. "What gives you the right to—"

Curly hit him. The right-hand punch was instantaneous—Lucas never saw it coming. He was hit flush on the forehead, just above the brows. He staggered backward into the counter and slid the length of it. As he fought to gain purchase and set his feet, a second driving fist hit him in the chest.

Lucas crashed into the wooden bins at the end of the aisle and collapsed onto the floor. As he painfully struggled to his feet, Dolph Stickney and George Petts jerked him upright. Lucas's feet never touched the floor as the men hauled him through the back storage room and out onto the loading dock. With maligned intent, they hurled him off the dock, sending him cartwheeling head over heels into the dirt. He landed with a body-slamming thud and passed out.

Clem Dowden, the proprietor of the hotel, happened through the alley just as Lucas bounched off the ground. Clem rushed to the prone figure, not privy to what had just transpired. He glanced up in time to see Dolph's broad shoulders disappear inside the storeroom.

"Hey, help me here!" Clem shouted after the man. Jumping to his feet, Clem rushed up the steps of the dock and ran for the closing door. His well-intentioned quest for assistance was misconstrued by Dolph as a confrontation. Dolph violently kicked the door shut as Clem reached for it.

Clem's outstretched hand was slammed in the door and two fingers were broken. The remaining fingers were badly smashed. He screamed in agony, unable to pull his hand free.

Dolph spun, with feral savagery, threw his weight against the door. Clem's fingers were further damaged, and he nearly blacked out from the blinding pain. Dolph suddenly jerked open the door and lashed out furiously at the hunched figure. His brutal, pummeling blows drove Clem off the dock. Clem's efforts to protect himself by raising his hands in front of his body failed. One of Dolph's wild blows hit his damaged hand. Clem was brought to his knees by the burning, searing pain. He fainted. His body hit face-first in the dust, within arm's reach of Lucas. Dolph smiled between gapped teeth and went inside feeling good about his accomplishments.

By the time the doors of the Mercantile Store were closed, Wilbur Palsy and Amos Compton were gloriously inebriated. They had earned a combined three dollars and had voted a total of six times. They didn't know George Petts or particularly cotton to him—it was his money they liked. After buying two rounds, George had made them a most attractive offer. Four bits every time they voted. By some strange coincidence, the two lovely dames at the polling place were only too happy to oblige them in exercising their right to vote.

Still at the bar, Wilbur and Amos were interrupted as a boisterous crowd of rowdies burst through the batwings. Curly Hall was celebrating as the unofficial winner of the special election.

"Harry," the jubilant candidate shouted above the uproar, "drinks are on me!" Even while playing the good ol' boy, Curly was sober and keenly aware of Colburn's expectations of him as sheriff.

There was a stampede for the bar, and The Rose was in full swing. Shouts of joy were soon replaced by calls for a speech. A foot-stamping, hand-clapping cadence built in tempo until the building shook. Curly relished the attention and basked in it for the better part of a minute. Then he raised both hands, hushing the crowd. "Please, my friends, please!" Several catcalls and whistles continued, but Curly quieted them. "I want to thank you law-abiding citizens for your support. I promise a return to law and order starting tomorrow morning. I'll do you proud as the new sheriff. Another round, Harry!" Curly hollered to the barkeep as he worked his way to the bar. Harry joined the festivities and downed a whiskey.

The county clerk snaked his way through the throng of revelers and ultimately reached the bar. Diminutive and hesitant, he attempted to talk with Harry the bartender, but it was impossible with all the commotion in the saloon. Harry realized the plight of the clerk and took matters into his own hands. He reached under the bar and produced a sawed-off 12-gauge shotgun. Taking the cleaning rod in hand, he stuck the brush down the right barrel of the shotgun, twisting it several times. With a delicate touch, Harry pulled the loosely packed wadding out of the barrel. Then dipping the barrel, he rolled the nine 00 buck pellets into his hand. After pocketing the pellets, Harry cocked the hammer, aimed the barrels skyward, and touched off the trigger.

The thunderous deep-throated shot silenced the crowd. Harry glanced sheepishly up into the corner. He had punched a plate-size hole through the ceiling. Small pieces of ceiling and sawdust sprinkled his head and shoulders. He grinned at the stunned crowd. "We have the official results of the election. Mr. Goodwin?"

The clerk cleared his throat and read in a loud but unsteady voice, "The vote tallies are as follows: Rutherford Hall, 117 votes; write-in votes for Big Lil, the bar matron of The Rose, 29; and Hayes Jacobson, 12 votes."

A rousing cheer drowned out the clerk. He attempted to continue but could not.

Once again, Harry raised his shotgun and fired. The subdued boom of the powder charge silenced the room. Harry choked as he implored through the cloud of smoke, "Please, let the man finish."

This plea rankled the crowd. They proceeded to hoot and holler until Curly stepped forward to quiet them. Mr. Goodwin reluctantly took the floor.

"I must point out that since there are only ninety registered voters in the town, Judge Williams has impounded the ballots. We will recount immediately. Expect the results within the hour."

With the hurried departure of the clerk, a new round of drinks was ordered by one of the patrons, followed by the Big Lil second-place round. Big Lil was right in the thick of the drinking. This beefy, buxom Irish gal could "raise an elbow" with the best of 'em. Not only could she dance, but the lady played a wicked hand of poker, too.

Big Lil was mingling with the barflies when Mr. Goodwin returned through the batwings. He threaded his way to the bar. Harry, with two more drinks under his belt, reached for the scattergun. Big Lil was a step ahead of him and put two fingers to her lips. A shrill, piercing whistle dampened then quieted the cowboys.

"Give us the good word, Mr. Goodwin!" Big Lil shouted toward the clerk.

Uneasy as the center of attention, the clerk read the slip of paper that he took from his pocket. His hands shook like a leaf. "The official results of the election are—"

He was cut short abruptly by a well-primed cowboy. "Cut the fancy gabber, clerk! Just give us them numbers."

"Very well. Rutherford Hall, 49 votes; Big Lil, 29 votes; Hayes Jacobson, 12 votes."

A spontaneous outburst from the crowd stopped the clerk. He waited patiently as the party renewed its gusto. Big Lil bellied up to the bar and led the boys in a sacrifice at the shrine of Bacchus. Eventually she realized that the hovering clerk still had more to say and hushed the boys.

"The votes tally with the register. The results will stand." Mr. Goodwin appeared pleased with his presentation. "Judge Williams has invalidated the terms of office of all who served under Sheriff John Tibbetts. This decree has the full support of the mayor and the council." A sigh of relief escaped from Mr. Goodwin as he finished his speech. He couldn't get out of that house of ill fame fast enough.

Curly fought back a smile at the knowledge that he was now in charge of Jacob's Well. Thank you, Judge Williams, he thought with pleasure. Good-bye, Royal Ballou.

CHAPTER
3

Royal Ballou broke through the dense cedars on the mesa top. He reined up short of the edge and gazed down upon Jacob's Well, nestled snugly against towering red and yellow-gray sandstone cliffs. The Puerco River snaked through the valley floor, its steep, lush green banks contrasting vividly against the gray sage and the red soil. From this vantage point, it was an hour's ride to town. Royal followed the trail of descent with his eyes. It traversed off the mesa top and clung to the steep cliff faces before it reached the wide sloping hills that gently melted into the valley floor.

The local cattlemen bragged that their stock could look at the grasslands and get fat. The river bottom held some of the best farmland in the New Mexico Territory.

Royal off-horsed and walked to the edge of the mesa. He stretched his weary legs and rubbed his saddlesore butt. Hunkering down beside a gnarled, wind-twisted cedar, he built a smoke with deft, absentminded fingers. He cupped the match against the breeze and watched a rancher cut his field. He coughed, then choked on the smoke. With disgust he ground the half-smoked cigarette into the dirt. "Nasty habit—I quit." The moist smell of freshly cut hay wafted up on the thermals. The aroma pleased him.

Santa Fe had been unseasonably hot and dusty. Royal had been miserable there. Now he was fully recovered from his wound. A purplish nipple-size scar slightly in front of his left armpit was the only trace of the bushwacker's bullet that remained.

After the shooting of Royal that night, Sheriff Tibbetts's comment had been "You put your saddle on the right horse." Luckily, Royal had turned just as the gunman shot him. Otherwise he would have been hit squarely in the heart. Royal owed his life to Sheriff Tibbetts and Doc Shu. Tibbetts had brought down one of the gunmen and pulled Royal to safety. Doc Shu had kept him from bleeding to death. The doc had suspected possible shoulder joint damage and had personally escorted Royal to Santa Fe. There Royal had been treated by one of the best damned bone doctors in the territory. That doctor happened to be one of Shubael's old classmates in medical school. The day-long trip in a buckboard had been far worse than getting shot and Royal had pleaded several times with Doc Shu to put him out of his misery. But Doc Shu had mothered him 'round the clock and pulled him through a touchy bout of fever. Royal was indebted to the doc for his efforts.

His anticipation of seeing Tibbetts and Doc Shu hurried Royal off the mesa. Thoughts of Libby Dowden's home-cooked meals at the hotel also spurred him ahead. He realized, too, how much he had missed Abbie's company and their gab sessions. As he trotted past the cemetery on the outskirts of town, Royal took note of the recent activity. I wonder who passed away, he thought. He murmured reverently, "Rest in peace."

Royal was dark of face, sun beaten. His hard brown eyes set in a square-jawed face gave him a look of determination. Windblown, unkempt black hair tufted out from beneath his battered Stetson, and a scruffy two weeks' growth of beard covered his face. He was looking forward to shaving the itching, uncomfortable shag. His quick sense of humor and ready smile had helped him through his time with Sam Houston. A brief stint with the Texas Volunteers stationed at Fort Defiance had educated him in life in the West. Doc Shu referred to Royal's build as "deep rooted, not over tall, thick ribbed yet sinewy." Sheriff Tibbetts had measured Royal with a glance. "Mulish, impervious to reason, but a damned good hand."

The Ballous had been a Pennsylvania farm family, a close-knit clan with three boys to work the land—Royal was the middle of the lot. The farming life had been flushed with success for the hardworking Ballous. Nevertheless, stories of adventure and exploration in the West had tempted the eldest son, Jason, away from Pennsylvania. Royal had pleaded his own case to accompany his brother so successfully that Papa Ballou had reluctantly capitulated and sent the two boys on their way.

The brothers, accustomed to hard work, found some six months later in the Panhandle herding cattle.

Jason became embroiled in the struggle for Texas independence and soon was riding with Colonel Bill Travis. He was among the Texas Volunteers who had reinforced the men at the small fort known as the Alamo. Royal was allowed to ride along with the soldiers on the understanding that if heavy fighting broke out, he would be sent to the rear—Jason was determined to protect his brother.

The speed and size of Santa Anna's thrust toward San Antonio had caught the Texans off guard. Hard decisions were made. Travis vowed that the Alamo would be defended to the last man. Several men volunteered to report on the movements of the Mexican Army—Jason was one of those men. On the night of February 21, 1836, Jason Ballou and two others had been killed in a surprise raid by Mexican dragoons on the outskirts of town.

On February 24, Colonel Travis honored a pledge he had made to Jason. Royal would carry Travis's final message to Colonel James Fannin in Goliad. Jason had feared for Royal's life and had known that if Royal weren't sent from the battlefield, he would die there. Royal scouted for Colonel Fannin at Fort Defiance and was captured near Goliad with the Texans. He escaped from the San Antonio River massacre, although twice wounded. He made a slow recovery and worked his way back to the Pennsylvania farm.

Papa Ballou drank himself dead over Jason's death. Mother Ballou held the family together until she died of a broken heart within six months of her husband's quietus. Royal and his younger brother Grady sold the farm and left Pennsylvania.

A year later, the brothers were lawmen in Salina, Kansas. The two kept a tight rein on punchers and drifters and knocked heads on drovers and sodbusters. Law work in Salina was good honest work although fraught with unexpected dangers. The brothers stuck by each other through gunfights and brawls. Royal and Grady were well respected by men on both sides of the law—apparently too well respected.

On one sticky, humid Kansas night, two men ambushed the brothers. Grady was gunned down, Royal slightly wounded. Royal shot and killed Peter Hoose, one of the assailants. The other man escaped. The following day, Grady was buried in

Kansas and Royal retired from his position. He spent the next two years hounding Grady's killer, Dallas Detweiller. Royal killed him in Hobbs, New Mexico.

Then Royal drifted without purpose. He worked for a spell as a ranch hand near El Paso, then packed his belongings into his saddlebag and traveled throughout the Southwest. His wanderings brought him to Jacob's Well, where a want ad for a deputy lawman caught his attention. He spoke with Sheriff John Tibbetts and liked the man. He was offered the job. Jacob's Well was a pleasant town. The people were neighborly. For the past two years Royal had worked with Sheriff Tibbetts.

As Royal cantered into the outskirts of the town, he reflected back on the night he had been shot in Jacob's Well. He and Sheriff Tibbetts had started to cross the dark alley beside The Rose when shots rang out. In the furious exchange, Royal had been hit once. Tibbetts killed one of the gunmen, Lefty Hallahan. John was convinced that two men were involved in the set-up and ambush. His reasoning was that the four or five shots aimed at Royal had been too closely spaced to have been fired by one man. Although there were neither footprints, nor hoofprints to support his belief, he was certain that two men had shot at them. Rumor had it that the gunmen had been imported by a wealthy landowner. No one wanted to step forward to point a finger—the five-hundred-dollar reward wasn't worth dying for.

Royal led his horse toward the corral of the livery stable. He purposely rode in behind the stable so as not to announce his arrival. He wanted to surprise Sheriff Tibbetts. Royal knew the old man would be sitting in front of his office with boots propped on the railing. Tibbetts liked to give the impression that he was simply out "warmin' himself," but his express purpose was to see who was coming into town for the evening. This watch was a ritual. Farmers and working folk were not a problem—a few drinks, a card game or two, and they were on their way. But the cattle ranchers were another matter. Range riders and cow camp boys were here for only one reason: to raise hell. If a trail crew or two were in town, trouble was assured.

Royal left his mare. Joe Mex, the stablehand, knew to rub down and grain her. Royal hefted his saddle over his shoulder, snagged his saddlebags, and headed for the sheriff's office. As he eased around the corner of the jail, he looked for his friend at the railing. Not there. Maybe the old man's inside, he thought, getting some coffee. Weighed down by his gear, Royal unlatched the door with his knee. Awkwardly sidestepping the door, he caught sight of the sheriff bending over the stove brewing coffee. With his foot he swung the door closed. As he dumped his gear in the corner, Royal spoke over his shoulder.

"Well, Sheriff, how are ya?"

The man glared as Royal turned around. "Fine. Who in the hell are you?" a rough, unflinching voice demanded.

Royal was urgently snapped out of his casual entrance. The man facing him was not John Tibbetts. Royal sized the man up with a quick scan; big, confident, and aggressive. An ominous feeling welled up inside Royal.

"I asked you a question, mister. Who in the hell are you? What do you want in my office?" The man moved to the desk and set his cup down. He placed both hands on the desk top, leaned forward, and confronted Royal.

Cover yourself. Fake it. Royal dallied, playing for time while his mind raced for a ploy. He wiped his nose on his sleeve, then thumbed his hat back. "Sheriff, I'm Wendell Slocum. Up from Watesville." He tarried as his eyes searched the office. His Pennsylvania rifle was still in the gun rack. Lucas Boothe had customized it to his specifications. "I come up here to buy a rifle from Tibbetts." Get out of here fast, he thought.

"Tibbetts is gone" was the blunt reply. "I'm the new sheriff, and I don't have no guns to sell. So get out." It was an order, not an answer.

"That's a shame," Royal drawled as he sought more information. "Best be on my way. Tibbetts be back later?"

"Nope" was the dead-end answer. The sheriff continued to glower at him.

Royal desperately wanted more information about Tibbetts, but the man offered none. Picking up his saddle and bags, Royal stole another look at the man. A behemoth. A bullet-shaped head and a thick neck set on massive shoulders. Stout arms and huge hands. Royal struggled with his gear and the door. The sheriff strode to the door as Royal cleared the frame and slammed it shut. Royal caught the graceful movements of the lawman. Don't be fooled by his size, he warned himself.

Royal quick-footed back to the stable. He wanted to be out of town before the sheriff started asking questions. Joe Mex was nowhere to be seen, and Royal learned nothing about Tibbetts. He would ride out and double back in order to reach Doc Shu's corral unnoticed.

The mare was disinclined to gallop—she was tired. Royal pushed her hard, wanting to show his heels to the sheriff. He didn't understand the situation, but he knew not to trust the sheriff any farther than he could throw him. "Throw him, hell," Royal chortled with a laugh. "I couldn't even pick him up." Royal retraced his path out of town. He rode at the foot of the red bluffs that bordered the outlying houses. After he left the main road, he chose his route with great caution. A telltale trail in soft or wet sand would be a dead giveaway. Royal searched for hard pack or rocky terrain. He was confident that he had left no prints.

He cut through the bluffs and backtracked to Doc Shu's corral. The corral butted against the steep cliffs that surrounded the southern approach to Jacob's Well. The ride took Royal a full hour to complete.

With the mare secreted in the corral, Royal slipped around the front of the drugstore and let himself in through the door. The infernal bell clanger announced his entry. Doc Shu glanced over a pair of half reading glasses precariously perched on the tip of his nose.

"Evening, sir," he stated, then studied the face closely. "Royal! Damn, boy, am I glad to see you!" The doc was on his feet, moving out from behind the counter. The friends greeted each other with back-slapping abrazos.

"Lad, you need some home cooking," the doc fussed. He stepped away and appraised Royal as only a doctor could. "You look out of health. Still feelin' poorly?"

"Doc, please," Royal begged, "don't mother me. I needed to get out of Santa Fe. Soon as I start working, I'll be fine. I'm fully mended."

"Fine, glad to hear it." Doc Shu was aglow. "Let's have some medicine to celebrate your homecoming." He headed toward the back room. "What took you so long?"

"What do you mean?" Royal was puzzled. "I left when I was ready."

"Didn't you receive any of my telegrams? A letter?" Doc Shu asked him through the open doorway.

"Not a word." Royal shook his head.

"That's strange," the doc replied as he returned with a bottle. "I sent two separate telegrams on two different occasions." He couldn't fathom that his messages had not reached Royal. He was discouraged, sullen. He sank slowly into his chair.

"Doc, listen to me." Royal motioned to the old man. "I didn't receive a thing from you. Not by post or by wire. I've been traveling for the better part of a week. Why did you need to reach me? Does it have something to do with the man I encountered in John's office?"

"Sit down, Royal." The doc pointed to a chair beside his desk. Two shots were poured and raised in a half hearted toast. They sipped their drinks. Doc Shu reneged on his effort to talk.

"Doc, what in hell is going on here?" Royal pleaded. "I walk into my office and confront a bear. I get thrown out. I stop here, and you have fallen prey to melancholy. Where is John Tibbetts?" He had posed the inevitable question to his closest friend. He looked Doc Shu in the eye—he was not to be denied.

The doc would not meet Royal's eyes. He started to speak, but he choked. His hand shook slightly as he poured another shot. This drink he downed in one gulp.

"John is dead." Royal spoke with forced calm. The doc bobbed his head. A dread, empty feeling weighed on him. "And that hooligan is our new sheriff. Right?"

Doc Shu agreed while absentmindedly polishing his smooth head.

"To add insult to injury, I'm without an office or a job," Royal added.

"Correct on all accounts," Doc Shu whispered, his voice quivering with emotion. Then he cleared his throat. "The election—and I use the term loosely—was two days ago. You are out! Mr. Curly Hall is in. Backed by our esteemed mayor and council." The doc's words were harsh. And sarcasm tinged.

"What happened to John?" Royal couldn't quite believe his mentor was dead.

"He was gunned down," the doc said painfully. "Curly Hall claimed it was self-defense, but it was a set-up plain and simple. Curly put his little brother Perley out front, then double-crossed him in order to get John." Doc Shu related Perley's misreckoned squabbles with John, the name-calling and insults. He detailed what he saw of the shoot-out and afterward, in the alley. "Royal, the man is a cold-blooded killer. He sacrificed his own kin. The rogue requires considerable watchin'."

"I agree, Doc. Sounds to me like a hell-born outlaw now wearing a badge."

The men were silent. They remembered John Tibbetts and how he had influenced them. To Royal, John had been a second father. A man he respected. A proud lawman. Royal mused, then smiled. Hell, Tibbetts had forgotten more about law work that I'll ever know, he thought.

Doc refilled the empty glasses. Shubael had liked John because he was a man of his word, with no lame excuses or windies. It was ten minutes before either man spoke.

"Doc, you mentioned two attempts to reach me. You sure you addressed them properly?" Royal asked.

"Right address? Hell," he fumed, "I took you there! Remember?" He stared defiantly at Royal. The old-timer was sharp, ireful.

"Check your blood pressure, Doc." Royal ribbed him with a wide grin. "Who sent those telegrams?"

"Let me think." The doc shined his head. "Elihu Jones the first time. When I got plum desperate, Paul sent them again."

"Elihu Jones. Uh-huh. Wasn't he in hock up to his ears several years ago to the land company? Over the ranch he bought?"

A sly smile crossed the doc's face, and wrinkle lines creased his head. "I do seem to recall the situation, now that you mention the land company."

"Correct me if I'm wrong, Doc, but he seems to have cut himself a fat hog now that he's grazing H bar C beef."

"I don't think in those terms, Royal. You tend to look at the law from a different angle. It does make sense." The doc complimented Royal.

"What would you say, old man, if we sent Mr. Jones on a fool's errand in a few days?" Royal glanced inquisitively at his prospective partner in crime.

Curiosity bested the doctor. "What do you have in mind?"

"Two nights hence with Elihu on duty . . ." Royal detailed his plan to Doc Shu. Then he said, "Might be wise for me to lay low for a few days—I want to avoid Curly. Know of a place where I can stay out of town?"

Doc Shu was silent for several minutes. "I've got it." He

slapped his palm against his thigh. "Clem Dowden has a broke hand. I was fixin' to go out there day after tomorrow and visit. You can stay out there. He'll be glad for help with the chores."

"What happened to him?" Royal asked.

"One of Curly's strongarms smashed Clem's hand in a door. One hundred percent vicious." The doc grimaced. "Clem was trying to help Lucas and was soundly thrashed. I set his hand. Two fingers broke, three badly tore apart. I doubt he'll have full use of that hand again." The doc demonstrated on his own hand as he spoke. A look of consternation set deep around his mouth.

"Why was he helping Lucas? Neither's a fighter," Royal asked, baffled.

"Curly beat the fire out of Lucas. Seems Lucas questioned the sheriff's intelligence. That was a mistake. Lucas saw double for a full day. He's back at work, still a little shaky." Doc Shu smiled in sympathy for Lucas.

"For goin' contrary to that sheriff, I'd have to question Lucas's intelligence also. Sounds like this lawman is here for the duration, and he brought his own help. If he has the blessings of the mayor and the council, he's Ham's choice. Right?"

"I'm 'fraid so. At the moment, I don't know what we can do to change it either."

"And tell me about Abbie. Where is she? Is she well?" Royal grew excited thinking about that young lady.

"She's doing as well as can be expected. I sent her to visit with some old friends for a spell in Sedalia. It hasn't been easy on her. Tibbetts was like kin to her," Doc said tenderly.

Royal was momentarily silent. "Your back-room cot available, Doc? I've got a batch of thinking to do." Royal ran his fingers through his unkempt hair.

"Go ahead, lad. I'll bed your horse in the corral. She'll be safe and out of sight."

Royal's knock was barely audible on the rear door of Boothe's Saddlery and Gun Shop the next day. He was expected. Doc Shu had spoken to Lucas earlier. The door was unbolted, and the padlocks removed on the inside. Lucas stepped aside to let Royal into the storage room. They shook hands and talked in hushed whispers.

"Doc mention I need powder and a rifle? I'm pinched for cash at the moment." Royal searched Lucas's face for approval.

"Not to worry, Royal," Lucas reassured him. "Take what you need. We'll settle later."

Their conversation was interrupted by the bell on the front door. Lucas motioned Royal to stay put while he minded the shop. Royal overheard the confrontation.

"What do you want?" Lucas demanded rudely.

"My, my, ain't we on the prod today. Still have a headache, Lucas?" Dolph Stickney asked with mock concern. A gapped smile furrowed his features as he glanced at his companion.

"State your business," Lucas mandated. "If you aren't here to purchase something, get out." He indicated the front door.

"Hear the man, Georgie Boy?" Dolph turned to his friend. "He told us to get out. Not very neighborly, is he?" Dolph knew Lucas was afraid of them. Lucas vividly recalled the election-day beating administered by those two roughs.

"Mr. Boothe"—George winked at Dolph as he moved to the counter—"we're here to make you a business proposition."

Outright extortion is more like it, Lucas thought.

"We're forming the Jacob's Well Improvement Commission. For a meager monthly contribution, the sheriff's office will provide protection for your business establishment. Check windows, lock doors. Make sure no one enters your store after dark." George finished his discourse, satisfied with his presentation.

"And if I refuse?" Lucas challenged him, his jaw set.

"Why, Mr. Boothe," George Petts painfully excused, "that would be most unfortunate."

As George spoke with Lucas, Dolph walked past the horseshoe bin and kicked the supporting leg out from underneath it. The bin crashed to the floor, and shoes cascaded into the aisle. The loud racket brought Royal forward. He peeked over the batwings that separated the two rooms.

"Perhaps you'd like to reconsider our offer?" George asked the infuriated store owner.

Royal knew he had to act. Lucas was short fused, and the merchant was overmatched with these two.

"Like hell I will," Lucas blurted out, and reached beneath the counter for his pistol. George anticipated the move and lunged across the countertop. He yanked Lucas against him before Lucas could clear the Colt from under the counter.

Royal parted the batwings, crouched, and angled toward the front of the store. He paused beside a barrel of ax handles and stealthily eased one out. George was toying with Lucas, by keeping him pinned against the counter. The bully's wide back completely hid Lucas. Royal grasped the handle with both hands and flung it violently at George. It lambasted him across the shoulder blades with a meaty whack. George dropped Lucas and recoiled, a look of shocked disbelief on his face. Dolph ceased his barrel-rolling destruction to glance at George. He followed George's eyes toward Royal. A spinning ax handle cracked him across the crown of his forehead. *Boop!* It sounded like a ripe melon. Dolph was cold cocked. He bowled over a barrel of shoe nails as he fell, and several hundred pounds of nails dragged him under.

George recovered from the blow and turned on Royal. He hitched for a heartbeat, then reached for his gun.

The loud click of a hammer being cocked, followed by hard steel pressed into the base of his skull, stopped him short.

"That's as far as you go," Lucas warned as he reached over the counter and relieved the tough of his pistol. "Pick up your friend and pack him out of here." Lucas encouraged George with a nudge of the pistol barrel.

George, his face masked with hatred, sought out Royal, but he could not see him in the dimly lighted aisle.

"Get goin', I said." Lucas brandished the pistol at George. Petts rubbed his sore shoulders as he stumbled through the nails and horseshoes. He pulled Dolph to his feet, then steadied him as they scrambled over the debris. When they reached the front door, Lucas called to George.

"Here, you left this." Lucas slid Petts's pistol across the floor. It hit George's right boot. He knelt and groped for the pistol. He found it and managed to keep Dolph on his feet. As George raised the pistol, he noticed that the percussion caps were gone. Lucas had removed them. The fighter violently holstered his useless pistol and exited with Dolph in tow. He nearly slammed the door off its hinges.

Royal came forward out of the shadows. "Seems your election day luck still holds, Lucas," he kidded.

"Those vultures," Lucas said in disgust. "They're shadows

for Curly and do whatever he commands, no questions asked. There isn't a lick of sense between the two of 'em."

"I wonder what hate and discontent they'll spread next?" Royal said.

For the next quarter hour, Royal and Lucas picked up and put together the shelving and restocked the bins. Pleased with their work, they rested on a pile of saddle blankets and tried to anticipate Curly's next move.

"Clem's the one," Royal said. "He's back at work, right?"

"Sure as hell is. As of yesterday."

Royal was on his feet and headed for the back door. "That's where those thugs went next."

"Go ahead, Royal," Lucas called after him. "I'll get help and join you."

Royal sprinted from the shop and ran full out for the rear of the hotel. He stayed behind the Main Street buildings. Panting hard, he slowed to a walk at the hotel's loading dock. He smothered all noise and stepped onto the dock. The sound of breaking china greeted him from inside the kitchen. Palming the latch with a feather touch, he cautiously cracked the makeshift cheesecloth screen door. Rusty hinges announced his entry. There was silence from within. Royal peered inside and saw two men frozen in position. George Petts had been dumping the contents of a flour bin onto Clem's prostrate body. Dolph Stickney had been smashing china plates against the cook stove.

"Party's over, boys." Royal stepped inside and toe-hooked the door closed behind him.

"Devil take." George looked at Royal, and a demonic smile twisted his mouth. "If it ain't our sneaky back fighter from the saddlery store. We got a score to square with you, mister." George hurled the flour bin aside. Dolph dropped the stack of dishes with a biting crash and moved away from the stove, trying to flank Royal on the right.

"Here, Dolph," Petts called as he plucked a meat cleaver from the cutting block and threw it gently to his partner. Dolph caught the cleaver with tender caution, then smacked his open hand firmly with the heavy, flat blade. George pulled a thin-bladed butcher knife from the side slot of the block.

"We're going to teach you a lesson, stranger," Petts threatened. "Don't nose into other people's business." George inched closer, and both men converged on Royal.

The stilled atmosphere of the room was shattered by a woman's shrill voice. "You vile sons of bitches!" Libby Dowden boomed from the dining-room door. The men turned to address this unexpected threat. "I'll kick you both a new ass for this mess. What have you done with my Clem?"

Neither man knew how to deal with the overwrought female. "Ma'am, we didn't mean no trouble," George feebly explained, a honeyed grin on his face.

"Horse manure!" she hollered. "Where's my man? Oh, Clem," she moaned in distress as she spotted Clem buried beneath fifty pounds of bakery flour.

"We'll explain everything," Dolph offered as he wisely distanced himself from this big-boned woman. He hadn't finished his sentence before Libby let fly with a pastry rolling pin. Dolph, caught in midstride, was helpless. The pin hit him solidly under the rib cage and sent him sprawling toward the kitchen door. Within an eyeblink, Dolph was on his feet and with his arms shielding his face, crashed through the screen door to temporary safety. Libby rushed to the stove, yanked her apron loose, and grabbed the pot of boiling water. She hefted the pot with no effort and steamed toward George. Seeing the oncoming danger, George angled for the tattered door.

George stutter-stepped and threw the knife as hard as he could at Royal. Instinct sent Royal into a belly-flop dive to the floor. *Thud!* The knife buried itself deep in the shelving directly above him. Libby Dowden completed her mad charge and threw the boiling contents at George. Fortunately, George and Dolph were ahead of the water. They escaped, battered but unhurt.

Libby turned lightly on her heel and rushed to her husband. She dropped beside him and gently lifted his head out of the flour. With tenderness that belied her size, she cradled his face to her ample bosom. Royal knelt beside them.

"God bless you, Royal Ballou." Libby clutched Royal's hand as tears streaked her floured cheeks. Clem moaned and delicately touched the bruise beneath his chin. At that moment, Lucas and Doc Shu barged into the kitchen. Lucas, rifle in hand, warily approached the broken rear door and checked behind the building. Doc Shu helped Clem to his feet and inspected his splinted and bandaged hand. It was undamaged. The doc breathed a sigh of relief.

Libby rounded up the kitchen help, and they cleaned the floured china mess out of the kitchen. Then she made time to greet Royal. "Come here, you big hunk." She smothered him with a bear hug as they stood shoulder to shoulder. "You can't begin to know how happy we are to see you."

Royal put his arm around her waist. "Looks like I'm back in the nick of time. Well"—he shrugged—"close enough." They laughed together.

"You better hightail it away from here, Royal." Doc Shu herded him toward the back door. "Wait for me in the store. I'll be back as soon as I'm able."

Lucas escorted Royal to the doc's shop and returned to the saddle shop. Over dinner, Doc, Clem, and Libby worked out the details of Royal's pending stay at the Dowden Ranch.

Doc Shu finished his coffee with Clem and Libby. At quarter past nine he left the hotel and walked to the telegraph office. As he came through the door, Elihu Jones looked up from his paper work.

"Evenin', Doc" was the heedful greeting from the telegrapher.

"Elihu," Doc Shu said as he stepped to the counter, "I want to send two telegrams." He drew two separate slips of paper from his shirt pocket and handed them to Elihu.

"First thing in the morning, Doc" was the clerk's brush-off answer.

"They're mighty important, Elihu." The doc's expression was grave. "Have you time to send them tonight? I would greatly appreciate it."

"For you I will" was Elihu's strained answer.

"Thanks, my boy." The doc nodded with pleasure but didn't leave.

A deadlock. Doc Shu wanted to stay. Elihu wanted to be left alone.

"Any problem, Doc? I'll get right on these." Elihu was out of humor with the doc's presence. His suspicions surfaced so he asked, "Ever done code before?" He was cautious, covering his ass.

"Nope" was the doc's straightforward answer. "I can barely write, let alone understand a damned bunch of clatter on a wire. I wanted to watch you send them out. I hear tell that telegraphers can identify each other by the manner in which they send messages. Truth?" He looked at Elihu for an answer.

"True enough." The clerk brightened. He was more at ease knowing that the doc was interested in his profession. "Give a listen, and I'll call Harlan Wilcox. He's in Watesville. He has a real sweet touch. His characters flow." Elihu was secretly jealous of him.

The clerk straightened around, set himself properly in front of the key, and began to tap out letters. Moments later, the reply clicked over the sounder.

"Ain't that somethin'? Smooth as ice," Elihu commented on his fellow telegrapher's skill at the keys. He picked up the first telegram. "This one goes to the U.S. Marshal's office in Tucumcari. Correct?"

Doc Shu nodded. He watched and waited as the clerk worked his way through the message. The reply was lengthy. "What's he saying, boy?"

"Just confirming the names and addresses—that's all, Doc."

"I've seen all I need to. Thanks, Elihu."

Doc Shu waved good-bye and left the cluttered office. Within twenty minutes, Royal tapped lightly on the doc's back door. Over coffee the men discussed the telegrams that Elihu had just sent. The doc was pleased to know the telegrams were on their way.

"A relief." Shubael smiled confidently. "The marshal's office will now start looking into the background of Mr. Curly Hall. You satisfied, Royal?"

"Ya" was Royal's unenthusiastic reply.

Doc Shu was taken aback by Royal's nonanswer. He wondered if he should press the matter or drop it. But before he could broach the topic, Royal spoke.

"How's the second hay cutting, Doc?"

"That's a damned fool question to ask a medicine man. Go talk to Clem." He was irritated by Royal's lack of interest in the telegrams.

"Just answer the question! How is it?" Royal pressed him.

The doc relented a shade. "Rumor is that it's a good crop." A sly smile wrinkled his cheeks.

"What a coincidence. That's exactly what Elihu and Harlan

were discussing not more than twenty minutes ago. I was listening outside the telegraph office window."

"What?" Doc Shu was on his feet, headed for the telegraph office. Royal lunged at him, snagging his arm and holding him back. "Sit down, old-timer, before you go off half cocked." Doc Shu sat filled with misgivings. "Doc, when I was a deputy in Salina, I studied to become a telegrapher. Came within a hair of being qualified."

"The hell you say!" Doc Shu replied with unbelieving surprise.

"Mr. Elihu Jones is trying to save his worthless hide and salvage his ranch. I'm guessing that H bar C cattle have something to do with his situation. Now I understand why none of your messages ever reached me—or anyone else for that matter."

Doc Shu volunteered his opinion. "I venture to say that Ham Colburn figures prominently in the picture. He never gives nothin' away for free, 'cept his high-mettled advice—which doesn't amount to a pimple on a gnat's ass."

Royal leaned away from the table, balancing on the hind legs of his chair, and marveled at the doc. Doc's ecstasy of rage continued until he ran out of breath. He paused in his tirade and caught sight of Royal.

"What you lookin' at?" he frostily demanded.

"You old windbag. Why don't you hush up before a vein pops in your hard head?" Royal's wily smile amused the old man, who laughed. "You through?" The doc laughed again and agreed that he was finished. "Good. Now let me stew over Elihu Jones, our misdirected telegrapher. I believe we can use his services at a later date."

Doc Shu shuffled to the stove and fussed up a pot of hot coffee. As he carried the cups to the desk, Royal broke the silence.

"Doc, when is Abbie coming back? I'm wantin' to set eyes on her real bad."

"I don't have a firm date yet. But soon—within the week." He smiled a knowing grin. "Miss her, do ya?"

Royal ignored the remark. "How'd she take John's death?"

"Not well," the doc replied sadly. "That man was her life. Just like kin. But that young lady has spunk." He smiled widely. "She'll pull through with some help."

"I won't be in town when she returns. Give her my best. When things calm down, I'll stop in to visit. She still work with Clem and Libby at the hotel?"

"Yep" was the doc's immediate response. "It makes my day to see her sunny face. You better look after that sweetheart," he playfully cautioned Royal, "or I'm gonna take her right out from underneath your nose."

CHAPTER
4

Four weeks had passed since the death of John Tibbetts. The dust-up concerning the sham election had blown over. By and large, the town had accepted the new lawman. A few hard-heads continued to resist the Improvement Commission scam and voiced their dissent.

Royal was laboring as Clem's ranch hand. He relished the hard work. Between irrigating the fields and doing the chores, he had little time for anything else.

One night in the fragile light of a fingernail moon, two men secreted their way up the hindside of the knob and dismounted. They eased forward to the edge of the crest and looked down upon the Dowden spread. A small cabin nested against the hillside with fields fanning out to the valley floor. A corral and three small storage sheds clustered next to the cabin.

The men focused their attention on the reservoir that was built into the slope halfway down the hillside. An underground spring supplied the water for Clem's irrigation system. The network serviced a hundred acres of the richest farmland in the valley.

"Can you do it, Dolph?" George Petts asked nervously. "Got 'nuff powder?"

"Relax, Georgie Boy," Dolph reassured him. "When we get done here, there won't be enough ranch left to fret about. Help me carry this box."

The men hefted the box and angled off the knob. They hugged the side of the grassy hill and gradually worked their way over to the reservoir. The moon cast ample light. As they crouched on top of the dam, they could see the ditches in the distance reflecting the moonlight. Clem had labored years to build this system.

"Aim for the sluice gate, George." Dolph indicated with his

head. "That will be the weakest point of the dam. We'll place the charges there."

The men struggled across the face of the earthen dam. They dug their bootheels into the soft earth, which allowed them to traverse the steep bank. The steel sluice box was firmly anchored into the dam with timber ties. The mouth of the gate was ten feet wide and four feet high. A steady flow of water flushed down into the spillway.

Dolph pried the lid off the box. He had capped two fuses earlier. Gently inserting one of the capped fuses into the center of a dynamite stick, he readied the first charge. With a helping hand from George, he bundled nine sticks around the fused one. Then they repeated the procedure. Soon another ten-stick charge was ready. Dolph placed the charges, one beside the sluice gate, the other at the base of the timber retaining wall. His plan was to buckle the wall first, then bust the gate loose and let the water bring the dam down.

"Light yours now, Georgie Boy," Dolph whispered downhill to his partner. He fished a match from his vest pocket and waited patiently. A bright flare momentarily silhouetted George as he thumbnail-struck the match. George cupped his hands and lit the fuse. It sputtered for a brief second, then went out.

"Blow on it," Dolph snapped. Seconds later, he heard George blow on the fuse. A dim flicker of flame, a loud hiss, and the fuse caught. George stepped away quickly and clawed his way up the bank. Dolph struck his match and lit the end of the fuse. It took with a flash.

"Quick! Get the hell on top!" Dolph ordered as he stood. "We've got two minutes."

They scrambled up the steep earthen face of the dam, cresting the top on their hands and knees. Both were sucking wind and gasping for breath. Unexpectedly, Dolph rose to his feet and clipped George underneath the chin with his shoulder. The blow stunned George and knocked him off balance. He lurched backward and toppled off the dam into thin air. George fell without a murmur and hit the black water with a loud splash. He disappeared. Dolph dropped to one knee, frantically searching the surface for any trace of his friend.

"Georgie Boy!" Dolph called, fear spilling from him. Silence. "Georgie," he pleaded. Still no response. The sound of water lapping against the dam was the only reply. Smoke burned in Dolph's nose. Thoughts of the pending blast and flood urged him to his feet. "Hellfire, I gotta run." He sprinted the length of the dam and had nearly reached safety when the ground underneath him shook. Down he went as the muffled roar of an explosion buffeted him. His knees touched the ground for a heartbeat. Then unadulterated fear had him on the run again.

A strange groaning escaped from the dam. Dolph watched in awe as the sluice box slowly settled, then self-destructed in a twisting, wrenching mass of steel. Dolph's hat was blown off by an unnatural gust of wind. The entire right-hand side of the dam collapsed with a frightening roar. The crashing thud of boulders and timbers being swallowed up was deafening. Dolph half ran over the knob to the horses. He unlooped the reins of George's horse and tied them to one of the saddle strings. Fuming mad, he yanked his reins off a small sage and whipped them over the head of his horse. He mounted in a scramble, wanting to put ground between him and the terrible destruction of the broken reservoir as soon as possible.

"Damn you all to hell, George Petts!" he cursed as he spurred his horse.

Moments before he lay down on his beckoning bed, Royal heard a muffled explosion. He fumble-searched for his boots and yanked them on. Blindly groping for the table, he stumbled over a chair and sprawled full length onto the floor. He felt for the wall. As he stood, he arm-hooked his pistol belt off the wall peg and opened the door. In a low crouch he ducked outside and pressed against the log wall. The monstrous roar from upstream instantaneously sent him running for high ground. Fear of death from the wall of water panicked him. He hurtled the porch railing, landed on the run, and nearly decapitated himself on the clothesline.

The mass of debris, rocks, and timber had gained unimaginable momentum as it wrought havoc throughout the ranch. The corrals and outbarns were obliterated. Royal was terrified. He was tiring badly. Only the deepest bottom of his will made him go on.

Finally unable to punish himself any longer, he fell to the ground. His sides ached, and his chest pained at every breath. The burning in his lungs nearly doubled him over. The roar of the flood receded like a freight train going away. Royal was not sure if it was really lessening, or if he was slowly losing consciousness.

The pounding in his temples diminished, though not without a fight. He was able to breathe with a semblance of normalcy. Royal sat on the hillside until his mind gave his body approval to move. The valley was quiet. Walking at half speed, he eased off the hill. He knew what to expect; the ranch would be rendered null—total annihilation. If any part of Clem's ranch was still standing, he would be astonished.

At the base of the hill, he could make out the dim outline of the cabin. The sight cheered him considerably. He pressed against the logs of the cabin as he walked its length. Shy of the corner, he stepped off into emptiness. A frantic backward lunge —luckily he grabbed the corner post of the porch. As he muscled himself back onto solid ground, he heard pieces of dirt falling into the new stream bed. The last step off Clem's porch was twelve feet deep. Climbing over the railing, Royal stood on the porch and tried to visualize the destruction in front of him. Only daylight would reveal the extent of the demolishment.

Later that night, Lucas Boothe's dog growled as he lay beside the cabin. A noise spooked him. The next sound, *twang,* was the last he heard. An arrow hit him between the shoulders, piercing him completely. The dog crumpled in a heap.

"Nice goin', Willis," Curly whispered. He was impressed. "Where in the hell did you learn to shoot like that?"

"Indian territory," he replied with pride. "My father served as an agent. My growin'-up pals was all Injuns. They was good for somethin'."

"Ya," chuckled Curly. "Shootin' dogs."

Willis bristled at the jest. "Got a better way?" He rubbed his broken nose and breathed deeply through his mouth.

"Slack off, Willis. We're too close to mess this. You know what to do?" Curly was burdened, although they had hashed over the plan a half-dozen times.

"Yep" was Willis's lukewarm response.

"Give me ten minutes. Then torch 'em."

Willis nodded as Curly disappeared into the night. He had four arrows ready. He had covered the shaft behind the arrowhead on each with pine tar and straw. The straw was secured with strips of cloth. In the bottom of the draw that paralleled the cabin, Willis kindled a small fire out of dry grass and scrub twigs. He poured a mixture of kerosene and coal oil onto the pile and lit it. The fire flared brightly, then died to low flames. A few twigs would keep the fire burning. Sidestepping up the bank of the draw, he took a final look at the barns.

The hay barn was a mere fifty yards away. Both doors of the loft were wide open. He could hit that blindfolded. The other barn was thirty yards farther downhill. Its open doors would be an easy target too.

Returning to the fire, Willis poured the mixture over the straw and rags, soaking them thoroughly. He touched two arrows to the fire. *Poof!* Both burst into flames. Scampering up the bank, he set one arrow on the dirt and notched the other. Then he drew back smoothly and loosed the arrow. His shootin' eye didn't fail him. The burning arrow disappeared with a fading glow into the open loft of the main barn. Forthright, the second arrow was in the loft of the smaller barn. Yellowish red flames illuminated the interiors of both buildings.

The straw, tinder dry since the first cutting, exploded into flames. With the speed of a wind-whipped prairie fire, the barns were engulfed. Willis couldn't resist the temptation to fire the cabin. He slid off the bank and quickly lit the other arrows. Shooting from the rim of the draw, he watched as the third arrow sailed clear of the cabin and missed the cedar-shake roof by inches. The fourth arrow was a mite puny. It clipped the porch overhang and lodged in the cabin door. Within a half minute, the door was partially cracked, then slammed shut. Seconds later, a cloth-wrapped hand emerged from the door and snapped off the flaming shaft. It hurled the arrow to the ground, and the door banged shut.

Willis waited for the door to reopen. Nothing happened. Impatiently, he stood and pushed his hat back. His hand reflected an orange tint. At first he thought it was from the burning barns, but then he realized the glow was coming from behind. A glance showed that the small fire had flared and ignited a clump of dried grass. It'll burnt out shortly, he thought.

Perchance Willis saw the muzzle flash from the hillside behind the cabin. If he did it was too late. Lucas Boothe shot him through the chest with his Mississippi .58 rifle. Willis was swept from the rim and landed flat on his back in the draw. The small fire he had kindled now licked at his clothing.

Shots rang out from the pasture of the Boothe ranch. The cattle, on their feet as a result of the fires, now stampeded. Curly pushed them toward the lower fence and ravine. His shots were at the cattle. He killed or wounded six with his first loaded pistol. The following six shots from a second pistol were on the mark. In full flight, the cattle slashed through the bob-wire fence like a runaway locomotive. Many of the panicked critters plunged into the boulder-strewn bed of Hardscrabble Wash. Others plowed into the thick tangled underbrush. Cattle were scattered to all four points of the compass.

Lucas and Sarah watched as their barns collapsed. Swirling spirals of cherry red sparks lighted the dark sky. The Boothes' dreams went up with the smoke.

Of Lucas's sixty head of prime beef, twelve were shot dead or were dying from wounds inflicted by Curly. Sixteen more were gone from the plunge into Hardscrabble Wash. Four died from injuries in the underbrush. Eight head had been so badly cut in the bob wire that Lucas had to shoot them. That made forty known dead. The next day, range riders from the H bar C rounded up fifteen strays on their range. They were rebranded so quickly, they hadn't had time to recuperate from their run of the night before. Lucas had five head left, huddled in a tight cluster in a corner of the pasture.

"Hello the house!" The call startled Lucas. He reached for his rifle out of habit. The rider reined his horse next to the fence and awaited a reply. Lucas squinted through the early morning haze and recognized Royal. He bade Royal to the cabin and set the rifle next to the door. Royal nudged his mare forward through the main gate, halted at the hitching post, and slid out of the saddle. He did not bother to tie the horse—he knew she wouldn't spook but would wait for him to come and get her.

"Had a fire"—Royal coughed on the smoke—"last night?"

"You might say that" was the frosty reply.

Royal surveyed the smoldering ashes. "Seems like natural disasters were the order of business last night."

"This wasn't no natural disaster"—another blunt answer from Lucas.

After several seconds of awkward silence, Royal spoke again.

"The Dowdens had a slight flood last night. They're hurtin' bad."

Sarah opened the cabin door with her hip and eased out onto the porch. She carried a tray with fresh biscuits and hot coffee.

"Oh—Royal." She too was startled. "I didn't hear you ride up."

She placed the tray on the table next to Lucas. Then she turned her back to Royal and wiped tears from her eyes. Royal walked to her and attempted to hug her, but Sarah's bulging waistline prevented it. They both laughed at the failed effort. He finally hugged her sidesaddle. Sarah buried her face against his chest and let out more of her emotions. Deep racking sobs shook her solid frame. Royal held tight, trying to soothe her.

"Royal, don't look at me," she complained. "I'm a mess." She tried to pull away, but Royal wouldn't let her.

"It's of no concern." Royal reassured her. "We'll beat 'em. It'll take time, but by damn, we'll do it." Moments later, Sarah's crying ceased and she gently pushed away from him.

"I'll fetch another cup and some butter" was her excuse to make an exit.

Lucas motioned Royal to a chair. He poured coffee and offered a biscuit. Sarah reappeared and sat down near Lucas. She squeezed his hand tenderly. He winked in return. Nothing was said during this shared moment.

"We won't quit, Royal," Lucas stated defiantly. His mind was set. "A lifetime of work has gone into this ranch. I'll be go to hell if they force me out of business."

"Keep fighting," Royal commented sympathetically. "Too much love and caring in this spread to throw away."

They sat and enjoyed the remaining pleasures quietly. Royal smiled as he looked to Sarah. She had balanced a cup and biscuit on her tummy. Soon the Boothes were talking about rebuilding their barns and buying replacement cattle. Royal was a patient listener.

"I have something to ask of you, Lucas. May I borrow your buckboard?" Royal was skittish about begging a favor so soon, but he needed the wagon badly.

"Sure can." Lucas brushed off the request. "At least it wasn't burned to ashes last night. When do you need it?"

"Later this afternoon. I have a body to drop by the sheriff's office," Royal explained.

"You got one too?" Lucas's face brightened up. His interest was immediately aroused.

"Lucas, Sarah." Royal was deadly serious. "Clem's reservoir was dynamited last night. Everything that didn't wash away was flooded. Every acre of his field is under a foot of mud. I found a fellow jammed against some cottonwoods at the far end of the spread. Don't think he just happened by."

"The whole farm?" Sarah asked in anguish.

"Not entirely," Royal added with a touch of humor. "You need a ladder to get off the front porch, but at least the cabin was spared."

"Why was this done to us, Royal?" Heartbreak touched Sarah's face as she searched his for an answer. "It makes no sense."

"Hush, Sarah." Lucas softly chastised her. "We've been over this already."

"Lucas, I know why you and Clem stand against the Improvement Commission, and I know how vehemently opposed you are to that crooked bunch in town. What's the connection?" Royal pounded his fist into his hand. "We need proof. Something solid to go on."

"Proof you want. Proof you got!" Lucas replied confidently. "You know who I found in the draw?" Lucas paused, teasing Royal with suspense. "Mr. Hammond Colburn's private bodyguard. None other than Willis Clampett. He's slightly well done. Seems that he fell into his own fire. But you can recognize him." Lucas grinned like a possum.

"We can't prove that he wasn't acting on his own."

"Damn. Hadn't thought of that." Lucas's face dropped. His trump undercut, he grew pensive. "What strikes me odd is that he had a hundred dollars stuck in his pocket. Ten double eagles. A payoff?"

"Sounds like one to me." Royal supported Lucas's suggestion.

"Describe your dead man to me," Lucas asked. "I suspect I can give him a name."

"It'll be tough." Royal hesitated. "He was pretty beat up. I'd say five feet ten, medium build. Lean, no fat." Royal grimly recalled the man's characteristics. He used his hands in the description. "Sandy hair and a moustache."

"Sounds like that fella who hangs around with Curly.

Dolph? No, not him." Lucas was stumped. "Hell, I can't recall his name. Bitts, Betts. Aha!" Lucas became wrought with excitement. "George Petts. That's him! You met him last week in my store. He's the one you hit in the back with the ax handle."

"You're dead right, old man." Royal knew him immediately. "Also met him in Clem's kitchen. He tried his level best to kill me with a butcher knife."

"This could be a most difficult situation for the new sheriff to explain." Lucas took heart from Curly's predicament.

That afternoon, Royal drove the buckboard into town. Two blanket-wrapped bodies kept him company. Weren't much for conversation, though. Acting upon Lucas's suggestion, Royal rummaged through George Petts's pockets and found seven double eagles. The idea of a payoff looked better all the time. Lucas rode into town and broke the news to the Dowdens about their ranch. The Boothes minded the hotel while Clem and Libby hurried home to confront the ruins. The closest fields to the reservoir were boulder strewn, with uprooted tree trunks jutting grotesquely through the devastated landscape. The lower fields were as smooth as Doc Shu's head. Stubble cornstalks stood in three feet of soupy mud.

Royal eased the buckboard next to a feed shed in the alley. He was directly behind the jail. From previous conversations with Doc Shu, he knew that Curly made an early evening round at six o'clock. Kicking his feet onto the boot, Royal waited for the sheriff. Right on schedule, Curly stepped from the porch and headed down the boardwalk. Five minutes passed. Royal flicked the reins of the team, nudged them up the alley, and stopped shy of the street. With the brake set and the reins looped over the lever, Royal hopped from the buckboard and checked the street. Clear. He hustled to the wagon and pulled one of the bodies upright. Then he dipped his shoulder and hefted the body onto his back. Staggering under the weight, he walked to the porch. *Thud!* He dumped the dead man onto the porch. A repeat performance, and Curly had two bodies on his front step.

Royal put a foot onto the wheel hub, grabbed the side of the wagon, and pulled himself into the seat. A quick kick with his foot released the brake. He snapped the reins, and the team was in motion. With his collar turned up and his Stetson pulled low,

Royal entered the street, drove away from the business district, and headed out of town.

Thirty minutes later, Royal hid the team in the thick underbrush along the Puerco River. With a leafy branch, he obliterated the wagon tracks and hoofprints. He unhitched the mare from the rigging. Now that she was no longer a team horse, she was playful and wanted to run. Royal stepped into the saddle and let her fly. Lucas would recover the buckboard later. Now Royal rode for Doc Shu's store.

"Royal, I'm not certain if that was a smart move or not." Doc Shu pondered as doubt lines creased his forehead. "We probably should have buried 'em and been done with it."

"It'll give Curly something to worry about." Royal was smug about his delivery.

"Sure will—on how to get even with you. That man don't take lightly to being made a fool of," Doc Shu warned Royal.

"What's done is done, Doc." Royal accepted his decision. "I want some more information on George Petts. I don't recall the name of the other fella."

"Willis Clampett. A four-flusher from Texas. Waco, to be exact. Horse thief and a confidence man to boot." Doc Shu gave the rundown on him.

"I still have friends in the law business." Royal reflected back on some long-standing friendships. "I'm going to dig up some facts on George Petts. Maybe now is the time to pay Elihu Jones a visit and find his real worth. What do you say, old man?"

The doc wanted to even the score with that crooked telegrapher. "Good a time as any to smoke him out."

"Evenin', Elihu," Royal whispered to the telegrapher as he slipped inside the small office. It was 10:30 P.M. The young man looked up, a shocked expression warping his face.

"Roy—Roya—Royal!" he stuttered in disbelief. "Uh, how are you? Been a long time since we've seen you in these parts. All mended?" The clerk was flustered and talked off the top of his head.

"I'm fine. Yes, it's been a while. I'm well, thank you." Royal answered all three questions in one breath. "I need some information, Elihu."

"All right" was the guarded reply. "How can I help?"

"Do you know what happened to those telegrams Doc Shu sent me? I never received a one," he complained with token distress, staring hard at the clerk.

The clerk balked for several thorny seconds. "I sure don't. They were sent! I've got the receipts on file—time, date, destination, and who sent them." He was confident in his answer. He knew he was covered.

"Glad to hear it," Royal assured him. "You have a few minutes to spare? I have a couple of telegrams that must go out—tonight, if possible." It was more a statement than a plea. Royal reached for them in his pocket.

"Golly, Royal, I'd love to, but"—a quick, evasive answer—"the other end might be signed off."

"Go ahead, Elihu. Ring him up," Royal encouraged. "It won't take more than a second."

The clerk realized he was caught and acquiesced sullenly. With creeping dread, he set himself at the key. The code went out smoothly. Then the staccato reply flashed back. "Let me have 'em. I'll send 'em now."

"Thanks, Elihu. I appreciate your effort." Royal smiled warmly. "You go ahead. I'll do some quick work on the corner desk."

Elihu read the telegrams as Royal walked to the small slant-top desk. With one eye on the door, Royal readied himself to copy down every letter that Elihu sent and received.

As expected, the first telegram Elihu sent was not the message Royal had handed him.

```
h/c yrlng sale. salina sat am. hi bid.
21cnts hoof. 2000 head 4 sale. delv 11-12.
advs chas. w. rsvp soonst. ej
```

The reply from Watesville clicked over the wire.

```
will do. reply wthn 24 hrs top $. chas. w
regds. ww
```

Elihu glanced at Royal and breathed a sigh of relief. His back was turned, and he continued the paper work. Elihu faltered at sending his second message. "The hell with it," he mumbled under his breath. "I've proven my worth." The message he typed read:

advs chas w. info now 80-20%. ej

Minutes later, the reply came from Watesville.

cautn advsd. good luck. ww

Elihu felt confident. He had informed Mr. Charles Wiggins that the price of inside information had just increased by ten percent.

Charlie Wiggins, armed with the information provided by Elihu, would outbid his competition at cattle auctions and resell the livestock for a handsome profit. Once again, Elihu scanned the telegrams Royal wanted sent. Colburn would pay well for the information in these telegrams.

Royal leisurely approached the desk. "How's your ranch doing?"

Elihu was surprised by the question but answered calmly. "Fine." Then doubts began to surface within Elihu.

"Good calf crop this year?" Royal looked him in the eye.

Elihu was scared. Sweat dampened his armpits. "Not bad." He was reluctant to volunteer more information.

Royal took note of the underdetermined reply. He kept the pressure on. "Grass lookin' good?" He quizzed the clerk.

He's getting at something. What? Elihu wondered.

"Want to lose your ranch, Elihu?" Royal tossed the question.

"Lose it?" The suggestion was an affront. "It won't happen. It's mine. Too much work has gone into the spread. I intend to be buried there."

"I like a man who sticks to the land." Royal smiled. "A man with roots." Then Royal turned serious, and the forced smile vanished in a flash. "You probably will be buried on your land, Elihu. Maybe as soon as next week, when Charlie Wiggins settles down enough to have you killed. Ham know you're selling inside information to his main competitor? He'd slit your throat if he did." Royal laughed. "Maybe together the two of them will bury you on your ranch."

Caught! What would the price be? The ranch? The cattle?

Maybe the bank account? Elihu's mind raced. He mustered enough courage to speak. "I was—"

"Shut up!" Royal's yell cut him off. "Don't you say a word until I'm finished. Understand?" Royal jabbed him painfully on the chest with his index finger. "I know why none of Doc Shu's telegrams were delivered. You never sent them. Right?" A meek nod was the clerk's reply. "I have an idea how long you have been messing with the system. But this bullshit stops right now. You got it?" Royal demanded an answer from the terrified man. Elihu opened his mouth. Royal pressed his finger against Elihu's lips, preventing him from speaking. "Not a word, remember," Royal hissed at him.

Elihu looked at Royal with wide, fearful eyes. His knees buckled, and he headed for the floor. Royal broke the fall and plopped him back into a chair. The clerk slumped forward, sitting motionless in front of his key. Royal filled his hand with water from the desk pitcher and slapped Elihu's face. He squatted beside the revived telegrapher and threatened him. "I'll say this only one time, you craven sneak: Send my telegrams out letter perfect. Got it? And if word of these telegrams gets back to Curly or Colburn, I'll personally haul your worthless carcass all the way to Santa Fe. We'll talk to the federal judge there."

Elihu was silent. Wisely, he elected not to speak.

Royal headed for the door. There he stopped, turned, and warned Elihu, "Remember, you don't need to worry about your ranch if you stay straight. If not, you'll be an old man by the time you get out of prison."

Elihu sat becrippled. His destiny had once again changed hands. He had no more control this time than last. Royal returned to the counter. "I want answers to those telegrams. Give them to Doc Shu. No one else. Understand?"

"I'll have replies by tomorrow at the latest," Elihu answered to defuse Royal.

"You better hope I hear by then," Royal threatened. "You haven't seen me or know where I am. Got it?"

Royal stayed at the Dowden ranch. This ranch was special to him—he had stayed here when he had first hired on with Sheriff Tibbetts. For the present, he was purposely keeping clear of Jacob's Well. Trying to salvage what remained of Clem's ranch kept him busy. But the repairs were only symbolic. No amount of work could reclaim the land, although Clem said he could plant corn next spring in the lower fields. The flood waters had carried tons of rich soil downstream. The major expense would be seed. Clem had lost all his planting seed when the waters demolished his sheds. The hay fields were a total loss. They would have to be planted with ground cover to keep wind and soil erosion to a minimum.

Resting on the porch, Royal watched as Clem punished his team in a mad dash for the cabin. He wasn't being chased, but he was puttin' the leather to the horses. They stumbled and nearly went down on that sorry excuse of a new road, and Clem was almost thrown out of the wildly bouncing buckboard. He finished the last fifty yards with a single rein in hand. Using his good hand, he yanked the team to a skidding halt. Out of the seat with a quick leap, he two-stepped the newly hewn log stairs to the cabin porch.

"Boy, have we got trouble, big trouble." He addressed Royal in passing as he banged open the cabin door.

"Let me guess," Royal joked from the porch. "Curly's been elected mayor."

"Damn it, Royal!" Clem yelled. "Get serious." He went directly to the corner cabinet and plucked a bottle and two glasses from the shelf. Back on the porch, his hand shook as he poured drinks.

"To your health, my friend. You'll need it." Clem didn't see whether Royal raised his drink or not. He had downed his own in one gulp.

"My health?" Royal shrugged and knocked back his whiskey. He intercepted Clem's hand as he poured another drink. "Easy now. Let's not get out of control."

"Out of control?" he scoffed. "I'm the only damned one who's in control. Everything else has gone straight to hell." Clem was agitated, and his bluster compounded the problem.

"Take it easy, Clem." Royal calmed him. "Tell me what's goin' on."

"Remember our discussion about burying those two thugs?" Clem got a nod from Royal. "Your luck has taken an ill turn. Curly has a wanted poster—oh, wait." He cut short his sentence and fumbled through his pockets in search of the paper. On the second go-round, he pulled it out and handed it to Royal.

WANTED

DEAD OR ALIVE

ROYAL BALLOU
for the murder of George Petts and Willis Clampett.
$250.00 REWARD
Considered Armed and Dangerous
Contact Sheriff Rutherford Hall, Jacob's Well.

Royal, unwarned, was silenced. For a long minute he sat and reread the poster. Fear gnawed his gut, and a hot flash of embarrassment warmed him. How could he have been so boneheaded?

"Goddlemighty, Clem," Royal moaned in disbelief, "did I ever step into a cow pie on this one!"

"We both did" was Clem's acid comment. "The question is, how do we step out of it?"

"I honestly don't know, Clem. I've never been on the left-hand side of the law here before. $250 dollars—that's cheap." Royal forced a laugh.

Clem ignored the joke. "I'll tell you one thing, lad. We were wrongheaded with Curly."

"I'll drink to that." Royal poured another.

"Curly claims both men were shot. That you buried one and tried to burn the other one."

"Both shot? Any damned fool knows that isn't true," Royal defended himself. "The one I found was drowned like a rat. Yours had the bullet hole."

"They both been shot." Clem reported the facts as Curly stated them. "Want to venture a guess as to caliber and type of rifle?"

A crystal-clear flashback: Royal's Pennsylvania rifle in the sheriff's office. The fancy brass butt plate with the initials RB engraved on it.

Royal fully realized his misjudgment. "Oh, Clem. Shoot me right now between the eyes. Put me out of my misery."

"Don't tempt me, boy. I've given it serious thought. Where in the hell did he get your rifle?"

"The day I came back from Santa Fe, I tried to buy it from Curly. He wouldn't budge and threw me out of the office."

"We're in a box canyon now, Royal. Our best efforts brought to naught."

CHAPTER
5

Ellery Albee, the mayor of Jacob's Well, was meeting with his councilmen, Lem Tilden, Hervey Brown, and Asa Hemmingway, to talk shop in the back room of The Rose. Their twice-a-month business meeting dealt with monies received from the tables, the bar, and the girls. Any outsider's impression of this collection of reputable businessmen would have been favorable. After all, they were leaders in the community. In truth, power and corruption were alive and well in that room.

The routine entry of Hammond Colburn, preceded by his new body guard, Dolph Stickney, brought the gab session to an abrupt halt. The loyal court all rose to greet the king—like Johnny-jump-ups after a summer shower, Albee thought bitterly. As he struggled to heft his bulky frame, he realized he was no different from the others.

Colburn brought with him an added surprise: Curly. The sheriff strode boldly into the room. A confident bastard, mused the mayor.

"Please, gentlemen"—Colburn motioned to them—"be seated." He smiled at the council, pulled up a chair, and sat at the poker table. He measured each individual with a hard look. As joint owners of the saloon, their common interests were strictly monetary. "Let's get down to business. Asa, an accounting to date, please." Colburn made himself as comfortable as his busted hip would allow.

Asa, the meat market owner, was a wisp of a man. He fetched a folded paper from his coat pocket and presented his report with precise detail. Colburn's power intimidated him. The memory of the cattle poisoning was fresh in his mind. Beneath his henpecked appearance, Asa was a weasel—clever and greedy. As he spoke in the stifling room, his familiar meaty smell grew slightly pungent.

"Ham, for the two weeks since our last meeting, the saloon's combined earnings were exactly eight hundred and forty three dollars." Asa droned on with facts and figures. Each of the men let his mind wander and paid scant attention.

"Can't we get a better return on the ladies?" Colburn expected more from them.

"It's hard work, Ham. The girls don't last long." Asa smiled at his comment.

"You mean they get wore out?" Colburn volunteered. The men laughed at the joke. "Thanks for the figures, Asa. With a five-way split, we pocket one hundred sixty-eight dollars each. Correct, Asa?" Colburn had a way with numbers—he had done the division in his head.

Asa hurriedly worked the numbers on a scratch pad. "Not a bad profit for two weeks' work." Asa was delighted with the revenue and smiled at his business partners.

"Ham, it will get better," Hervey commented, up beat, as he blew a series of smoke rings toward the ceiling. "Trail crews are here, with more arriving every day."

"Downtown business brisk?" Colburn looked at Lem and Asa. They nodded. Colburn rubbed his hands together. "Excellent. Since we're on the topic of downtown business, Curly will enlighten us on the success of the Improvement Commission."

The sheriff reached into his shirt pocket and plucked out a slip of paper. He took his time as the businessmen anticipated the report. He cleared his throat. "I'm proud to say that roughly seventy-five percent of the businesses have voluntarily joined our organization." Voluntarily my ass, thought Asa. With a gun to their heads, is more like it.

"Does anyone have any concerns about the Improvement Commission's membership drive?" Colburn looked around the table. No one spoke. "If there are no further questions . . ." Colburn paused and waited. In other words, the subject was dropped. "I have some news concerning our late deputy sheriff. Curly, please escort Judge Williams in."

The judge, a tired old man, tottered into the room and slumped into the first empty chair. He measured his every word and presented each statement with a lawyer's caution and legalese. "Concerning the warrants issued last month—"

"Last week, Your Honor," Colburn corrected.

"Ah, yes, last week. Concerning the untimely deaths of Mr. Betts and Mr. Clampett."

"Petts, Your Honor," Colburn corrected again.

"Thank you, Mr. Colburn." The judge slurred his words. "I must reluctantly inform you that we are no closer to an arrest now than we were at the time of issuance."

"Please, Your Honor. Permit me to explain. If you gentlemen are not aware, two days past, Judge Williams issued arrest warrants on Royal Ballou. Double murder." A wicked grin slashed Colburn's face as he spoke. "For the murder of George Petts and Willis Clampett. He is wanted, dead or alive." A stir of excitement circled the table. The thought of having free rein in the town was cause to celebrate.

Curly spoke next. "There are over a hundred wanted posters territorywide. Mr. Ballou is living on borrowed time. The bounty hunters will be on his trail real soon." A look of satisfaction rested on Curly.

"That's all I have." Colburn nodded and stood. The councilmen followed suit. Dolph headed for the door, with Colburn on his heels, and Curly brought up the rear.

As Colburn and Curly sauntered down the boardwalk, Colburn talked business. "What about the businesses who haven't contributed yet?"

"Don't know, Ham. There are three we can't break—Lucas Boothe, Clem Dowden, and that old medicine man. He continually bad-mouths us." Curly was clearly aggravated with Doc Shu. "I'd like to thump his head—maybe it would change his mind."

"Well, lean on them a little more," Colburn instructed the sheriff. "That account in the bank will look real sweet in a year's time. Maybe we won't have so many splits. You understand what I mean?" Ham's conspiratorial nature surfaced momentarily.

"Nice talkin' with you, Ham." Curly was all smiles as the two parted company.

It was long after midnight when Dolph, the last of Curly's territorial prison friends, dawdled down the boardwalk. He made little noise as he stepped deep into the shadows. Across from Clem's hotel, Dolph stopped and tugged a slingshot from his hip pocket. He fished two rounded river rocks from his shirt and cupped one of them in the leather pouch. He checked both directions on the street—it was graveyard quiet. He pulled back and loosed the first rock. *Crack!* One of the plate-glass windows collapsed in a cascade of broken glass. The second rock shattered the other. Dolph stuck the slingshot back into his pocket and walked into the alley. A lantern flickered in the lobby of the hotel.

Dolph cut behind the stores and quietly approached the rear of Boothe's Saddlery and Gun Shop. On the dock were two half-kegs of lead. Lucas had his gun shop in the basement. There he melted down the lead and cast bullets from it. Dolph muscled one barrel onto its side. He sat down, braced against the second barrel, and scrunched his feet up against the keg. Turning and aligning the keg with his feet, Dolph violently kicked his legs straight. The two-hundred-pound keg lumbered across the dock and hit the bottom panel of the back door. The keg shattered the door with a loud crash, took out the stair railing, and plunged to the basement floor. It self-destructed on impact, lead flying in all directions. The second keg rumbled after the first but brought the doorframe along with it. As Dolph walked away, a candle was lighted inside the back of the shop. Its light shone through the gaping hole that used to be the back door. Dolph congratulated himself. *"Keep the pressure on"*—those had been Curly's words.

Curly waited until the next day to approach Doc Shu. The sheriff knew he would have his hands full if he didn't finesse the old coot. Doc Shu had threatened to shoot Curly if he ever set foot inside his business establishment. Curly vowed he wouldn't let the doctor rile him.

The sheriff climbed the boardwalk steps and walked into the doc's store. He feared no man, but the doc unsettled him.

"Mornin', Doc." Sore against his will, Curly greeted the man as he shut the door.

The doc, busy behind the counter, partially raised his head and surveyed Curly through the half-spectacles. "It was," he rudely replied. He never took his eyes off the sheriff.

Curly let the insult pass and walked to the counter. He rested his beefy forearm on the smooth oak top and tried to reason with Doc Shu. "We're butting heads, old man. Why don't you get off your high horse and talk sense? I'm easy to get along with."

"Listen to me, sonny boy," the doc shot back. "I've seen the likes of you everywhere I've been. A dime-a-dozen gunfighter. Sheriff. Lawman. Ha." He laughed contemptuously. "Your kind is an insult to those very words. When I think back on the man you murdered in cold blood, I want—I want to puke. Then I want to shoot you on sight. Get out of here, *now!*" The venomous words had spilled from the doc's mouth. He was shaking, trying to control himself, the veins in his shiny dome bulged.

"Calm yourself," Curly implored. "I'm trying to get along with you."

"You can get along with me," Doc stated boldly. "Right along out the front door. Don't let it hit you in the butt on your way out."

"Why, you moth-eaten old reprobate!" Curly uttered viciously as he grabbed for Shubael. The doctor had anticipated Curly's move and stepped back out of harm's way. As he leaned away from Curly's pawing mitt, he reached for the pistol he kept in the drawer of his counter.

Curly, desperate, knew the old man would shoot him. He grabbed the first object at hand and hurled it at the doc. The heavy, leather-bound medical reference book struck Doc Shu in the upper chest, with a punishing blow that staggered him back into the shelves of medical supplies. He cracked his head on the corner of a shelf and was knocked out colder than a January morn in Colorado. As he fell to the floor, he dragged half a dozen shelves of patent medicine and cure-alls down with him.

Curly cursed himself for losing his temper but felt the move justified. That mule-headed medicine man had been trying to kill him. Curly stood on tiptoes and looked over the counter at the crumpled figure lying on the floor. The stench from the numerous broken bottles was overpowering. Curly's eyes smarted and watered. He fled the store and headed for The Rose. He needed a drink to settle his shakes.

The sound of approaching horses startled Royal and Clem. Royal was setting posts for the new corral while Clem was pestering him. Clem's hand was on the mend but not yet usable; out of habit he went for his rifle at the sound and cradled it on his arm.

Stepping onto the porch of the cabin, they spotted two riders headed their way. The horses fought the rough rubble-strewn road. They easily identified Libby Dowden as the lead rider, but the second rider was a mystery. The woman had a large-brimmed hat tied securely with a silk scarf, the ends tucked in around her face. Neither Clem nor Royal could identify her. Clem eagle-eyed Libby as she approached, then turned and went inside the cabin. Clem knew his wife was outraged. Royal could hear him pour one drink and then another. Clem exited the cabin, shot glass in hand, and headed for the corral. Libby rode by the cabin and dismounted at the corral fence. She stormed angrily toward Clem. Royal hopped off the porch and trotted toward the Dowdens. He took the horse's reins, ducked under the neck of Libby's Morgan, and bumped into the other lady.

" 'Scuse me, ma'am," he mumbled, and stepped aside.

"Royal!" Abbie shrieked, and threw herself at him with open arms.

Royal caught her lunge and hugged her tightly. They held each other for a long time. Then Royal drew back. "Look at you, little lady." He grinned as he admired her. John Tibbetts had called her that since he first set eyes on her.

"Mercy sakes, Royal. I've missed you." She traced his cheek with a fingertip. "Not having you around at the sheriff's of-fice . . ." The talk died. Royal reached for her and tried to stop the silent tears with his fingers. It didn't work. Abbie failed to keep her composure and buried her face in her hands. Royal pulled her to his chest and let her cry. Abbie trembled in his arms. He stroked her long hair, holding her gently. Clem and Libby had retreated into the cabin.

Minutes later, as the sobs subsided, she tried to dry her eyes. "I look a sight. I'm sorry. I got your shirt all wet." She daubed at Royal's chest with her handkerchief.

"A pretty sight, I might add." He smiled at her. "I apologize for not coming to see you at the hotel. As you well know, things have gone to hell around here."

"Yes, Libby told me. We sure are in a pickle." She lovingly circled his waist with her arms.

"Hey there, young 'uns," Libby hailed them from the porch. "Come up here and settle in. I'll whip up something to eat."

Libby went inside the cabin, with Clem following close be-hind. As Abbie and Royal topped the stairs, Clem darted out the door and slammed it shut behind him. *Thud!* A cast-iron skillet bounced off the door, then clattered to the floor.

"Curly's really done it this time," Clem offered.

"Damn that transgressor, Lord! Curses on that miscreant!" Libby hollered at the top of her lungs. Her voice carried through the walls. Clem cracked the door as she looked sky-ward. Guilt etched her face as she talked to her unseen protec-tor. "Beggin' your pardon, Lord. I had a spell of temper."

"What's all that about?" Royal whispered as he hid behind Clem.

"Ask Abbie." He motioned with his thumb. "She's smack dab in the middle of it." Clem slipped inside to try to defuse Libby as he talked.

"Let's walk. Do you want to?" Royal reached for Abbie.

"I'd love it. I used to spend many an hour on the dam watch-ing the fish jump." She took his hand and walked beside him. Abbie looked winsome. She remembered growing up in Sedalia, Missouri, when it had been a sprawling, exciting cow town. She'd lived with her Aunt Sally and Uncle Jim after her father pulled up stakes and left. Missouri hadn't been kind to her father. He'd lost two sons in a riverboat fire. Ten months later, scarlet fever claimed his wife. His hollow promise to return for Abbie had been exactly that—hollow. She had written and re-ceived letters from him over the years, but the close bond had faded.

Her childhood under the firm but fair thumb of Aunt Sally had been an adventure. The school friends, outings, horseback riding, and parties gave her much to joyfully recall. Sedalia had grown in size, and Abbie had adapted well but longed for days gone by, days when she could ride from dawn till dusk and never see another person, afternoons of swimming in the cool river, of knowing only solitude.

Her aunt and uncle had urged her through a finishing school, all the while secretly grooming her for a "nice young man." Abbie would have nothing to do with it. As a matter of fact, she'd run the prospective bridegroom off the property. Put out and at wit's end, Uncle Jim had contacted his old medical school friend, Shubael Cates. Shubael had agreed to help cure Abbie of her foolishness. He had brought her to Jacob's Well two years before. Abbie had liked the people in town and stayed.

The two crisscrossed the hillside, avoiding the deep, freshly carved gully, and reached the hard-packed top of the dam. A shallow pool was all that remained of the once-full reservoir.

"What are you smack dab in the middle of?" Royal asked innocently.

"Oh, nothing really." Abbie dismissed the question as she sat on the edge of the dam.

Royal was silent. It was obvious that Abbie didn't want to discuss it.

His small talk put him in trouble. "Libby thought it was important. She was swole up like a bullfrog." He laughed. "That's as mad as I've seen her in a long spell."

"Royal, please," she begged. Her tone cut short further discussion.

Royal sat quietly beside her, aimlessly throwing pebbles off the face of the dam. Suddenly he stopped, his arm frozen in midair. He scrambled to his feet, motioned Abbie to stay put, and slid down the loose dirt bank. Testing the edge of what had once been the spillway, he knelt slowly. Belly on the ground, Royal extended his arm and tenderly tugged on a dynamite fuse. The bundled charge came loose. With the gentle touch of a midwife, he carried the charge to the top of the dam and set it on the ground.

"A dastardly gift from George Petts," he told Abbie. "May he rest in hell."

"What are you talking about?"

"The blackguard who blew up this dam." He tapped his foot on the ground. "He got caught somehow and drowned. I found him over by the cottonwoods."

"I see," Abbie added. "He's one of the presents you left for Curly."

"Oh, that hurts." He chastened himself lightly. "The move that backfired completely in my face." They both smiled at the mistake.

"I'm thankful this charge didn't go off. It would have busted the dam at ground level. Then the whole ranch would have been lost," Royal explained to Abbie.

He delicately pulled the fused blasting cap from the center stick of dynamite. With a fluid sweeping throw, he flung the cap into the rock-strewn gully. There it detonated with a sharp, crisp crack. Abbie jumped, startled by the healthy explosion.

The cabin door was jerked open, and Clem's long-barreled rifle poked out.

"You all right up there?" Clem shouted as he showed himself.

"One of Georgie boy's leftovers!" Royal waved and held the bundle of dynamite aloft.

Abbie, in low spirits, stared at the water.

"What's the problem, little lady?" Royal touched her chin.

She smiled at the endearment, then turned to face him. "Royal, I owe you an apology."

"An apology? What for?"

He watched Abbie. She was a good-looking young woman of twenty years. She was tall, with none of the plain and rugged boniness that seemed a mask of survival in most of the women hereabouts. She was whole, and bloomed with vigor. Her brown hair was braided in a thick tail that fell near upon the sway of her back. Her green eyes sparkled, despite having seen some of life's cruelties. A flowered cotton blouse and three-quarter-length riding skirt outlined her slender figure. But any idea of a frail and helpless woman was quickly dispelled by her carriage. Abbie was resolute, self-willed. A full-lipped smile graced her wide but feminine face.

She snapped Royal out of his daydreaming. "I owe you an apology for not telling you why Libby is furious with the sheriff. Curly started a rumor that I was working in The Dusty Rose Saloon."

"Doing what?" Royal asked in complete surprise.

"You know." She shrugged, slightly embarrassed. "One of the bar ladies."

"Why, I've never heard a dumber untruth!" Royal retorted, shaking his head in disbelief.

"I know, but several of the matrons in town are lending credence to his lie."

"Would I be mistaken if I mentioned the honorable Mrs. Albee and several of her petrified friends?" Royal looked at her with eyebrows raised.

"How do you know so much?" she asked, surprised at his insight.

"I've worked around those old hens for the past two years. If you ever want to see the power behind our town government, attend one of Mrs. Albee's teas. But you don't seem terribly put out by Curly's lie."

"It's lip wisdom," she commented. "Besides, what can I do?"

"You've got a point. It's not worth the aggravation."

"Well, I'll be out of the gossip now." She looked relieved. "Libby thinks it best I stay here for a spell. Let the rumors die a natural death."

Royal felt a race of excitement. Abbie was pure joy, and he delighted in her company.

"You don't think we'll start our own gossip out here, do you?" She met his eyes and and held them. Royal blushed and turned away. Abbie laughed playfully at him.

The cabin door opened, and Libby stepped outside, shading her eyes against the setting sun. She yelled at them, her voice booming off the hillside, "Come on down! I've outdone myself for supper!"

Royal stood and helped Abbie to her feet. Then he leaned over and lifted the dynamite off the ground. Together they walked toward the cabin.

CHAPTER
6

Royal and Abbie rode through the cedars that speckled the base of the cliffs. The fresh, sweet smell rekindled a deep appreciation for the beauty around them. This was where they longed to be—away from Jacob's Well, its rumors and prattle. The dun-colored cliffs reflected a clash of red rocks and yellow tierra. The greens and grays of sage and mesquite complemented the rust color. To an outsider, this was a tawny, desolate land. But natives found charm and beauty here.

As they cut across loose scree, two does and a buck bolted in front of them. The deer bounded down the grassy hillside in long graceful leaps and disappeared into the underbrush.

"We didn't spook them, Royal," Abbie said in a soft voice.

Royal motioned her to be silent with his hand. He halted his mare and slipped out of the saddle in a single move. Surefootedly, he crept to the edge of a small rise, reached his hat off, and bellied onto the ground. Gingerly, he peered over and immediately spotted a posse of twelve men. They were spread out in a ragged picket line that covered the breadth of the valley.

The metallic *clink* of a shod horse brought Royal to his feet, in a dead run for his mare. With a half-stepping jump he mounted the mare, yanked her around, and charged headlong down the hill. Abbie was right on his heels. They rode recklessly off the grassy hillside, praying their horses kept their footing. Royal's horse nearly tumbled into a small crevasse that slashed into the slope. He turned his horse and urged her into the cut. The mare, winded from the frantic dash, was skittish as she plunged into stifle-deep water. Abbie's mare balked at the mouth and wouldn't venture into the cramped grotto. Royal leaped from his mare and plowed through the water.

He stepped behind Abbie's horse and smacked her on the rump. The horse panicked and bolted. Abbie, caught leaning the wrong way, was pitched violently out of the saddle. She landed with a loud flop in the pool of water. The mare charged past Royal and fled the creek bed, then vanished into the thick brush. Abbie surfaced, blew water from both nostrils, and choked on the water. Royal waded to her as she caught her breath.

They were on the verge of laughter when Royal's mare nickered, pointed her ears forward, and looked toward the mouth of the cut. There, astride his horse, sat Elihu Jones, rifle across his lap. He raised his rifle, cradled the butt plate against his thigh, and slowly reached into his coat pocket. After fumbling for a few seconds, he threw a folded paper onto the rocks. With a final look at them, he heeled his horse in the flanks and rode downstream.

Royal holstered his Colt .44 and breathed again. As he looked at Abbie, he could not distinguish her tears from the water that streaked her face.

"I guess you know what that paper is," she told him. Her voice was barely audible. Royal splashed to his mare, snagged the reins, and led her out of the grotto. Abbie followed. Her boots sloshed as she joined him. Before she mounted to sit behind Royal, she pocketed the paper. The five-hundred-yard ride from the cravasse mouth to the underbrush was a prolongation of time, an eternity. They waited for a shout or a rifle shot that would signal the chase.

Deep in the thick brush, Abbie unfolded the paper. It was the wanted poster.

"But, Elihu? I don't understand," Abbie questioned Royal.

"Either he's sweet on you, or—" Royal paused.

"Or what?" Abbie demanded.

"Or my talk changed his mind. Elihu is on Ham's payroll, has been for years. Let me rephrase that: Ham has Elihu over a barrel. Doc Shu and I discovered a problem with Elihu's responsibilities and duties as a telegrapher." He smiled knowingly. "We got things straightened out."

"You mean you threatened to kick his butt?" She put him on the spot.

"Put that way, yes," Royal replied.

"I'd say you're even," she offered. "What do we do now?"

"Head back to the Dowden spread." He pointed with his

head. "I'll leave you with Clem and Libby. You dry enough to ride?" His voice expressed concern.

"Do I have a choice?" she countered.

"No. Just thought I'd ask," Royal ribbed her. "Let's ride."

The return trip was tedious. Riding double slowed them considerably. And being on constant watch for the posse added an extra dimension—tension. Abbie had her hands clasped around Royal's waist. She was asleep, her head resting against his back. He placed one hand over hers, holding her securely. With his coat draped over her shoulders, she was pressed close to him. Her warmth felt good on his back. The half-full waxing moon cast the countryside in a soft, silvery light.

It was night by the time they rode into Clem's corral. "Clem!" Royal called out, leery of riding upon any cabin after dark. That was a surefire way to get shot. Abbie stirred. A shadowy figure emerged from the darkness next to the cabin.

"Hello, kids," Clem greeted them, relief in his voice. "Am I glad to see you. We was worried when Abbie's mare come home riderless."

"You didn't need to wait up," Abbie told him sleepily.

"Hell, neither one of us could sleep," Clem told her. "Libby has some fresh-baked bread and hot coffee. Come on inside."

"We had a close call with a posse, but I think we've found a friend in Elihu Jones," Royal said to Clem as he loosened the cinch and slipped the halter from the mare's head. She went into the corral and directly to the feed trough.

"I know about the posse," Clem told him. "Had a run-in with that lynch mob earlier this afternoon. I run 'em off. Told those scoundrels to come ashootin' next time, 'cause I sure as hell intended to." Royal smiled. Clem was feisty even at this ungodly hour.

Over coffee, the four discussed Royal's options. All agreed that he should make himself scarce for a spell. The cow camp cabin was an ideal place. Located in the mountains, it was out of the way and difficult to find. Everything Royal needed was there. The shelves were well stocked, wildlife was abundant, and a spring ran beside the cabin.

Clem took a sip of coffee, then joshed Libby. "Damn, woman! What you servin' here—sacred water?" He got to his feet, fetched a bottle, and returned to the table. He poured two glugs into the cup. Then he tasted the coffee. "Now, that's more like it. Good coffee, ma'am." He smiled at his partner.

Libby presented her idea. "Royal, what if you ride south, past the Harris spread, then cut back west. You would circle behind the cabin without leaving a trace."

"Good idea, Libby," Royal complimented her. "I was wondering how to get there without being seen."

Clem, now deep in thought, said nothing. Suddenly he banged the table with his fist, startling everybody. "Know how you can do it?"

Royal watched him closely, not knowing if the coffee was getting to him or if he had a solid idea. "How?" Curiosity bested him.

"Take my shoe nippers, rasp, nails, and hammer. After you get above the Harris place, travel into the foothills. Without horseshoes on that smooth sandstone, no one could follow you." Clem leaned back and sipped his coffee.

Royal smiled. He approved the idea. It might give him the time he needed. "That's the last move the posse would expect. You've got a deal, Clem. I like it. Remember Mr. Smith. I watched him lose Nogales Ned that way. Ned wrapped his horse's hooves in rags. That sneaky bandit made Mr. Smith look like a fool." They laughed at the story.

"You will also recall," Clem pointed out, "that Mr. Smith caught Ned nine months later. Superstition Mountains, I believe."

Royal nodded his head. "Nogales Ned should have known better than to shame an Apache—especially Mr. Smith."

"You ever have dealin's with that Apache, Royal?" Clem turned serious.

Royal sipped his coffee. "Yep. Long time ago, when I served with General Stoddard. We were jumped by a band of Mescalero Apaches raiding out of Old Mexico. I dug a bullet out of Mr. Smith's back." Royal leaned forward and pointed to the spot. "Ungrateful lout. Never bothered to thank me. I guess it's to be expected."

"He's a hard one. Hope I never have him tracking me," Clem said honestly.

"Me neither. That man could give you sleepless nights."

* * *

The following morning Royal left the Dowdens' and Abbie with sadness. He wanted to help Clem watch the ranch and the women. After skirting the Harris spread, Royal rode into the rolling foothills. Those undulating sandstones formations, sculpted by ceaseless winds and rains, offered him a safe haven. He understood this land and used it to his advantage.

He had made preparations on the mare. He had filed and trimmed her hooves before leaving the Dowdens'. Now, in a secluded hollow of the foothills, he pried loose and removed her shoes within fifteen minutes. He led her on foot and carefully avoided soft spots and washes. After two hours of tedious travel, Royal felt confident that he had covered his trail. The soft sandstone had not worn the mare's hooves. With a little rasp work and fine trimming, he quickly reshod her. The long ride to the mountains southwest was ahead of him.

It was late afternoon when he arrived at the camp. The cramped low, log roof gave Royal a secure feeling. He hung a chunk of beef, compliments of Clem, in a corner, covered it with cheesecloth to keep the flies off. After a meal of steak, potatoes, and corn, Royal sat in the lonely solitude of the setting sun. A chorus of coyotes serenaded him.

For two days Royal rested, fixed his gear, and fussed about the cabin. This break in the tension of the past several weeks was welcome. One evening, a change in plans brought Abbie and Clem to the cabin. Along with supplies, they brought foreboding news. While Abbie and Royal walked in the moonlight, he had her repeat the information.

"You're dead sure?" Royal asked afresh. He felt a creeping apprehension settle over him.

"Yes, positive," Abbie replied firmly. "Curly made a big hoop-de-do over it. He said Mr. Smith was the best and would have you caught within the month." Abbie looked at him with trepidation.

"He's right on one account," Royal commented, his face a mask of seriousness. The thought of Mr. Smith tracking him made Royal incredulous. "How in the hell did Curly get him to join the search? That Apache doesn't owe him a damned thing."

"Doc Shu said Colburn did some fancy talking with Colonel Miller. He's the commanding officer at Fort Buchanan. Told him how dangerous you are. The citizenry needed protection. Colonel Miller promptly volunteered Mr. Smith's services."

"Ham probably offered him horses or cattle in trade," Royal said with disgust. "That's how he works."

Abbie was as concerned about this latest development as he. "What will you do, Royal?"

"Don't rightly know. I'll tell you one thing." He was defiant. "I'm not going to sit here and wait for Mr. Smith to find me."

The next morning, after Abbie and Clem had gone, Royal set out for the northwest side of the mountain. Anyone searching for him would have to come through the Puerco River canyon. As soon as he rode clear of the pines, he sensed his blunder. He stopped and searched the boulder-strewn canyon below. Four riders were converging on the trail that led up from the canyon floor. Royal pulled back on the reins. The mare fought him momentarily, then backed into the pines. As he slacked off the reins, the mare's ears perked forward, and she looked uphill. A horse snorted off to the right in the underbrush. Royal froze. He leaned forward and covered the mare's nostrils.

"Don't you make a sound," he whispered to her.

A shot rumbled like an afternoon thunderstorm off the cliffs. Royal was pounded out of his saddle and hit the ground. He landed heavily on his side, momentarily stunned. The mare ran a short distance, then stopped. Royal tried to breathe, but pain stopped him. With short, panting breaths, he managed to fill his lungs. A soothing warmth bathed his right side as the sharp, biting pain gave way to a dull, aching throb.

Royal looked in the direction of the shot and saw a crouching figure warily approaching him. The rifleman, with slow-paced, languid movement, reloaded his rifle: powder, patched round ball, both firmly tamped down. A cap and the inevitable second shot. *Crack!* Rolling thunder once more. The force of the shot stunned Royal. His chest burned, not with a sharp stab of pain but with a slap. He didn't realized that the second shot had hit a tree branch that lay in front of him. The bullet slammed the branch into his chest but did no further damage.

Before the rifleman could come forward, he was clubbed from behind by a short, stocky figure who emerged from the fringe of the jack oak. The rifleman dropped to the ground. As

Royal gradually lost consciousness, he watched in fascination as Mr. Smith walked toward him.

The Apache dragged the rifleman to his horse and muscled him into the saddle. He leaned the man forward and tied his hands underneath the horse's neck. A portion of a cut rein looped around each foot held the man tightly in the saddle. With luck, Dolph Stickney would stay in the saddle.

Royal came to as Mr. Smith was leading Dolph's horse out of the pines. The Apache smacked the horse violently across the rump, and the horse lurched forward and raced downhill. Mr. Smith cocked Dolph's rifle and with considerable self-command waited until the horse approached the clustered riders on the winding trail. Then he fired a single shot at the riders.

The four men were on the narrow, exposed stretch of trail when Dolph's horse bore down on them. The single shot had primed them and added to their fear of slipping off the steep slope. Dolph's horse galloped around a sharp corner of the cliff face and sideswiped one of the riders. Both horse and rider went down. The second and third riders in line had difficulty staying on the trail. They fought to bring their horses under control. The last rider calmly raised his rifle and shot Dolph. The solid blow knocked him partially out of the saddle. This threw the horse akilter and caused him to broadside the last rider. The man tried desperately to get clear of his horse, but his boot got hung up in the stirrup. Both horses tumbled off the trail. The animals pawed the air frantically as they fell. The man screamed until he hit the rocks four hundred feet below. His shriek echoed off the cliffs and faded into silence. The three men remaining on the trail were unnerved. They abandoned the chase and hurried down the trail. None of them were prepared for the gruesome sight that awaited them in the boulders.

Mr. Smith trotted over to Royal and gently rolled him on his side. The Apache pulled Royal's neckerchief from around his neck and wadded it. He pressed the pad over the deep gouge wound behind Royal's shoulder. The Apache unbuckled Royal's belt and with considerable effort pulled it free. Gently he ran the belt under Royal and cinched it tightly around him, applying pressure to the wound.

Struggling with the half-dazed Royal, the Apache supported him up the gentle face of a boulder. He clicked his tongue to call his pony. He grabbed the pony's ear and firmly pulled him against the rock. Then he slipped beneath Royal's arm and sat on the pony's rump while keeping one hand on Royal. The Indian gently pulled Royal forward. He took one half step and fainted.

Later, Royal regained consciousness, and with great expenditure of effort looked about. The familiar interior of the cabin greeted him. His back ached and his head throbbed every time his heart beat. A slight rustling caused him to move his head. That move elicited a groan from Royal. Mr. Smith was kneeling beside the bed. Inch by painful inch, he peeled off the bloodied bandage and examined the seeping wound. Royal caught a glimpse of the Indian's face: a slight grimmace and an upturned nose. Before Mr. Smith discarded the bandage, Royal saw the yellow stain and knew the wound was infected. He spoke to the Indian.

"Get Doc Shu here, or I'll die."

Royal was drained from the effort. Mr. Smith redressed the wound with pieces of cloth. He felt the Indian lash him to the bed. A leather strap secured his ankles, and another bound his chest. Mr. Smith left the room as Royal faded into unconsciousness. He didn't hear the Apache ride away.

Royal was soaked with sweat. A burning fever gripped him. He was delirious, talking gibberish.

"I'll get through, sir." Royal spoke to his commanding officer, Colonel Bill Travis. He was back in the Alamo, February 24, 1836. Travis had handed him a message to be delivered to Colonel James Fannin in Goliad.

"You understand the importance of this message." Travis measured the gangly lad who stood before him. "Impress upon Colonel Fannin the urgency for reinforcements. Without his help, we will be defeated. You understand what I'm saying, son?"

"I understand, sir."

Those words spoken aloud startled Royal awake. He forced himself to breathe deeply. His shirt was wet; his hair was damp and matted on his forehead. This is crazy, he thought. The Alamo was twenty years ago.

Royal cooled from the warm, prickly fever. A slight chill coursed his spine, making him shiver and raising goose bumps on his arms. The damp shirt speeded the process. Soon he was shaking uncontrollably. He attempted to curl tightly as he sought warmth, but the leather straps prevented it and hurt him as he pulled against them. He yelled for Mr. Smith to cover him with a blanket. His throat was parched.

Exhausted from fighting the shakes, Royal relaxed. His legs ached from straining. At a snail's pace, he stretched out full length and felt comfortable, warm again. But with disquieting dread, he continued to heat up. Minutes later, he was burning hot. In his struggle to sit, he sensed the first wonderful feelings of unconsciousness. The searing heat that scorched his brain gradually diminished, replaced by a foreboding blackness. Before he passed out, memories from twenty years ago flashed into his head. Goliad! That terrified him.

In Goliad, Texas, Colonel James Fannin, the commanding officer of Fort Defiance, dallied too long in his withdrawal from the fort. Not known for his leadership, Colonel Fannin vacillated between fight or flight.

Royal, a scout for Colonel Fannin, kept the colonel abreast of Mexican General José Urrea's relentless advance.

Royal was a strapping young man, full of self-confidence. He knew his direction—he had earned the respect of the Texans in Goliad with several daring scouting forays against the Mexicans. He confronted Colonel Fannin and, risks be damned, challenged him into action.

"Sir, we have to leave immediately. We are badly outnumbered. Escape north is our only chance." It was more of an ultimatum than an explanation.

"Mr. Ballou, I take offense to that Mexican general's attitude." Here we go again, thought Royal. "Who does he think he is, marching up here like he owns the place? I want to stay and fight. That honor rests with me."

"Sir." Royal's frustration rose. The colonel did not understand the gravity of the situation. "He *does* own this place. And if we don't leave soon, we won't be alive to have any honor."

"I'm not convinced" was the unconcerned reply. "We could give him a good fight. This battle could be the turning point of my career."

"Sir, at the moment I wouldn't be as concerned about your military career as much as your life," Royal caustically replied.

"We are outnumbered three to one. I've heard the general has *zapadores* with him."

"*Zapadores*—what's that?" the officer asked in complete ignorance.

"Combat engineers." Royal took the time to explain. "We do not stand a chance in hell if we hole up in the fort. They made quick work of the Alamo, as you know, sir."

The colonel relented. "Be ready to march at fifteen hundred hours."

"Sir," Royal pleaded, "we don't have that kind of time!"

"It will be difficult," he whined.

"Colonel, Sam Houston ordered the fort destroyed, not to let it fall into Mexican hands. I'll have the men place the explosives."

"No time for that. We march immediately." It was an order.

Colonel Fannin and his four hundred soldiers fled Fort Defiance in an early morning drizzle and thick fog. Their march was hindered by cumbersome wagons and excess equipment. The soldiers, well aware of the approaching Mexicans, were anxious to distance themselves. Out on the open plains, they felt relieved to be marching again. To a man, they questioned Colonel Fannin's leadership abilities. Royal scouted ahead of the column. He was convinced they had waited too long to leave Fort Defiance.

Partially obscured images masked by fog played tricks on Royal's eyes. He thought he saw mounted riders. Once he wheeled his horse around to ride after them, but the thick fog bank stopped him. He lagged back and waited for the forward riders to catch up. Hearing the approaching wagon, he fell into line. Colonel Fannin was riding with several of his officers.

"How does it look, Ballou?" Strain was apparent on the colonel's face.

"Not good, sir," Royal said bluntly. "I'm stone blind in the fog. Can't see nothing. I got a rank feeling this fog is our undoing."

"Why do you say that?"

Royal told him the truth. "I'm not in dire need of eyeglasses, but I could have sworn I saw riders in front of the column."

"Get back out there. I need to know if anyone is ahead of us," Fannin bruskly ordered. Fear marked his voice. He appeared to fully comprehend his errors in judgment.

Royal spurred ahead. Sore against his will he entered the fog bank. A slight breeze swirled and lifted the fog, momentarily granting him a clear field of vision. On the horizon were mounted Mexican soldiers—gray coats, white pants, and white hats marked them clearly. Surrounded.

Royal yanked his horse around and whipped the animal into the bank of fog. He shouted at the top of his lungs, "Fannin, Ballou coming in!" Three times he hailed the colonel and patiently awaited a response.

"Ballou!" came the faint reply. Royal rode toward the source.

Bursting through the fog, Royal violently jerked his horse to the side to avoid a collision with Colonel Fannin's aide. "Where the hell is the colonel?" Fear of capture and defeat was uppermost in Royal's mind.

"Beside the second wagon." The man was startled by Royal's demanding bark. He pointed to the colonel. "Over there."

"Sir," Royal shouted as he rode up to Fannin, "we're surrounded. There are mounted Mexicans in front of us. I'll lay odds we're flanked also." He indicated their positions.

"Impossible!" Colonel Fannin refused to believe what he feared most would happen. "We left in ample time."

A distant bugle ended all conversation and doubt. An answering bugle signaled encirclement.

"Withdraw to the fort. We'll make a stand there." Colonel Fannin's tough talk had been a ruse—retreat was now his order.

"Sir, we can't outrun cavalry, not with wagons," Royal dissuaded him.

"What must we do?" Colonel Fannin begged, as perfect fear overtook him. "Use the wagons. Make barricades with them. It's our only hope." Fannin answered his own question.

"Do it, sir," Royal encouraged the hapless colonel.

"Captains Miller and Cooper, get the wagons! Make a defensive square with room in the middle for the horses and mules." When pointed in the right direction, Colonel Fannin was a competent officer. He demonstrated what he expected from the officers as he snapped out orders with firm control.

The two captains deployed to their respective commands. As the wagons came in, Colonel Fannin positioned them. The teams were unhitched and picketed in one corner. The smaller wagons were turned on their sides, offering more protection to the soldiers and horses. The sergeants ordered their men into positions, desperate to beat the Mexican assault.

Colonel Fannin and his men survived the next two days on pure guts and mule-headed stubbornness. The rains stopped, and the fog lifted. The men baked under the Texas sun and sweltered in the humidity. Water supplies were short to begin with and soon were critically low. The Mexican assault in the late afternoon of the first day was driven back. Another attack before daybreak was repulsed also. The casualties on the Mexican side were staggering; two hundred and fifty were killed, and over three hundred wounded. Although the Texans lost only seven men, they suffered over sixty wounded. These men were tormented due to lack of treatment, little or no shade, and scant water.

Colonel Fannin, himself wounded, knew the soldiers could not hold out much longer. That evening he called a staff meeting to discuss the situation. Royal was requested to attend the meeting. The officers talked late into the night. Colonel Fannin thanked and dismissed them. He knew the final decision was his.

"You were rather quiet tonight, Royal. What do you think?"

"Sir, I'll be plain spoken. You are selling out," he told the officer frankly. "The Alamo was less than a fortnight ago. How can you surrender to the Mexicans? I would fight till I dropped. If I'm ordered to stop fighting, I will—under protest. But surrender? Never." Defiance darkened his young face, and he set his jaw.

"Royal, if I didn't have the wounded to think of, I would die fighting here. I have no choice. I am responsible for my men." Colonel Fannin spoke with compassion.

"Very well, sir. I'm at your service, but I want you to know that I would rather fight and die here than give in to them."

On March 21, 1836, Colonel Fannin surrendered to General José Urrea. The colonel, haggered and overspent, addressed the Mexican general, "Sir, we are agreed. I will surrender on the condition that we be treated with honor and paroled to the United States."

General Urrea, as a professional soldier of Spanish background and tradition, was a man of honor. "You have my word, Colonel Fannin. I will personally guarantee your protection and that of your men."

"I graciously accept your offer," Colonel Fannin replied with a deep feeling of relief. He had saved his men further suffering. "I reluctantly relinquish my command. I await your orders, sir."

General Urrea returned to Goliad and Fort Defiance with the captured Texans. Royal, at Colonel Fannin's side, was stunned by the quick turn of events.

For seven days, the Texans were treated well. General Urrea dispatched his personal physician to treat the wounded. He was not hardened to the suffering of soldiers. But Colonel Fannin lived with the brutally hard consequence of his failure to depart sooner.

General Urrea had given his word and worked tirelessly for the release of the captured soldiers. They were a burden on his supplies, and it sapped his manpower to guard them. The general respected Colonel Fannin's decision to surrender. That gesture had saved both sides tremendous casualties.

On Palm Sunday, March 27, the Texans were mustered together and marched from the fort. Rumors flew. Some said they were on their way to the United States via New Orleans. As the men neared the San Antonio River, seven hundred Mexican soldiers escorted the Texans to the riverbank. A Mexican officer shouted in broken English for the Texans to kneel. As the soldiers knelt in the hot sun, the Mexican officer shouted orders to his troops.

Royal understood enough Spanish to know what was coming. "No, don't shoot! Don't sh—" His words were smothered by the crashing shots of the first volley. The Mexicans killed the Texans where they knelt. General Santa Anna had issued orders to General Urrea to kill the prisoners. They were a hindrance and an expense to him. General Urrea had opposed the order but had no recourse. He carried them out under strong protest.

Of the four hundred Texans, only sixty survived the slaughter. Royal, twice wounded, reached the opposite bank of the river and escaped with two other men. The river scene haunted him for years. He felt burning shame for not having fought the Mexicans to the death, and guilt for having abandoned his fellow soldiers there. He thought he should have done more to save them.

Royal's fever broke, and he regained consciousness. He was in the cabin tied to the bed. He struggled feebly to free himself, but Mr. Smith had tied the knots well. His clammy shirt began to cool him as the chills returned. Dread thoughts of the San Antonio River massacre alarmed him. He hoped that Doc Shu would arrive soon.

CHAPTER
7

"Don't shoot—" Royal moaned. "Don't sh—" He lunged to one side to avoid the rifle fire from the Mexicans.

"Royal, lie still. Please." Firm hands held him. "If you don't, you'll open the wound." A woman's voice broke sharply into his head. Gradually Royal relaxed and became aware of his surroundings. The log cabin greeted him. Abbie was sitting on the edge of the bed, holding him down. He closed his eyes for several seconds, then opened them as she placed a cool cloth on his forehead.

"Howdy, stranger" was his feeble greeting. "What are you doing here?"

"Hush." She mussed his unruly hair and chided him, a full smile on her face. "I don't need to listen to you any longer. These past days have been crazy, what with you ranting and carrying on. I came here with Mr. Smith. He has gone for medicine and supplies." She released him, and he settled onto the bed.

"Could I have something to drink? I'm parched." Royal jokingly reached for his throat, relieved to be no longer tied to the bed.

Abbie dipped a tin cup into the wooden bucket beside the bed and helped him to sit up for a drink. Royal gulped the water, nearly choking in haste. "Wonderful," he commented as he lay back. "One of my fondest memories of this place is the spring water."

Abbie walked to the stove and added new wood. "You hungry? I've made soup and coffee."

As if on cue, Royal's stomach growled. They both laughed. "I'm famished. Feels like I haven't eaten in days."

"Four days," she told him.

"No, it can't be! I passed out last night—not four days ago."

"You're wrong." She pointed at him to underscore her point. "Mr. Smith came down on Tuesday. He said you had been shot. I've been here since Thursday." She tested the broth, mindful not to burn herself. "You were crazy with fever. A lady shouldn't have heard some of that talk."

"You're probably right. I apologize for whatever I said." He looked sheepish.

Abbie busied herself at the stove preparing Royal's soup. She turned to speak, thought better of it, and went about her task.

"Go ahead." Royal knew she was troubled. "I'll try to answer your question."

"Royal, no." Abbie declined, shaking her head. "It's none of my business."

"Speak your mind," he encouraged her. "If you don't, you'll worry it to death."

"Fine. Here we go." She ventured with trepidation, "Who was Dallas Detweiller?"

Royal didn't answer. Memories of the night in Salina flooded him. That particular evening, Royal and his brother Grady had been walking their rounds together. They stepped off the boardwalk and started across the alley. Four shots rang out from the shadows of the building. Grady went down immediately. Royal dove under the boardwalk and waited. Seconds later, he saw the vague outline of a man hugging the wall. As the figure approached Grady, Royal shot at him. The man staggered and fell in the dusty alley. Peter Hoose was dead. Royal rolled over and got to his knees as two shots from above smashed through the planks. Royal shot blindly at the other gunman. Pounding footsteps retreated. By the time Royal crawled from beneath the boardwalk, the street was deserted.

"Why do you ask about him?" Royal was testy.

"You cursed the day Detweiller was born. He killed Grady, didn't he?" Abbie was not one to mince words. Royal was silent. Abbie felt him stonewall and gently nudged him. "You killed him later in Hobbs, New Mexico, didn't you? They were in it together, right?"

"Yes and yes. Even after some ten years, it's hard to fess up to it. I hope this puts the last chapter on it. I admit it and come clean."

Abbie brought a tray to the bed and sat beside him. She would not let it rest. "The night you were shot in Jacob's Well, you and Sheriff Tibbetts were walking together. You and the sheriff were side by side as you stepped off the boardwalk. Correct?" Abbie challenged his silence.

"Yes," he replied softly.

Abbie leaned forward to hear his answer. "Don't you see it, Royal? The same set-up as in Salina, the night Grady was killed. Bushwacked at night in an alley. Royal, there is a connection. Think back to the night you and Sheriff Tibbetts were ambushed." She nudged him along. "What was the name of the man John Tibbetts killed?"

"I don't have to think on it," Royal shot back. "Lefty Hallahan. Means nothing to me."

"It should, Royal," she reprimanded. "The last name. Spell it out."

"H-a-l-l . . ." Abbie held up her hand and stopped him. "Hall. Lefty Hall. Damn it, Abbie! Who in the hell is Lefty Hall?" Royal's temper flared.

"Does the name Rutherford Hallahan ring a bell?" she asked with interest.

"Nope" was Royal's deadpan answer.

"Drop the last four letters."

"You mean like Curly Hall?" He smiled. A blush of red colored his pallid cheeks. "Lefty was Curly's brother?"

Abbie nodded. "And add to the soup Perley Hall. He was a set-up by Curly to get back at John Tibbetts for killing Lefty. The three were brothers."

Abbie pecked him on the forehead. "You're well at last."

"Oh, bless me," Royal blurted out, cheered by this knowledge. "I've been waiting for this news."

"The way you been going with Curly Hall, the lord better be watching over you." Abbie served him notice. "That man has been a step ahead of us since day one. Be careful with him."

"You, my dear, are absolutely right."

"Royal, listen to me. Sheriff Tibbetts was following a lead that tied Curly to the ambush that wounded you. Rumor had Curly linked to a wealthy landowner. John had no proof, but he was on to something. Doesn't it seem strange that both Halls appeared in Jacob's Well at the same time?

"Another tidbit." She baited him. "The three brothers have prison records in Texas and Oklahoma, and as you realize, changed their names."

Royal listened to Abbie's revelations. "I wish John were here to help us along." He missed his old lawman friend.

"So do I" was Abbie's wistful reply. "Turn to your side. I want to change your dressing." She tugged at him and brought hot water and a clean cloth to the bed. She gently soaked the old bandage and easily peeled it off his back. The dressing was clear of infection. For twenty minutes, Abbie applied hot compresses, then dressed and wrapped the wound. "Doc Shu will send me new bandages and medicine tomorrow night with Mr. Smith."

"Good. I want to get out of here."

The next day, Abbie had Royal on his feet and outside the cabin. Royal sat against the log wall and basked in the sun like an old groundhog. The day was lazy, and they did little but enjoy it.

After Abbie had seen Royal off to bed, she heard the nickering of a horse. She moved quietly toward the door. Her skirt brushed against a storage shelf and knocked a tin to the floor. "Who's there?" Royal called out sleepily.

"It's me, Royal" was Abbie's whispered reply. "Mr. Smith is here. I'll be back in a few minutes."

Royal fell back asleep. Suddenly, he sat bolt upright. Abbie had not returned. Royal struggled to pull his boots on. He wanted to see what was happening outside. Pistol in hand, he felt along the wall and partially opened the door. The top hinge squeaked. Two shots drove him back inside. The heavy slugs had splintered the door.

From instinct, Royal knew to get out of the cabin fast. He shuffled past the table, hooked his jacket from the back of the chair, and headed for the woodbox. With his good arm, he crouched in front of the small chute. A dull thud inside the cabin made him look around. In the middle of the floor was a four-stick bundle of dynamite, its fuse hissing loudly. Royal dove for the hole, opening his wound as he slammed through the chute. He scrambled over the woodpile and crawled away from the cabin. Fresh air greeted him as he stood. He half lunged for the empty ditch beside the cabin and covered his head with his coat.

Boom! The deafening thunderclap lifted him off the ground. The concussion slammed him down, momentarily knocking his breath out. As he gasped for breath, he choked on the acrid smoke that drifted from the cabin. Looking over his shoulder, he saw faint orange flickerings as the coals burst into flames. Royal slithered the length of the ditch until he was out of the circle of light. Whatever hadn't been blown up was now burning. He watched as the blazing cabin consumed itself. Bright swirls of cherry-red sparks danced into the night. Abbie was gone. Why in the hell would Mr. Smith grab her? Royal knew it was futile to search for her tonight.

Four miles shy of Royal and the burning cabin, in Little Dry Wash, Mr. Smith hunkered down beside a small glowing fire. His hands were securely tied behind his back. If he was afraid of imminent death, his battered and bloodied face did not show it. He showed no emotion or feeling. He was thinking about his family, his wife and two children. He had not seen them in a year. He remembered how peaceful life had been before the white man, traders, and railroad had destroyed it. He would go back to his people soon.

"Yessiree, Bob." Jim Slater laughed as he nursed a bloody nose and talked with two other H bar C riders, Elmer and Wesley Higgins. "I thought this here backslider was aworkin' fer us, lookin' for that outlaw Ballou. Don't seem that way." He spat blood from his throat and sniffed through a plugged nose. "This here Injun just rode past us bigger than life itself. Not a care in the world."

"He don't have a care now," replied Elmer sardonically. "He knows he's on his way to the huntin' grounds."

"Yep," Wesley chimed in, "the only good Injun is a dead one, and we got us a dead one here." Wesley glared at Mr. Smith through a badly puffed left eye.

Mr. Smith had been returning to the cabin with the promised supplies from Doc Shu. But broken fortunes were upon him—his bad luck took him to a chance encounter with four H bar C riders. They had killed a bottle of applejack and were whittled, sleeping off the effects of the liquor. Mr. Smith had taken the only route open to him. Sandwiched between sheer walls as the only access through the wash, he had hugged one side, trying to sneak past the dying fire and the drunken riders. The Apache had been abreast of the men when Wesley startled from his drunken stupor. Wesley, seeing double, had made a snap decision to shoot it out with the Indians. His fifth shot had creased

Mr. Smith across the skull, knocked him stiffer than a brandin' iron, and bowled him off his pony.

Elmer had lurched to his knees at the sound of the shots and witnessed Mr. Smith's exit from his pony. "Hot damn, Wesley!" he shouted excitedly. "You got him."

"No, I didn't," Wesley contested. "I was ashootin' at the other one. He got away 'cause I don't see him nowhere."

The H bar C riders rose to their feet. Seth Holt, the soberest of the crew, volunteered to chase after Mr. Smith's pony. He mounted his horse on the third try and rode into the night. Mr. Smith's pony, on familiar ground, headed straight for the cow camp cabin, with Seth following close behind.

The remaining H bar C hands captured Mr. Smith after a fashion. The Apache, briefly stunned, came to as the cowboys waylaid him. It was a knock-down-drag-out fight, with Mr. Smith dealing out as much punishment as he received. Partially blinded by blood and weakened from the loss of it, Mr. Smith finally succumbed.

"How should we do him, Elmer?" Wesley asked with growing anticipation. "I want to see that Injun suffer before he kicks off." A malicious smirk crossed his bruised face.

"We could stretch his neck like we done to that Mexican we caught rustlin' cattle." Elmer chuckled. "Remember how he danced on his toes till his legs just plum give out?" They laughed.

"Sure was a tough little bugger, I'll hand him that," Wesley respectfully conceded.

"Come on, you two." Jim was on his feet. "It's necktie time. That tree'll do. Right there." He pointed with his chin to a mesquite on the side of the draw.

Elmer went to his horse, untied his lariat from the saddle tie, and walked under the tree. With a smooth flick of his wrist, he threw one end of the rope over a thick limb. Grabbing both ropes, he hefted himself off the ground and jerked his weight against the tree. It was stout.

Jim and Wesley yanked Mr. Smith to his feet and half-dragged him to the tree. "You know how to tie a hangman's noose?" Elmer asked Jim.

"Hell, yes," Jim answered with chilling finality. "Thirteen loops—but no call for that. We ain't gonna break his neck. We'll choke him slow," Jim patiently explained.

"Just wrap and knot it," Wes instructed his brother. He laughed. "The Injun won't care."

Elmer stepped forward and adjusted the rope around Mr. Smith's neck.

Boom! A wide swath of ground to Jim's left erupted into a storm of 00 buck pellets, broken sage, and splintered sandstone. The throaty explosion from a shotgun stopped all movement and talk. "Step back from the Indian. Now!" A woman's voice cut into the night. The three men sobered up and stepped away from Mr. Smith.

"No damned woman is gonna—" Elmer spat out the words as he reached for his pistol. Wesley lunged for his brother and caught his arm just as the pistol cleared leather.

"Don't, you stupid fool!" he screamed as he struggled with his younger brother. Elmer fought for several seconds more, then ceased. "She'll blow your dumb ass away! Don't do it." Fear set Wesley's tone as he looked at Elmer.

"Smart move, Wesley," the woman complimented him. "Now, drop your gunbelts at your feet. I warn you, don't do anything dumb," she said in a stern voice.

The three hesitated, then unbuckled their belts and let the pistols drop. "Step back. Way back." Jim Slater looked at the woman. A jolt of recognition stunned him as he placed the voice and the face together.

"This ain't your fight, Libby Dowden. Keep out of it," Jim threatened her.

"Like hell you say, you miserable little shit! You made it my fight when you hooked up with that crooked sheriff."

"There ain't nothin' wrong with him," Jim defended Curly.

"Jim, you weren't smart enough to pour piss out of a boot when I tried to teach you the three R's," Libby berated him. "You haven't changed a lick."

"Big talk from a schoolmarm," Jim defiantly said. "Boys, we outnumber her three to one. Elmer, go 'round the left." Jim stepped forward, his confidence renewed.

The loud click of the second hammer being cocked gave him pause. "That puny sage by your left foot," Libby told him. "You step past it, and I'll kill you." She shouldered the 10-gauge and gently fingered the trigger. Jim, his cockiness checkmated, did not challenge the line. "Now, you three git. On your horses and ride out of here." Libby followed behind the trio, her shotgun steady all the while. "Ease those rifles out. Oh, so carefully. You can pick them up a couple days from now at the H bar C."

The disinclined men did as they were told and dropped their rifles. They knew that upon their return to the H bar C, they would face the wrath of Ham Colburn. Then they would have to explain to the trail crews how a woman disarmed the three of them. "Head out, and don't look back. I might sic that Indian on you." The cowboys dug hard into the flanks of their horses and were gone in seconds.

Libby cradled the shotgun and walked over to Mr. Smith. She fumbled in her dress and pulled out a small pocketknife. Within seconds, she had cut the rope from around his neck, then his hands. The Apache flexed his shoulders and rubbed his wrists. Libby looked at his head wound and dismissed any treatment. "Mr. Smith, I hope you will forgive me. I followed you when you left Doc Shu's store." She looked guilt ridden. She walked over to the glowing mesquite coals and warmed herself. "Call it a woman's intuition, but I felt something like this would befall you. I owe you for savin' Royal's life. Thank you." She nodded to him. "Go to your wife and young uns. They need you."

Mr. Smith trotted to retrieve the cloth bundle he had dropped when he was shot. He handed it to Libby. Without a good-bye or a single word of thanks, he picked up his shell belt and rifle and walked into the black night. Libby collected the guns of the H bar C trail crew, stuffed the pistols into her saddlebags, and wrapped the rifles in her blanket. She tied the bundle behind her saddle. For the first time in fifteen minutes, her knees began to shake. Survival out here had hardened her, but she still didn't like it—she tolerated it.

In the first flush of pewter morning light, Libby cautiously made her way downhill toward the cabin. For a big woman, she moved with considerable grace. Her 10-gauge was cocked and ready. She had smelled smoke for some time, but now it was strong and tainted. Something was amiss. The trees surrounding the cabin were singed, their bark blackened and their needles rust colored. All that remained of the cabin was rubble. As Libby stumbled forward, her attention on the smouldering ruins, she nearly stepped on Royal. He was curled on the ground, bundled in his heavy coat. "Royal!" she blurted out, and knelt beside him. "Are you hurt?" A moan was his answer. Concern creased her face.

Royal managed to sit up and look at her through reddened eyes. He tried to talk but could not. Libby got to her feet, rummaged through the rubble of the cabin, and found a cup. She went to the spring and brought him water.

"What in the dickens happened here?" She shook her head in disbelief as she surveyed the remnants. "I lend you my cabin and return to a bed of coals."

Royal spoke after several sips of water. "Libby, I had a visitor last night. I think Mr. Smith grabbed Abbie. Why, I don't know." He shrugged his shoulders. "She's gone."

"Mr. Smith? Horse manure," Libby scoffed. "I saved his scrawny neck from a hangin' last night. Some of the H bar C boys had him well-nigh strung up in Little Dry Wash. Besides, what would he gain by taking Abbie?"

"Then who took her?" Royal asked as he struggled to stand.

"Oh, Lord. In all your wisdom . . ." Libby looked heavenward and called on her helper.

"Libby," Royal cut in abruptly, "not here, not now!"

"Mercy me, you're hurt." She turned to him. "Sit down. I want to take a look at you." She pulled his shirttail up. "Hm, seen worse. Infection's gone. Good. With a tight wrap you'll mend. It won't be pretty, but neither are you." She smiled at him.

"What about Abbie?" Royal questioned over his shoulder.

"I'll have to heat water and somehow clean you up." Libby continued her one-sided conversation. She searched the ruins and spotted several cans that hadn't exploded in the fire. She collected the cans. "Let's have something to eat first."

Then she abruptly stopped. "Royal, I have to get back to Clem today. We have to find Abbie. I can't go on not knowing where that child is or if she's safe." Libby was wrought up.

She trudged to the spring to fetch water, then scampered back quickly. "Royal, we've got company. Look down valley." She pointed toward the Puerco River canyon. "I saw three riders in the cedars. What'll we do?" Fear laced her voice.

Royal squatted and checked the canyon. He turned and eyed the high country behind them. "You have your horse, right?"

"Why, yes. She's tied in the trees."

"I want you to ride like hell across the hill. Stay in the trees."
He pointed out her route. "We're being circled."

"How do you know?" She eyed the hillside.

"Makes sense, doesn't it? Riders sweeping the valley floor.
Surely someone headed for the high country to cover them.
We'll take a gamble on beating them there. When you get to
that break, next to those boulders"—Royal pointed out the
spot—"touch off a round or two in their direction. Hopefully it
will distract them."

"What are you going to do?"

"Stay here."

"But, Royal—"

He motioned her to be quiet. "Libby, listen to me. For one
thing, I don't have a horse. Secondly, I can't ride. I know a
good place to hide. If you do what I ask, I won't need help."
Libby had misgivings, but Royal herded her away. "Get going.
When you're clear of the timber, you're home free. I'll see you
in a day, two at most." His smile was confident.

"Oh, damn, I hate to leave you alone."

"I'll be fine. Please, go."

After Libby disappeared into the treeline, Royal scattered
the canned goods. He threw ashes over the table and the footprints on the floor. The wood chute was obscured with partially
burned logs and sod. Royal squeezed into the jumble of debris.
Using a half-burned broom, he obliterated his tracks. He
kicked at a table, and it collapsed in front of his hiding place.
The waiting began.

He heard horses, then voices. He scooted farther into the
chute. Two riders came and stopped at the ruins. Royal
couldn't see their faces.

"You look, Wesley," he heard one cowboy tell the other.

"Aw, hell, Elmer," the other complained. "I don't feel like it.
I'm tired. I wanna quit."

"Pard, I'd do it if I was you," his brother threatened. "Old
Man Hambone is hoppin' mad. If that outlaw is here and overlooked, we're down the road."

"I s'pose you're right, Elmer. Well, here goes nothin'."

Royal glimpsed the cowboy as he slipped from his horse. The
lad was young, raw, in his early twenties. He had a bulldog
look of determination and would see this job through. With
Elmer's admonition fresh in his mind, Wesley set about his

search with purpose. The cowboy headed straight for the pile of debris. He knelt on both knees and reminded Royal of a bloodhound. Royal tried to pull his left boot back, but the heel wedged tight against a log. "Hey, Elmer!" he yelled to his brother. "Either he's buried in here, or he left in such a hurry he forgot his boots."

Royal cocked the .44 against his body to muffle the sound. If the boy pressed much farther, Royal would have no choice but to blast him. A hand grabbed the heel of Royal's boot and pulled it. He curled his toes and strained to hold steady. Fortunately Wesley couldn't get a good grip and released it. Royal sighed with relief and peeked at the lad. To his mounting horror, he watched as the boy sat in front of him, legs astraddle the hole. The cowboy braced both feet against the debris, grabbed the boot, and pulled with all his strength. Royal held him to a standstill until he got a cramp in his foot and straightened his toes. Wesley tumbled ass over elbow onto the floor. "Hey, Elmer, looky here!" he shouted excitedly. "I got me one."

Royal jerked his foot away from the hole and impaled his knee on a nail. The stinging pain hurt, but he dared not move. Wesley bellied up to the pile and stuck his hand through the hole where Royal's boot had been. Royal suspended his foot above the floor, so Wesley felt nothing. With a final lunge the cowboy thrust his body, armpit deep, into the hole and touched the heel of Royal's boot. "Got the other one, Elmer," he shouted proudly.

Royal felt the bullet hit before he heard it. *Whack! Boom!* The shelf above Wesley's head splintered at the impact of the .58 slug. As Wesley dove for shelter, a second bullet exploded several cans on the charred windowsill. Wesley, still in motion, was covered with pork and beans, tomatoes, and corn syrup. He was safe behind the woodstove.

Elmer dismounted—that is to say, he somersaulted off the rear of his horse when it bolted—and sought shelter in the ditch. "Up the hill," Elmer pointed out to Wesley, "near those boulders."

As Wesley raised his head above the stove, a slug knocked the stovepipe off and showered him with soot. He was momentarily blinded.

"He's mountin' up!" Elmer yelled as he shot at the fleeing figure.

"Get our horses, Elmer!" Wesley hollered. "I'll be with you soon as I can see a damn thing." He stood and stumbled toward the charred doorframe. His eyes watered profusely, and tears streaked his face.

Royal could no longer see the men, but he heard them chasing after their horses. With both hands he pulled his knee up and off the nail. "Damn you, little bugger," he cursed the nail. "But guess I ought to thank you." A quick glance out of the rubble revealed Wesley and Elmer, both mounted, heading uphill. "Thanks, Libby. You saved my hide," he murmured.

Libby followed Royal's directions. She had watched the Higgins brothers search the cabin. When Wesley dropped out of sight, she had acted quickly. She laid the H bar C rifles out in front of her and shot at the cabin. The results were better than she had hoped for. She fired twice more and watched the circus below. Then she wrapped the rifles in the blanket and tied them behind the cantle. When she saw the two cowboys on their horses, she swung into the saddle. "Head for home, gal," she told her horse.

CHAPTER
8

Hammond Colburn was in the sheriff's office talking to Curly. He chewed on a stogie as he fumed. He was unhappy with the lack of progress in the search for Royal Ballou.

"I don't believe it. Half the damned town and most of my crew searching for one man, and we still don't have him." His face twisted in a scowl, Colburn paced. "Where in the hell is he?"

"He knows the country, Ham," Curly assured the landowner. "That makes a big difference. Relax—it's just a question of time before we get him."

"Ya? Well, I don't have time. Neither do you." Colburn pointed his stogie at Curly. "This town's docile now, but we have to keep the lid on it. If Ballou gets back and stirs things up, we'll be in serious trouble."

"Jail is more like it." Curly laughed, and added with black humor, "Our jail."

"Damn it, Curly!" Colburn slammed his fist on the desk top. "I want him dead!"

"I need more help, boss," Curly flatly requested.

"Why didn't you say so?" Colburn was relieved. "I've got twenty men on range crews. I'll give you all of them." He strode to the door, yanked it open, and called to his foreman, "Stoney, get in here!"

A tall big-boned man entered the office. He was sinewy tough, mesquite hard, and range wise. He thumbed back his Stetson, reached into his shirt pocket, and pulled out a packet of Bull Durham and paper. With practiced fingers, he built a smoke. After he licked and twisted the paper, he struck a match along his thigh. He eyed the boss through a haze of smoke. "What do you need, Ham?"

"How many men can we spare from the range crews?" Colburn asked his top man.

"Which sections do you want to use?" It was a confident response from the tough puncher.

"All," Colburn demanded. "You tell me what you need for a skeleton crew—I'll take the rest. Curly wants more manpower."

"Let's see." Stoney talked under his breath. He figured his manpower—names, faces, and sections were part of his everyday life. "Leave me Tibbs, Walls, Pluckett, and McHenry on the west four sections. Jacobs and Hawley, east section. Shoot, boss," he complained, "we'll be short-handed as hell. I can give you fourteen, no more. I'll have barely two men per four sections. If anything happens, we're in deep shit."

"What could happen?" Colburn countered. "We'll be hayin' within the week. Cattle are on the summer range. I don't see a problem."

"You best hope we don't have any," Stoney cautioned. "When and where do you want the men?"

"As soon as possible," Curly rudely cut in. "We want to comb Puerco River canyon again. I'm betting Ballou's holed up in the high country." A breath of confidence welled within the sheriff. "With the extra help, we'll get him."

"Your luck had better change, Curly, with the added manpower. That damned Indian threw us off." Colburn bitterly shook his head. "No doubt he's headed south?"

"He's in the Sierra Madre right now," Curly said as he leaned back in his chair, his hands clasped behind his head.

"You might join him before this is over with," Colburn added grimly. "Stoney, wait outside. I'll be right with you." He curtly dismissed the cowboy and pointed to the door with his head. The foreman got casually to his feet and let himself out.

"How we doin' with the Improvement Commission?" Colburn's enthusiasm returned when he discussed money.

"Fine, Ham." Curly grinned. "We're doin' good. With the exception of a couple businesses, we collect every week. Getting a tidy sum in the safe." Curly pointed with his elbow to the big safe in the corner.

"Let's split it soon. Keep the mayor and the council happy. Who knows the combination to the safe?" Wrinkles of concern creased Colburn's forehead.

"No one but me" was Curly's solid reply. He laughed. "The only other person who knew is six feet under. We're as safe as my safe."

"You absolutely certain?" Colburn sought reassurance.

"My money's in it. I checked with the company that sold the safe to Tibbetts. He was the only one who had the combination until they gave it to me. Royal was in Santa Fe when Tibbetts received the safe."

Colburn and Stoney rode for an hour through the rolling grasslands of the H bar C. Neither spoke as they passed by several thousand head of cattle. Colburn broke the silence to query his old friend. "Something on your mind, Stoney? You're quiet today."

Stoney effortlessly rolled a cigarette. He lit it and blew smoke through clenched teeth. "Hammond, what you're doing is contrary to the law. You've got everything in the world money can buy, yet you're goin' for more. And that sorry excuse of a sheriff—he's a thug, a damned killer with a dirty badge." Stoney spat.

"What's with this holier-than-thou attitude all of a sudden?" Colburn was miffed. "Stoney, we've been through a lot together."

"Yes, sir, we have. Twenty-six years next month, to be exact. Up until now, it's all been fair and square—hard work, long hours, and low pay. Seems like now we're thieving, scheming, working on the sly. It don't feel right."

"We do things we aren't proud of," Colburn reasoned, "but they've got to be done. You can't forget those land disputes with the Mexicans or the Indians."

"No, sir. They was done for survival," Stoney agreed. "We had to do it. But this new stuff—buying' people off, intimidatin', sneak thievin'—I don't like it."

"Sorry you feel that way, Stoney," Colburn lied. "If you ever want to leave, I'll see to it you never have to work another day in you life."

"Thank you, sir." Stoney felt Colburn's uncommitted rhetoric and mouthed the hollow words. "I'm still workin' 'long as you say so."

"Good man." Colburn's approval was forced.

Colburn touched a nerve in Stoney. He hadn't once encouraged Stoney to stay on. Colburn was buying time, and Stoney knew it.

Royal abandoned the burned cabin as soon as the Higgins brothers rode after Libby. He took the marrowbone stage and cut through the rocky cliffs. No horse could possibly follow him. Libby's tale about the Apache put his mind at ease. He was relaxed yet mindful of the possibility of being spotted. He knew the posse not would expect him to walk out of the canyon. At this steady pace, he figured on arriving at Clem's spread past midnight. Knowing Mr. Smith was in the Sierra Madre was settling, but Royal couldn't get Abbie out of his mind.

Cresting the hill behind Clem's ranch, Royal took a breather above the cabin. It was moonlit and quiet—too quiet. He had misgivings as he came off the hillside. He skirted the demolished reservoir and approached the cabin. As he searched the shadows, he cocked his rifle and brought it up across his chest. A slight movement at the corral caught his eye.

"Clem," he called gently, then cocked his ear to listen for the reply.

A muffled rustle beside the cabin sent Royal to one knee, rifle shouldered.

"Royal, that you?" Clem's voice called from the shadows. His rifle barrel reflected a beam of moonlight.

"Yes." He stood and approached the cabin. "I'm losing my touch. I thought you were by the corral."

Clem laughed quickly. "Nope. Libby!" he called. Royal detected Libby's less-than-petite frame as she approached with the 10-gauge by her side.

As she came near, Royal noticed her left arm was in a sling. "Libby," he asked with mock sympathy, "did your good arm give out throwin' a skillet at Clem?"

"Don't get smart-assed with me, Royal Ballou." She laughed at him. "I can still whip ya."

"You two are a fine-looking couple. Clem with his hand busted, and you with your arm tied up. What happened, love?" he asked with concern.

"Those two hooligans at the cabin. I had them so confused, they shot at anything that moved. My horse was nicked and ran me into a tree."

"You granted me a reprieve at the cabin. I thank you." He looked at her arm. "Is it bad?"

"Naw, I was lucky. Doc Shu insisted I sling it for a few days. Keep the stitches in place. How you mending?"

"Good. I been tender on it. Where's Abbie?"

Neither spoke. Royal searched their faces.

"No one's seen her, Royal." Clem shook his head and as he spoke, emotion quivered his voice.

"What do you mean?" Royal stepped closer, as if the movement itself would bring him nearer to the truth.

"We've looked high and low—everywhere. She ain't in these parts," Clem explained. "If someone has her, he ain't talkin'."

"She just can't disappear," Royal said in disbelief.

"It's serious, Royal," Libby answered, long in the face. "Half the town's looking for her. You know how people feel about her. The other half is lookin' for you." She laughed. "That damned sheriff has these folks buffaloed. People won't do a damned thing unless he tells them. We haven't made much headway."

"All we can do is wait for something to break," Clem volunteered with a trace of hope. "It hasn't been easy on us, I guarantee."

"Let's go inside," Libby suggested. "I'll warm coffee and pie."

Royal forced himself to put Abbie out of his mind. "Is the sheriff still collecting his donations, Clem?" he asked with a purpose.

"Sorry to say he is" was Clem's disgruntled answer.

"Does he do it personally, or does he send his toughs?"

"Curly collects personally every couple of weeks in the late afternoon. Then he finishes his rounds and heads for the office."

"S'pose he puts the money in John's safe?" Royal's voice broke with emotion.

Libby, on her feet for more coffee, patted him on the cheek. "I feel the same way, Royal. It's hard for me to accept his death too."

Royal sat wordless, as Libby served another piece of pie. He ate in silence. Then with forced effort, he spoke. "Who else besides Curly knows the combination to the safe?"

"Don't you?" Clem asked in disbelief.

"Not I. It was John's toy. 'Bout the time it arrived, I was wounded."

"Why do you want to get into it?" Clem knew the answer to his own question. "I think you're headed for trouble."

"It's the town's money," Royal defended. "They deserve to have it returned."

"So how are you going to do it?" Libby asked.

"I'll tell you how." They clustered around the table while Royal explained his plan.

While the posse searched the Puerco River canyon for Royal, Royal waited impatiently in Doc Shu's back room. He paced the floor, walking the time away. Eight o'clock was a long wait.

"Damn it, boy, stand still!" Doc Shu snapped. "That pacin' about is drivin' me to distraction." Tension gnawed at both of them.

Footsteps on the boardwalk chased Royal into the closet.

As he closed the door, the bell clanger announced Curly's entrance. He shouldered his way past his flunky and confidently strode to the counter. "Afternoon, Doc." He went through the formality of being civil.

Doc Shu glared at him silently. He went to the cash drawer and removed two double eagles and contemptuously slapped them on the counter.

Curly swept the money with a well-trained hand into a small canvas bag. "Pleasure doin' business with you." He tipped his hat, a sarcastic smile on his face. "Anytime we can be of assistance, please call us." The flunky smirked and stood aside as Curly made his exit.

Royal cracked the door and stepped into the room. Doc Shu returned to his desk, opened the bottom drawer, and produced a bottle on the desk. His hand shook badly, and he spilled more than he poured. With no further ado, he raised the bottle to his lips and took a respectable gulp.

"May the devil smite him down!" Doc fumed as he reined in his anger.

"Doc, I'm surprised at you," Royal scolded him lightly, "giving in to that bully."

"Boy, you have no idea how much misery that man has caused me. And money. Come here." He explained to Royal as he headed for the back door.

Royal followed the old man. Cautious about being spotted, he remained just inside the room as Doc Shu showed him three boxes full of smashed and broken bottles.

"Two of Curly's thugs came one evening and destroyed my entire stock. I lost over two hundred dollars worth of patent medicine alone." As the doc spoke, Royal saw the first signs of defeat in his friend. Doc Shu was caving in. He was testy as he explained his dilemma. "I can't make a livin' that way. So I pay that sorry son of a bitch to stay in business."

"Sorry, I spoke too soon," Royal comforted his old friend.

Inside the office, they discussed Curly's schedule down to the last detail. The sheriff was a creature of habit. He took an early evening stroll at six and had dinner at the hotel between eight and nine. He made a saloon check at nine-thirty and joined one of the card games. The sheriff's final round was at midnight, when The Rose closed for the night.

"It's fully dark by nine?" Royal asked.

"Yep." The doc's eyeglasses slipped farther down his nose. "You best do it within the week."

"Right," Royal replied with a grin. "Wish me luck. I'm doing it tonight."

"You sure?" Doc Shu was startled by Royal's quick decision. "Damned short notice."

"Tonight is as good a time as any," Royal said, creeping excitement gripping him. "Those boys in the hills are going to tire of finding nothing."

Royal left the doc's shortly after eight. Long shadows fell on the ground, the harsh browns and greens were muted soft oranges and yellows. The day's heat was broken, the evening pleasantly cool. A breeze off the river was damp and refreshing. Royal followed the goosenecks of the meandering river that circled the town and approached the jail from the rear. The simple brick structure was set back from Main Street. It was the last building, separated from the others by an alley. The last time Royal happened through there had been when he dumped George Petts's and Willis Clampett's bodies on the front porch of the jail. That episode had proven disastrous.

Royal tied his mare in the thick underbrush and cautiously approached the jail. Blackbirds in the river bottom chattered among the cattails. Swallows swooped overhead in their final rush to catch insects in the fading twilight. A quick check before he left the cover of willows by the stream bank revealed no one in sight. Royal stepped on the short grass of the seldom-used trail to avoid leaving footprints in the sand. Then he picked up his pace and walked briskly to the back of the jail.

Pausing beneath the window, Royal listened for sounds within. It was silent. He edged around the building, hugging the west wall. The stones were still warm from the late afternoon sun. He stopped short of the corner, removed his hat, and quickly peeked into the street. It was deserted.

This was the moment of truth. He trusted that Curly would stick to his routine tonight. He hopped onto the boardwalk, stepped to the door, and opened it. The office was empty. He exhaled sharply and slipped inside.

Royal knelt in front of the safe. From his shirt, he removed two pocketknives and a slip of paper. He opened the blade of one knife and gently pushed to insert it between the number plate and the dial. It wouldn't fit. Quickly he snapped the knife closed and opened a thinner blade. With the point of the blade under the edge of the plate, he tapped sharply on the knife handle. The plate gave a fraction of an inch. Royal smiled. Now to work the blade around the plate and force it off the knob.

Millimeter by millimeter, Royal loosened the plate. He stayed calm as the minutes raced by. Royal pulled firmly on the handle. *Snap!* The blade broke.

"Pshaw," he hissed. "Slow down, take your time." He opened the other blade and continued to pry. The plate moved. Twist again. *Ping!* The number plate popped free and landed on the floor. It rolled in decreasingly smaller circles, coming to rest under the corner of Curly's desk.

A shouting, cursing voice signaled impending discovery. Royal snatched the paper and knives and scrambled across the wooden floor on his fingertips and toes. He scooted behind Curly's desk and squeezed into the well. A split second before the door opened, Royal saw the number plate beneath the desk. He twisted deeper into the well, reached under the desk, and pinched the plate between his fingers.

The door to the sheriff's office exploded open, and a drunken cowboy sailed into the room. He hit the floor with a fleshy squeak and skidded to the wall.

"You stupid rube!" Curly cursed the kid. "You're too drunk

to play poker with yourself, let alone with Smitty and the boys!
I'm gonna let you sleep this one off here."

"Come on, Sheriff," the cowboy mushmouthed as he lolled
on the floor, "I wanna play with them."

Curly ambled to the lad, grabbed his shirt lapels, and jerked
him to his feet. Holding the drunk with one hand, he hooked
the keys off the wall peg and escorted the cowboy to the interior cells. He steadied the cowboy against the wall with a beefy
forearm under his chin and unlocked the cell. As he shoved the
boy into the cell, he smoothly relieved him of his pistol and
deposited him safely on the cot. "Sleep it off, kid," the sheriff
admonished him. "I saved you two months' wages tonight."

"I'm gonna play." The boy lunged toward the door. Curly
set his feet and hit the cowboy. The boy slammed back against
the wall and slumped out cold on the cot.

"Damn, that lad has a hard head." Curly laughed as he
locked the cell and walked into the office. He flipped the keys at
the peg—a ringer. He smiled contentedly and headed for the
door and dinner.

Royal listened as Curly stepped off the boardwalk. He waited
several minutes before easing out from the desk. His right leg
was numb and starting to tingle with thousands of pins and
needles. Stooped over, he limped back to the safe. He stopped
breathing when he saw that the broken end of his knife blade
was still stuck to the dial. Fortunately, Curly had not seen it.

Royal pocketed the blade, took the paper from his shirt, and
smoothed it on the floor. With the number plate on the paper,
he carefully cut out a circle slightly smaller than the plate. A
notch on the paper lined up with the zero on the dial. He stuck
the paper on the front of the dial, then tapped the plate in
place. After a close inspection, he found no traces of tampering.
He pocketed the knives, double-checked the room, and stealthily approached the door. He cracked it, got a clear view of the
street, and stepped outside. As he walked away from the jail, he
fought an impulse to sprint for the river.

"Hey, you!" someone shouted from the jail.

His heart froze. In a single motion, he turned to face the
challenge and drew his pistol. Curly or one of his deputies? No
—the drunk in the jail was standing at the barred window.

"Hey, mister! Get me out of here," the boy pleaded.

Royal fastfooted it to the river. He found his mare and

headed for Doc Shu's store. After a brief visit he rode back to Clem's ranch.

Later that evening, Curly returned to his office. As he sat with his feet propped on the desk, the cowboy in the cell called to him, "You back again, Sheriff?"

"What the hell you mean *again*?" Curly rudely demanded. "First time I've been back all evening."

"Like hell," the cowboy contested. "You was out there 'bout an hour ago."

That's strange, Curly mused. None of my deputies are on duty. No one else should have been in. He quickly glanced around the office. The gun rack was untouched. Nothing missing. The safe? If anyone got inside the safe there was enough information there to hang him three times over.

Curly slammed his chair down on all fours and hurried to the safe. With quick spins, he hit the three-number combination and opened the safe. He saw immediately that no one had been inside. He shut the door, turned the handle, and gave the knob a good spin. Then the sheriff poured a cup of coffee and settled down at his desk. That dumb cowboy in the cell had given him a scare. "Aw, what the hell. He's still drunk," Curly excused, and walked back to the cell to have a chat with the cowboy. As he approached the cell, a glance told him to wait till morning. The lad was passed out on the hard wooden floor and snoring like an old hound dog.

Royal awakened before dawn and slipped out of Clem's cabin. He saddled his mare in the flat gray light, slipped his rifle into the scabbard, and tied his bedroll behind the saddle. As he stepped back to check his work, he felt someone watching him and slowly turned around. Clem, blanket wrapped, sat on the steps scrutinizing his every move.

"What in the dickens are you up to?" Clem asked.

"Clem, I'm goin' lookin' for Abbie. Maybe you're content to sit around, but I'm not. I have to find her." Royal swung into the saddle and pulled his mare around. He rode up to the porch.

"Royal, listen to me," Clem pleaded. "You can't go lookin' for her. Half the damned town is searching for *you*. You'll spend more time ducking them than you will finding Abbie."

"Someone has to look for her," he angrily replied.

"Just a damned minute." Clem stood, dropping his blanket.

He took hold of the mare's reins and pulled her closer. "Who in the hell do you think you're talking to? What do you think Lucas and I have been doing since the day she turned up missing? And the Harrises, the Culpeppers, and the Beaucamps?" Clem shook his bandaged hand at Royal.

"I don't know, Clem," he replied sheepishly.

Clem laid into Royal. "We've been riding from dawn till dusk searching for her. Hell, I've covered more of this country than you'll ever dream about. You can't go showin' yourself about these parts. Let us handle it, boy. The folks concerned for Abbie are doin' something about it. I know it ain't easy, but let it be."

Clem was startled by his own outburst. He paused and realized that his worry for Abbie had made him take his frustrations out on Royal. "Come on in, and let's eat breakfast. We'll figure us out a plan."

Sophie Fallan, the wife of Big Red, the stage driver, was waiting for Royal in the back room of the Needle and Thread Stitchery. "There you are, Royal. Good to see your face." She closed the door and moved with a grace that defied her husky size and gave him a hug. Men fought for the opportunity to dance with her. Being cushioned against that ample bosom was an added attraction to her flowing steps. Quick to smile, her features were accented by a mane of gray hair. Her easy manner was in sharp contrast to that of her other half, Big Red.

"How you doin', Sophie?" Royal asked with true intent. He floated an innocent compliment. "You're lookin' fit."

"Lordy me!" She laughed. "If you call fit twenty pounds too heavy, then I'm in hog heaven."

"You been keepin' up with your old man?"

She looked at him and rolled her eyes at the probability. "Doc Shu tells me you're up to no good. What do you need, hon?"

"My credit's good with you, right?"

"Sure is," she answered immediately. "Not that you use it much here."

"I don't have time to order a dress, do I?" Royal colored a shade.

"For you?" Sophie gleamed. "That might be a special order."

She burst out laughing, then turned serious. "It would take at least three, maybe four weeks."

"Pshaw," Royal sounded off in disappointment.

"I might have one here in stock. I could build you one in one week," she proudly stated.

The old Ballou smile surfaced, and Sophie loved it. Royal teased her. "I want the prettiest, fanciest, frilliest dress you have in the store."

"I have just the ticket!" she said with excitement. "Received a new shipment last week. No one has laid eyes on it. The best out of Kansas City."

Royal dropped the bombshell. "One about the size of Millie Tilden, our esteemed councilman's wife."

Sophie grinned like a possum and was quickly involved in the plot. "You little devil, Royal! How soon do you need it?"

"Tonight?" Royal didn't want to push his luck.

"I'll have to unwrap it. It's still in the original box."

"Sophie, can I ask a favor? Would it be possible to gift wrap it? Slip a card and rewrap it in the original box?"

"You bet. Give me about half an hour. What else?" She searched his face.

"Big Red still change teams at Apache Springs?" Royal needed to confirm his plans.

"Sure does," she bragged. "Stage arrives there at nine-thirty and leaves at nine-fifty. You can set your watch by it. New teams, and folks all fed."

"Do the ladies of Jacob's Well still have their Saturday luncheon?"

"Yes," she offered with mock sorrow. "And I still haven't been invited."

"Good. I'll work out the delivery date and time with Big Red. This dress will arrive by 'special post' on the day of the luncheon."

"Nice touch." Sophie clapped her hands together with glee. "And a loving card from her adoring husband. I'll get a sample of Lem Tilden's handwriting from my file. 'Bye" was Sophie's last word before she disappeared into the basement.

It was after dark before Sophie delivered the dress to Doc Shu's store. Royal wrapped the boxed dress in his blanket and tied it behind his saddle. As he stepped into the stirrup and swung up, he turned to Sophie. "Wish me luck."

"Be careful, Royal. Curly has riders everywhere."

"Thanks, Sophie. Oh—who's riding shotgun with Red?"

"Hank Reardon. Why?" She looked at him in surprise.

"Just wanted to know in case I don't get to Apache Springs in time. I'm off."

Doc Shu and Sophie waved and watched Royal ride away. Then they went inside Doc Shu's together.

"He'll be all right, won't he, Doc?"

"Ya, he'll do just fine."

Sophie saw through his bluff. "We'll pray anyway," she offered as a final gesture.

"Good idea." The doc laughed, then nodded with approval.

CHAPTER
9

The terrain changed from farmlands hip deep in grass to high-plains desert as Royal headed south. The sandy desert was sparsely covered with scrub grass, scattered cedars, and occasional clumps of sagebrush. Royal liked the desert, even though he baked in the daytime and froze at night. It was a most unforgiving land. Although not pleased with the half moon, he rode hard and made good time. The deeply rutted stage road was easy to follow, so he gave the mare free rein. She set a measured pace and covered a considerable amount of ground. Royal didn't like riding on the stage road, but time was important.

As they rode toward the Carizzo Mountains, Royal thought back to Curly's office and the safe. When Curly opened the safe, the notches on the dial would imprint each number on the slip of paper. The combination would punch through it. After that, it would be a question of retrieving the paper and noting the combination.

The mare, trotting slowly after her long run, suddenly stopped, ears perked forward. Royal saw a cluster of riders about a quarter-mile away. They were talking and sharing cigarettes. Royal cursed himself for not leaving the road sooner. He quickly looked toward the distant Little Colorado River, trying to find a gully to use as cover. He pulled the mare to the right and put several large sagebushes between himself and the group of riders. The mare was antsy, wanting to run. Royal held back until he felt there was enough cover to risk it.

A shot boomed into the night. A quick glance over his shoulder told Royal the chase was on. The six riders had fanned out in earnest pursuit. With blistering speed and surefootedness, the mare raced through the sage-covered country. The damp smell of water ahead encouraged her. Royal spoke to her in the dash for the river. As they neared a barrier of thick willows and cottonwoods, he slowed and searched for a break in the bluffs. He spotted a low dip and urged the mare toward it. She faltered on the edge and stepped back, but the bank gave away. As she fell, she kicked against the face to regain her footing. Those strong kicks thrust her away from the crumbling mass of dirt and into deep, still water. She and Royal landed in one of the few pools, hitting the water with a loud splash. The noise flushed a pair of owls from their treetop perch.

Royal, thrown from the saddle, kept a death grip on the reins. He kicked hard and bobbed to the surface. After a quick gulp of air, he was yanked under. He pulled on the reins and surfaced again. The mare was swimming strongly. Royal pushed away from her rump to avoid a kick from her powerful hind legs. With a lunge, he grabbed the saddle and let her do the rest. She grounded on a sandbar, and Royal matched her step for step out of the water. He led her beneath the undercut riverbank to rest. They were both winded from the swim.

"Come here," Royal said softly to his mare. She turned her head and nuzzled against him, nearly knocking him over. As he rubbed both ears, the mare leaned against him.

A shout from upstream alerted them, and Royal swung into the saddle. He did not want to be trapped in the river bottom. He rode downstream, then followed a small game trail that led up the steep riverbank. In several places, he lay against the mare's neck to avoid being brushed off by low tree limbs. Once on top of the bluff, the trail blended into the desert.

"A little more, gal, and we'll be safe." The mare responded to his words and touch. They rode through the lee side of a small hillock, angled across it, and eased into the open countryside beyond. The mare found her natural gait, and Royal relaxed. He liked his odds better in the desert.

"Oh, no! Sophie's dress!" he exclaimed in distress, horrified at the thought that he had lost it. "If that dress is water soaked, I'm wasting my time. All for naught."

Safely distanced from the riders, Royal slowed the mare and twisted in his saddle. He felt for the dress box and breathed a sigh of relief. Now to open it and check the dress. The leather tie was slippery and difficult to undo. After a struggle, he had the box in hand and the wet blanket draped behind the saddle.

Sophie had gift-wrapped the dress before placing it back in

the original box. She had used heavy paper on the box and sealed the seams with candle wax. The box was watertight. "Phew!" Royal exclaimed with a smile. "I love that woman." He thought fondly of Sophie and of the help she had given. He ran a fingernail down a seam, cracked it open, and eased the box partially open. He unfolded a corner of the wrapping and pulled the dress out.

"Hold still a minute there, gal." He stopped the mare.

He stuck the paper under his thigh and tenderly unfolded the dress. "Please be dry," he pleaded, and ran his hand down the length of the dress. Dry as a duck's back. The small lilac potpourri pinned to the bodice gave off a lovely scent.

Royal burst out laughing and startled the mare. He reprimanded and steadied her. As he talked to her, his voice was laced with humor. "Gal, this could be difficult to explain if we're caught. Out here in the middle of the desert at midnight holding up a dress for size. Maybe it's the moon." He scratched his head in disbelief. "Old John Tibbetts, God rest his soul, would turn over in his grave if he witnessed this!"

Folding the dress as best a man could, he rewrapped it and put it back into the box. He slipped the heavy paper on, then spurred the mare into motion. He headed for Apache Springs, with the box across his lap. It was a good three-hour ride. He would have to push it.

Apache Springs consisted of an adobe main building with two smaller outbuildings, a stable and corral. If you weren't looking for it, you'd miss it. It was nestled next to Dry Creek, a suggestion of a stream that trickled year round. The adobe buildings were built against low bluffs that shaded and cooled them.

Royal slipped behind the stable, staying in the dense underbrush. He slid stiffly out of the saddle and tied the mare to a bushy willow. He stroked her affectionately, and she nuzzled him. "I'll feed ya soon. We made it, gal."

Slicing through the underbrush with scarcely a sound, Royal reached the corral. A Mexican sprout was rounding up the fresh team as his compadre unhitched the other horses from the stage. When Royal ducked between the railings, he startled the youth.

"*Buenos días, muchacho,*" Royal greeted the motionless boy.

"Señor," the lad replied. He wasn't sure what to expect from this stranger.

"¿Qué tal?"

The boy yielded somewhat, not quite so guarded as he answered. *"Bien, gracias. ¿Usted?"*

"Bien. ¿Dónde está el señor Red?" The boy pointed toward the main building. *"Díga le que estoy esperando atrás del corral. Gracias."*

"De nada, señor," the boy replied as he went for Big Red.

Royal ducked through the railings, tucked the boxed dress under his arm, and walked to the creek. Minutes later, he heard Big Red mumbling about being interrupted during breakfast. Red marched through the underbrush, not around it. He was a big solid man, a nail keg wide and not much taller. A flaming red beard and long curly hair gave him the appearance of a wild man. When he saw Royal, his face lighted and he forgot about breakfast.

"Royal, you son of a gun!" He grinned widely. "How the hell you been?"

Red approached Royal and gave him a bone-crushing handshake and a spine-jarring slap on the back. Royal wondered if his pistol hand would still function after Big Red's ham-size fist had finished with it. Red stepped back and looked at Royal. "Damn, am I glad to see you." Red's feelings were genuine.

"You're lookin' a little rough around the edges, Red. How you keepin'?"

"Aw, hell. Can't complain," Big Red chortled, and his laughter shook his barrel chest. " 'Sides, no one would listen."

"I saw your better half last night." Royal realized his comment might be misconstrued and quickly added, "She's helping me stir up hate and discontent in Jacob's Well. I need your help. Would you mind?"

"Hell, no," Red replied immediately. "If'n she's in, so'm I. Whatcha need?"

"Two things. Could your Mexican gal reseal this box?" Royal handed it to him. "Then, can you deliver it on Saturday? Sophie knows all about it and will make a fuss over it. She'll talk to the stationmaster and have it delivered to Millie Tilden's Saturday luncheon." Royal waited for Red's reaction.

"That's all?" Disappointment cut Red's voice as he took the box.

"Now, don't go off half cocked," Royal reassured him. "You stop at Wicketts Junction and meet the train?"

"You damned betcha. Eleven forty-five on the dot." Big Red took pride in his trade.

"Good. When you get there, I want you to hand this telegram to Jim Banks. No one else, understand?" Royal gave the paper to Red. He nodded. "Go ahead, read it." Royal wanted to include Red in the effort.

Big Red opened the slip and slowly read the message. A smile worked its way across his face. He whistled and folded the paper before he stuck it into his shirt pocket. "This is gonna cause some problems for sure. Liable to piss off a few folks in the process," he added with peaked interest.

"Glad to hear you think so. Now, go finish your breakfast." Royal patted Red's massive shoulder. "Thanks for the help—I appreciate it."

Red crushed Royal's hand again, then turned and walked toward the corral.

"Oh, Red—have Jim send that telegram Friday night, 'bout ten." Royal had a twofold reason for sending the telegram then. He wanted the telegram delivered to Colburn in time for the Saturday afternoon poker game, and the telegram would also test Elihu Jones, the misdirected telegrapher. Red waved acknowledgment.

"My friend," Red called, "if you're stirring things up in Jacob's Well, I'm solid behind you." Royal's words were gospel to him.

"Thanks, Red. You haven't seen me, if anyone asks."

While Red finished breakfast, the cook's daughter pressed the wrinkles out of the dress and resealed the box. A Saturday delivery was noted on the schedule.

As he departed, Big Red's voice shattered the morning calm. "I'm goin', folks. You wanna ride, follow me." He headed out the door with four passengers tight on his heels. "Hank, check 'round back for sight-seein' passengers. We don't want any left behind."

Hank Reardon, the shotgun rider, a slip of a man, soft-footed behind the shed and scanned the corral. People said Hank was dying of consumption. He was shallow complexioned—an unnatural pallor touched his skin. With a minimum of motion he swept the area and spotted Royal. His look sparkled, and crow's-feet grew at the corners of his eyes as he grinned. With a casualness that belied his frailty, he eased over to Royal.

"How you doin', old man?" Royal asked with concern.

"Still kicking, if that's what you mean" was Hank's offhand reply. "Nice to see ya. You settle the score with that jackleg lawman yet?"

"Naw, but I'm working on it," Royal confided. "Ask Big Red 'bout it when you're movin'."

Hank liked what he heard, his offer was sincere. "If the need arises, say the word."

"You bet—thanks, Hank. Get goin', or Red will be ahowlin'."

Hank turned and headed for the stage, but spoke over his shoulder to Royal. "You be careful, lad. That sheriff's dangerous."

"I'll keep it in mind. Take care," he warmly told his friend.

Royal was amused as Hank threaded his way around the horse muffins in the corral. He shook his head and watched the skinny-framed cowboy walk away. Hank's clothes merely hung on his bony shoulders, and a belt kept his pants riding on thin hips.

The man did not appear to be a threat to anyone. But to think so would be a fatal miscalculation. Hank was as good with firearms as any man who ever pulled a trigger. He was a natural with shotgun, pistol, or rifle—it made no difference. The slow-as-molasses facade had fooled many a potential robber and highwayman. Several had passed him off as a tired old man, only to realize their mistake as they lay dying.

Big Red and Hank were a comical sight on the stage. Red, gregarious and full of life, dwarfed the taciturn shotgun rider. But they were a team. Each anticipated the other's move almost before it happened. Little if anything was said between them. Red wrapped two sets of reins from the lead team in his left hand. In his right hand were the reins from the wheel team. He drove with both hands because he didn't believe in a whip. Red commanded his teams, and they listened. He nodded to Hank, then kicked the brake loose.

"Loco, Patches—up! Let's go, you two." He snapped the reins. The two leaders pulled ahead. "Willie, Son, pick it up! *Pick it up!*" He talked to the wheelers. "Son!" Red yelled at the second wheeler. "Get your butt amovin'. I ain't babyin' you all the way to Jacob's Well." As the stage disappeared behind a wall of dust, Big Red's whistles and shouts cut the air. Royal reflected on why Red called that horse Son.

"It's easier than calling him Son of a Bitch every time," Red had laughed.

Royal couldn't understand it. "Why don't you get rid of him?"

"Lord, can that horse pull! We're talkin' strong." Red clenched his fist. "A little contrary, but a damned good horse. He could pull this rig all by hisself."

With the mare fed and rested, Royal left the stage station after midday. He was well stocked with Señora Sanchez's fresh-baked tortillas and tamales, and his mouth was still on fire from the chile rellenos. Now for the two-hour ride to Carl Enrough's ranch. Royal wanted to borrow a horse for a day.

Carl Henry Enrough's ranch was near the mountains and consisted of several hundred acres of grasslands and mesas thick with ponderosa pine. Snow-fed streams watered the ranch. The stream banks were lined with thick stands of aspen and cottonwood. The pastures were fenced, and horses dotted the valley. Hay fields were ready for a second cutting. The main house and barns were built on a small shelf that overlooked the entire spread. The CHE ranch reflected pride and hard work, the trademarks of Carl Enrough. He was a man of modest means but one hell of a sharp horse trader. He had an eye for horses and made a successful living by quality breeding. An Enrough horse was an excellent horse—guaranteed.

Royal rode the fence line that paralleled the ranch house. Carl was out in the corral walking a mare and her foal. A flock of kids were underfoot, playing, tripping, or fighting with each other. Carl glanced up as Royal dismounted and walked to the fence.

"Howdy, stranger," Royal greeted Carl, a wide smile creasing his rugged features.

"Royal!" Carl spoke in disbelief. "Royal Ballou! Long time no see. How you been?" He led the mare over to Royal and shook his hand.

"Fine, Carl. Thanks. I see you're still in the breeding business. Horses and kids." Royal broad-grinned as he watched three of the kids tussle by the trough.

"As my better half says, good studs are hard to find." He

laughed easily. Carl was tall, a shade over six feet, muscular and solid. Many years of hard work had toughened him. A mass of brown hair outlined his broad, craggy face, and his hazel eyes sparkled. Life to him was fun, a challenge, to be lived to the fullest. Nice white pearlies flashed when he smiled.

"Come on up to the house. We'll jaw for a while. Sorry to hear about John. What in the hell is happening over there?"

"Dirty politics and corrupt lawgivers," Royal answered with distaste.

They climbed the steps to the front porch. "What's this about?" Carl asked, and handed Royal a wanted poster.

"That, my friend, is a picture perfect frame-up. New style of lawmaker in town."

"I guessed as much," Carl replied with disgust. He met and held Royal's eyes. "Can you get out of it?"

"That's why I'm here," Royal explained, "I'm trying. With your help, I'll liven things up a bit."

"Holly, come out here!" Carl yelled through the partially opened door. "We got company."

"Be right out, hon," a woman's velvet-smooth voice answered.

Within a minute a tall, comely woman walked onto the porch. She was the "mare" of the family, Carl said. Her golden blond hair, neatly braided, framed a gentle face. Her blue eyes, soft yet all seeing, settled on Royal. He stood as Holly approached, a smile graced her face. She had a babe nestled in her arms, covered with a nursing blanket. She hugged Royal with one arm and kissed him on the cheek. "It's been a long time," she said with delight. " 'Bout didn't recognize you. You're looking good, considering the circumstances." An understanding smile dimpled her mouth.

"Your newest addition?" Royal asked, looking at the little one.

"Yep. And the last," she added firmly. "I'm going to cut the old man myself. With a rusty, dull knife." She glanced playfully at Carl. They all laughed.

"What did I do to deserve it?" Carl asked helplessly, enjoying his wife's humor.

They talked as only friends could. The stories and old lies were relived once again. Then Holly broke the spell. "Please stay for dinner. Another place won't be hard to set."

"You sure?" Royal questioned. "I don't want to barge in." Holly gave him a tender pat on the cheek and went inside to prepare the meal.

"Holly's still one of the best damned cooks in the territory," Carl bragged.

After dinner, Royal and Carl strolled past the corrals. One of Carl's young uns was feeding a mare and foal. Carl called to the lad, "Hey, Dude! Keep an eye on that mare. She's real protective."

"Your oldest?" Royal asked Carl as he watched the lad. He was the spittin' image of his dad. "Good-lookin' kid. Takes after his mother."

"So what's the favor you need? I'll help if I can," Carl offered.

"Let me tell you about the goin's-on in Jacob's Well." Royal gazed at the distant mesas with their deep purple shadows and pulled his thoughts together. "It's a complicated mess."

Royal and Carl continued their walk, checking horses, setting water, and closing gates before nightfall. When it grew dark, they returned to the porch. Royal had bent Carl's ear long enough.

"Sounds like we have a deal," Carl commented with pleasure. "I like what I heard. John Tibbetts was good to me." He was momentarily dispirited, and memories of the man threaded his voice with emotion. "He helped me several years ago with a rustling problem. The old man sat over there every night for a week before he caught the rustlers. I owe him a favor."

"So we are agreed." Royal looked pleased. "I'll return your horse in a day or two, depending on how things go."

"Fine. If it works, and I have every confidence it will, I'd be proud of my part in it." Carl smiled and shook Royal's hand. " 'Bout time someone cleaned house on that crooked bunch."

Royal left Carl's CHE ranch at midmorning with a two-year colt. The colt, a Thoroughbred, ran in a smooth, upright manner. Royal fussed over him all the way to Jacob's Well. To the colt, this was an adventure not to be missed, and he frolicked with abandon, causing Royal considerable trauma. What pleased Royal in particular about the colt was his stride, long and even. He was a runner for sure.

In the dead of night, Royal halted behind Joe Mex's stable.

He tied both horses to a post and walked quietly around to the empty front office. He glanced into the dark interior. Not a soul was to be seen. A note on the door explained the location and means of reaching Alex, the stableboy. Unless things had changed, Royal's unsuspecting "friend" had his stall at the rear of the stable. He squeezed through the partially closed stable door and walked carefully to the back. The last stall was empty. Good. Royal crouched in front of the stall, caught a glimmer of reflected light, and read the nameplate. A smile crossed his face.

Royal stood just inside the rear doors of the stable and searched the outside until he was convinced no one was about. Then he worked his way around the corral, found the colt, and brought him in through the gate to the last stall. With a scoop of oats and fresh water, the colt was content. As Royal dumped a handfull of hay into the feed trough, he spoke softly to the colt. "Do your part, little one, and we'll have some fun." The colt flicked his ears and kept eating.

The mayor and councilmen were having coffee together at The Rose. Business in town was down. Roundup time had not produced the expected revenues. Trail crews had stayed with their herds instead of coming into Jacob's Well.

"Money's tight now," Asa Hemmingway complained. A slight aroma of meat clung about him. "My meat sales have fallen sharply." The council ignored his drivel. "I had to put the brakes on the missus. She was spending me into bankruptcy." This last statement caught the attention of the others. They could relate to this problem.

"No easy task to whoa the missus," Hervey offered with tender concern as he spoke around the butt of his stogie. A chorus of guffaws followed.

Lem Tilden, the merchantile owner, added with sympathy, "Millie's been after me for weeks to let her shop in the big city. I flat told her we couldn't afford frillies at this time." The tic distorted the corner of his mouth.

"Be careful, Lem," Mayor Albee warned. As he spoke, his body seemed to shake. "Millie will be laying for you."

"I know, Mr. Mayor," Lem jokingly added. His smile was crooked. "I'm afraid I'll either get the rolling pin or henpecked when I walk in the door at night. Not much of a choice."

"Take the rolling pin, Lem," the mayor consoled him. "That way the pain is over quicker." The mayor's laugh jiggled his massive girth. The other council members joined in.

The laughter died as hot coffee was passed. Hervey relit his cigar. The meeting was then interrupted by the law as Curly walked boldly into the room. An uninvited guest, he did not belong to the good ol' boy clique. Resentment took over as all conversation ceased. Curly pulled up a chair and sat at the table. He poured a cup of coffee and leaned back in his chair. Not a word had been uttered since he entered the room. Curly looked around the table, eyeballing each member of the council. A hostile mood stifled the meeting.

"Nice-lookin' colt, Asa. Where'd you get him?" Curly looked directly at the meat market owner.

"Say what?" asked Asa. "What are you talking about?"

Curly, taken aback, challenged Asa. "I said"—he enunciated each word as he spoke—"nice-looking colt. Where'd you get him? The colt in your stall."

At a complete loss for words, Asa sat stone silent, growing flustered. As he perspired, the meaty smell grew stronger. "Mr. Hall," he begged off, "I don't have the slightest idea what colt you're referring to."

"Well," Lem interceded with barely concealed delight, "let's go see what Mr. Hall is talking about."

With a loud scraping and shuffling of chairs, the men stood and followed Lem.

"You coming, Asa?" the rotund mayor asked.

"Ah . . . yes," Asa answered falteringly. "I was just thinking."

A growing excitement touched the group as they walked through the interior of the stable and crowded around Asa's stall. Curly stepped forward, opened the gate, and approached the colt. The animal eyed him with reservation, sniffed his hand, and slowly moved forward. Curly rubbed him softly.

"Wow, isn't he a beaut," the mayor marveled.

"Fine-looking critter, Asa," Lem caustically commented. Even in a tight smile, his mouth was momentarily touched with a tic.

Hervey, the horseman of the lot, chomped the cigar into the corner of his mouth and knelt to the colt's level. He patted him with loving care. "That's as purebred an animal as I ever seen," he exclaimed with pleasure and gently traced the colt's legs with his hand. "What a dandy! Look at his long legs. He'll run like the wind."

Asa hadn't recovered from the original shock. To stand by his peers and hear their accolades was unnerving.

"Now we know why you put the skids on the missus. You needed the money to purchase this little bugger." Ellery prodded Asa with his elbow and shook all over. The other men laughed along with the mayor.

"But . . . gentlemen . . . this colt isn't mine."

"Nice try, Asa," Curly slashed at him. "Where did he come from?"

"People around here just don't have that kind of money," Lem added. "I want to be at your house tonight when you try to explain this to your wife. The hell, to your wife! Explain it to us."

"Take my advice, Asa," Hervey said around his cigar as he patted Asa on the back and tried to keep a straight face. He failed. "Back through the door tonight. That way you'll save your scalp."

Curly left the stall, followed by the others. They walked through the stable laughing and talking. Asa stood alone, irate. He found Joe Mex, the stable owner, and harangued him without mercy, which was out of character for Asa. Joe Mex put up with it for a reasonable amount of time before gracefully showing him out of the office.

Asa turned and emphatically pointed his finger at Joe. "This is final—I don't want that horse! Do whatever you want with him." Asa turned on his heel and stormed off the boardwalk.

Joe was in the stall when he was interrupted by Belle Fallan, the six-year-old daughter of Sophie and Big Red.

"Hi, Joe." She beamed. Her cherry-red cheeks were creased with a wide toothless grin. The dimples reached almost to her brightly ribboned braids.

"Hello, peanut." Joe squatted to her level and tugged playfully at her braids. "How's my favorite girl today?"

"Good." Again the quick smile.

Joe laughed, picked her up, and balanced her on the stall railing. "When you gonna get some new front teeth?"

"Pretty soon, Mom says." She shrugged with a child's resignation. "But I don't believe her. She talks about wishes and new teeth. You'd think by now she'd know that they just grow back."

A child's perspective on parenthood, Joe thought. "Ya, I know what you mean. Moms are like that." Joe acted serious, supporting her theory. "What can I do for you today?"

"I have a secret message for you," she confided.

"You do?" Joe stepped back in surprise, then moved close to her and whispered, "Who's it from?"

"Royal," Belle divulged. "He told me not to tell anyone but you."

"Good idea." Joe nodded his head, enjoying the innocence of this tomboy. "That sure was smart of him, huh?"

"You bet. He even paid me a *whole nickel* if I gave you this paper." She sparkled with joy and reached into her pocket to pull out a crumpled slip. Aglow with pride, she handed it to him. The message read as follows:

Joe, meet me at the swimming hole when you can

"My friend Royal said he would wait all day for you."

"Thanks, peanut." Joe tweaked her nose and got gales of laughter in return. He lifted her off the railing and set her on the ground.

As Joe worked in the stall with Belle on his heels, Curly's loud voice called from the office, "Hey, Joe, come here." Belle darted out of the stall and scooted around the corner into the corral before Curly appeared. The sheriff stood on the dock and waited impatiently as Joe came to him. Joe had popped the note into his mouth and badly needed a drink of water to wash it down. He hopped onto the dock, motioned Curly into the office, and poured a drink.

"What do you want?" he asked the sheriff with a minimum of civility.

"That colt in Asa's stall," Curly flatly stated.

Joe's heart sank. The thought of that little critter in Curly's hand riled him. "Did you ask Asa?" He stalled, trying to rescue the colt.

"He don't want him. Told me so on his way back to the meat shop."

"I guess if he don't want him, so be it," Joe said with resignation. "What do you think he's worth?"

"To you, Joe, nothing but a headache." Curly tried to intimidate him. "Since you know nothing 'bout the colt, I'll give you fifty dollars."

"Don't seem like very much."

"Forty-five" was Curly's snap answer.

"Hey, now." Joe contested the cut.

"Forty bucks," Curly interrupted with still another cut.

"The colt's yours. Take him," Joe blurted out. All he wanted now was to be done with Curly.

"Pleasure horse tradin' with you, Joe." Curly slapped him on the back then took him by the scruff of the neck. "I'll get you your money." A crocodile grin covered the sheriff's face. Joe had no choice but to go.

The two man walked briskly to the sheriff's office. Joe waited in the doorway while Curly opened the safe. The sheriff counted out forty dollars and paid him. With the money exchanged, they returned to the stable.

"This is between the two of us. Understand?" Curly threatened.

Joe acknowledged it with a nod. The sheriff tipped his hat and went through the door. He jumped off the dock and walked jauntily toward the stall.

"Hey, Joe!" Curly's voice boomed out with anger. "Come here! *Now!*" Joe sighed deeply and with a strong feeling of loathing went into the stable. Curly stood by the stall, his left arm on top of the railing. "I thought we had a deal."

"We did. Why?"

"Where's my horse?" Curly demanded, sweeping his arm toward the empty stall.

Joe was surprised. "I don't know." He shrugged his shoulders. "He was here when we left. I was with you the entire time."

"Don't fool with me, Joe." Curly was furious and stepped menacingly toward Joe.

"Curly," Joe told him forcefully, "I never left your side. Remember that?"

"Where's your boy?" Curly was grasping for straws.

"Alex? He won't be in till two o'clock."

"That horse can't just disappear." Curly could not believe this had happened to him.

"What can I say?" Joe pointedly asked the lawman. That should end it, he thought.

"Damn it all to hell!" Curly fumed, and stomped out of the stable. In an eyeblink he was back. "Gimme my money!" he demanded, and held out his hand.

Joe reached into his pants pocket and removed the coins. The big lawman snatched the money in a blur. "Pleasure doin' business with you," Joe muttered at Curly's back.

Joe Mex was puzzled by the disappearance of the colt. He sauntered slowly around the corral looking for clues. After a thorough search, Joe found the colt's prints mingled with other hoofprints. He knelt, studied the ground, and saw the telling clue. A child's footprint was beside the water trough, partially filled with water. Joe held back an impulse to ride for the river, but he didn't trust Curly and would bide his time.

The day dragged as he waited for Alex to show up for work. Then, shortly after two, Joe rode to the swimming hole. He eased his mule along the willow-lined trail. Several open patches of sand offered no trace of the colt. He spotted several lightly brushed areas and realized that Belle had brought the colt this way, covering his prints with a leafy branch. He hurried to meet Royal.

A man slipped out of the willows and blocked his trail. It was Sheriff Hall. Curly greeted him with barely concealed malice. "Goin' someplace, Joe?"

"Swimming, if it's any of your business," Joe bluffed.

"I thought you might be lookin' for something," Curly accused.

"Swimmin', sheriff," Joe told him again. "Now, if you'll excuse me." He squeezed past the lawman, trotted to the river, and headed upstream. The hole, deep and still, was shaded by big cottonwood and willow trees. The shore was sandy and sloped gently into the water. Joe slipped off the mule and tied him to a stump. He copped a quick glance toward the trail. Much to his dismay, he saw Curly slowly walking in his direction. Caught, damn it! Joe thought. A buried childhood fear of water welled within him. He would have to gut it out.

Curly sat on a log, one leg crossed over the other. He casually lit a cigar and blew smoke rings into the air. He taunted

Joe with twisted pleasure. "Go ahead, Joe. Nice day for a swim."

Joe Mex shucked his boots and reluctantly dropped his trousers. Next came his shirt. He looked a sight standing in his red longhandles, his white torso contrasting sharply against his sunburned arms and neck.

"Make the plunge, Joe." It was a borderline order.

Joe, disinclined to get wet, had no choice and toed the water. Many years ago his grandfather had thrown him into a ditch. "Learn him how to swim" had been the old man's words. Joe would have drowned if his older brother hadn't dragged him out. From that day on, Joe had been terrified of water.

"How's the water, Joe?" Curly's sardonic smile creased his cheeks.

"Nice," Joe managed to reply.

The loud cocking of a pistol heightened his fears. "Swim, Joe!" Curly demanded. Joe had both feet in the water when Curly shot.

The slug hit inches behind Joe. The noise seemed twice as loud as usual. Joe jumped and landed in deep water with a cracking splash. Curly watched the drama with delight. The sheriff would have bet even money that Joe's back never got wet, the way he thrashed and windmilled his way onto dry land.

"Do that again, Joe!" Curly roared as he raised his Colt again. He shot at Joe and missed. Joe staggered into the water and landed on his back. He sank from sight. A minute later, Joe erupted downstream, terror on his face. Curly hadn't moved a muscle as he smoked his cigar. Joe fought his way out of the chest-deep water and crawled onto the sand. Only then did he cough up river water. He retched half a dozen times, his body shaking uncontrollably. Curly stood, picked up Joe's clothes, untied the mule, and walked toward the trail.

"See you back in town, Joe." Curly flicked his butt into the water and left.

Joe, emptied, sat on his heels and glared at the disappearing figure. "I'll get you for this, Sheriff Hall." The man seldom threatened anyone, but when he did, it was a given that he would carry it out.

Joe stood shakily and headed for town. He wrapped his arms around his chest, seeking warmth. As he started up the trail, he stepped on a burr. This was a banner season for goat's-head burrs. As Joe pulled it from his bare foot, Royal stepped out of the underbrush.

"Sorry, my friend. I watched but couldn't do a thing to help. Are you all right?" He stepped forward and steadied Joe as he plucked another burr.

"Ya." He laughed. "I won't need a drink of water for about a week. Where's the colt?"

"On the other side of the river with Belle." Royal pointed. "She brought him down—said she didn't want that 'mean man' to have him. That kid is smart."

"I love her," Joe proclaimed. "She saved the colt from a life with Curly. Plus she did it all on her own." He shook his head in wonderment. To him, it was nearly worth the swim to see Curly outfoxed by a six-year-old. "Tell her I'll buy her some hard candy when we get together." He stepped back. "Ouch!" Another burr. He tenderly removed it and stuck it on his hatband. "This one's for Curly Hall."

"Can you spare Alex for the rest of the day?"

"Ya. Why?" Joe was concerned about leaving the stable unattended.

"I have to get that colt back to Carl Enrough." Royal filled Joe in on the details.

"So that's where you got him." Joe laughed lightly. "I should have guessed. Good stock."

"You're right there. And if I don't get him back, I'll be in hock for the next ten years."

"You can have Alex," Joe volunteered his stableboy. "He's a good hand. You won't have a worry about him. I'm on my way back to the stable." He took a step and found another burr. "At this rate I'll be there tomorrow morning."

"Here, Joe. You'll never make it that way. Tear this in half and wrap your feet." Royal pulled his shirttails out, and yanked on both lapels. Buttons flew in all directions. "What the hell, it was old anyway. I've got my vest in my saddlebag." He handed the shirt to Joe.

"Thanks, friend." Joe smiled in gratitude. "My feet thank you also."

CHAPTER
10

It was after dark when Royal returned to the jail. He tied his mare in the willows and cautiously approached the building from the rear. He had misgivings about going back and felt that he had pushed his luck last time. Would his luck hold on this venture? The paper behind the number plate was his ace to Curly's safe. If Curly stuck to his routine, Royal would have a clear shot at the safe.

A careful check of the street revealed nothing suspicious. Royal stepped onto the boardwalk with catlike grace and in soundless movements reached for the office door. Taking a deep breath, he gently opened it.

Click! Curly glanced up from his desk. It took him only a split second to recognize Royal. The sheriff jumped to his feet, knocked his chair over backward, and rushed the door. Royal slammed the door shut and grabbed the handle with both hands. He braced his shoulder against the doorframe. Curly yanked hard on the knob, only to have his hand squirt off it. The sheriff expected Royal to hold the door, so he wrapped both hands on the knob and jerked with all his strength. Royal had let go, a step ahead of the sheriff. The door swung wildly open. Curly stumbled backward, off balance, and fell to the floor. The door slammed solidly against the wall and banged shut.

Royal took a chair from the porch, set it in front of the door, and leaped off the boardwalk. Curly was on his feet in the blink of an eye. He threw open the door and with gun in hand burst outside. The lawman tripped over the chair, his momentum carried him to the railing. With his legs scythed out from beneath him, Curly slowly somersaulted off the porch and landed in the street. He touched off a round as he hit the dirt. Fortunately no one was hit by the stray bullet, but folks came outside to see who was shooting. Curly rolled from his back to his knees, then stood. He holstered his Colt and fell forward as he took a step—the wire bracing from the chair was tangled in his feet. He couldn't move until he had extricated himself, which took considerable swearing and effort.

"Who the hell you gawkin' at?" He glared defiantly at the crowd, then quickly searched the street in both directions. The people mimicked his movements and looked in both directions too. With the exception of the curiosity seekers, the street was empty.

"What you talkin' 'bout, Sheriff?" a voice called from the crowd. "All we see is you afoul of that poor, defenseless chair." A few onlookers laughed.

"Royal Ballou is in town," Curly addressed the growing crowd. "I'll personally give one hundred dollars cold hard cash to the man who brings him in. Dead or alive."

It took only one look to tell the sheriff was serious. The word spread like a wind-whipped prairie fire. The townies, bar patrons, and fortune seekers quickly formed a posse. Soon The Rose was empty, the tables and bordello deserted. A mounted posse gathered in front of the sheriff's office. Before Curly could issue orders, shots rang out from the far side of town, and the posse took off in that direction.

During the short ride to Doc Shu's store, Royal listened with enjoyment to the war in progress. It sounded like a siege. Shots were fired, followed by the thundering of horses and shouts of alarm. When Royal dismounted behind the sandstone formations that butted against Doc Shu's small corral, he heard the rumbling approach of horses. Fearing capture, he mounted again, ready to break for the foothills. The posse charged past the store on its way out of town. Random shots filled the night. As Royal guardedly approached the store, he heard metal scrape against rock. He stealthily dropped to the ground and bellied against a flat slab.

"That you, Curly?" a voice called from the darkness.

"Ya" was Curly's muffled reply. "Let's search the place. I'll cover you."

Royal heard footsteps crunch and molded himself into the rock. A shadowy figure stood above him, and pebbles pelted his face. The man stepped toward the rear of the building. Royal held his breath, afraid to move a muscle. He watched Curly sneak out of the corral, heading for the back door. As the deputy joined him, he stumbled into boxes of broken bottles.

Doc Shu fumbled with the back latch, then cautiously opened the door. "Who is it?" he called. Royal prayed Doc would not use his name. "I know you're there."

Curly moved forward into the light. "Lookin' for me, Doc?" The sheriff startled the doc, but Shubael concealed his alarm and held his ground.

"I thought it was a skunk rootin' through my garbage. Guess I was right." He swung the door shut, only to have it blocked by Curly's foot.

"I'm searchin' for Royal, Doc. Seen him?"

"Nope. I wouldn't tell you if I had, but you're welcome to search my place if you want."

"Be careful, old man. I'm keepin' an eye on you." Curly removed his foot, and the door closed.

Royal watched Curly and the deputy depart, then waited ten minutes before entering the store.

"Had a visitor a few minutes ago." Doc wiped his brow.

"I know. I just missed getting caught near the rocks."

The doc was on the prod. "You responsible for the fracas?"

"Guess I am," Royal admitted sheepishly. "I had some help from Curly. He offered a hundred dollars for my capture." Royal laughed. "Half the posse is too drunk to recognize me; the other half is too drunk to do anything about it. You heard and saw the rest."

The humor of the moment settled Shubael. "Come here." He motioned to Royal. In the dimly lighted front of the store, he pointed to three bullet holes in his window. "You want to buy me a new window?"

"Put it on Curly's tab," Royal joshed.

"Hell," Doc Shu retorted, "I oughta go into the glass business! Between you and Curly, I could make a fortune." His anger faded as he realized that Royal had been taunting the lawman. That suited him just fine.

"How am I going to get back inside that office? After tonight, it'll be watched closer than a faro dealer's hands."

"That's a tough one. Curly will be keeping a close eye for you. He'll no doubt tighten things up at the jail."

"You're right, Doc. What can I do?"

The doc reached into the bottom drawer of his desk and set a bottle of "prescription medicine" on top. He poured two shots. He grinned, then pointed his index finger at Royal, scheming now. "Maybe we have a way after all."

"What are you thinkin', Doc?" Royal pressed.

Doc Shu headed for the small attic above the storage room. He climbed a short ladder and called into the darkness, "Hey, boy! It's Doc. Wake up, son. You hear me?"

"Yes," a child answered. "I'm awake."

"Come down," the doc instructed. "I want you to meet a friend."

Doc Shu returned to his chair and waited. "With a little help from the offshoot, we just might get back inside the jail." A look of expectation shone on his face.

As the men sat and talked, a small Apache boy came down from the attic and walked over to Doc Shu. He was short, worn to a shadow. His trousers were tied around his waist with twine, and his sleeves were rolled yet hung to his wrists. The boy sized up Royal in a glance. He was suspicious but trusted Doc Shu when he said this was a friend. The boy leaned against the old man, resting his arm on the doc's shoulder. The doc put his arm around the lad's waist.

"Royal, I'd like you to meet Little Smith, one of Mr. Smith's many offspring. This young lad is every bit as good a tracker as his father." Doc laughed. "Where else could you find a better teacher?"

The boy came to Royal and shook his hand. "Mr. Ballou, I've heard of you from my father." Royal listened to the lad as he spoke in good English. He was the mirror image of his father. Missionary educated, the Smith family was an example of the Indians' ability to adapt to the white man's ways.

"Tell me your plans, Doc," Royal demanded. He was high mettled and ready to act. He steeled himself for a long, windy discourse, but the doc fooled him.

"I was on the town council when we built the jail. It's got a single flaw we might be able to exploit."

Only an hour after Curly's visit to the doc's, Royal and Little Smith were standing behind the jail. Curly was on the porch talking with his deputies. "Please, Mr. Ballou," Little Smith begged, and his small hand tugged at Royal's shirt sleeve. "I want to get even with the sheriff. His men tried to kill Father. Please?"

"All right. We'll do it. But if you're caught," he sternly warned, "you'll end up missing. Someone will find your sun-bleached bones in the desert two or three months from now. Still want to?"

The boy nodded.

Royal hunched beneath the rear window, his hands braced on his knees. Little Smith climbed onto his back, using the wall to steady himself. Royal slowly stood, and Little Smith walked up to Royal's shoulders. His fingertips touched the windowsill. "Can you reach it?" Royal whispered.

"Yes. Give me a boost."

Royal put his hand underneath the boy's heels and muscled him up. Little Smith pulled himself to the far right of the frame and squeezed between the bars.

Doc Shu had remembered that when the jail was built, the space between the last bar and the windowframe was wider than the others. An additional half row of bricks had been added, but the flaw remained. Doc Shu's hunch that Little Smith would be able to slip through easily was correct. Royal glanced up to see Little Smith's feet disappear into the cell. "Be careful," he whispered. They had discussed the removal of the dial number plate. Now Little Smith was on his own.

Footsteps sounded in the alley. Royal sprinted from the wall into the deep drainage ditch that ran from the jail to the river. He was afraid the noise of falling pebbles would give him away. A deputy, the portrait of slovenliness, bumbled around the corner, passed beneath the window, and continued his rounds. He checked nothing. His laxness reflected his attitude. He'd rather be out riding with the posse.

Inside Little Smith dropped onto the cot. The cell was dark, but he could see the open door. He secreted his way to the office and headed directly for the safe. The knob was just as Royal had described it. Fishing the knife from his pants pocket, he opened the blade and pushed it under the plate. It wouldn't budge. He heard muffled voices from the porch. Little Smith chose a smaller blade and, after several tries, forced the tip under the plate. He pried around the plate and forced it off.

Pop! The plate snapped off and hit the wooden floor with a loud metallic clank.

"What was that?" Curly asked.

"What you talkin' about?" one of the deputies asked.

Little Smith heard a chair scrape on the porch. He ran for the cell. On the way he scooped up the number plate, bobbled it, then caught it in midair. His feet cleared the dark cell doorway just as Curly's Colt preceded him into the room. The sheriff checked the office, then grabbed a lantern above his head and searched each cell. Satisfied that nothing was amiss, Curly returned to the office. "Want some more coffee, boys?"

"Yo, boss" was the reply. "Bring the pot. Too nice an evening to stay inside." One of the deputies held the door for Curly.

Little Smith crawled from beneath a cot and crept to the edge of the light. He peeled the piece of paper off the back of the plate then mounted the cot by the window. He uttered two soft dove coos and waited. Below, Royal hurried over to the wall.

"Here it is, Mr. Ballou." Little Smith stuck his hand between the bars and dropped the slip.

Royal caught the fluttering leaf and trotted back to the ditch. Shutting his eyes against the flare, he struck a match. He paused as the flame died, then read the paper. It was perfectly imprinted with the numbers of the dial. The three combination numbers were punched through the paper. So engrossed was Royal in figuring the sequence that he burned his fingers. "Ouch." He dropped the match and sucked on his index finger. Another match and he had the numbers. In a clockwise motion he counted 24 right, 9 left, and 15 right.

On his feet again, Royal hurried to the wall. "Little Smith, you there?" Royal couldn't see the boy in the window.

"Yes, Mr. Ballou," the lad replied. "I'm here."

"Good. Now, remember where the dial was. The position. Got it?" Royal knew the dial mark and the zero on the number plate had to line up.

"Yes, Mr. Ballou," Little Smith answered with childlike confidence.

"Here is the combination. Right 24, left 9, right 15. Remember those. Go in a clockwise direction."

"Yes, Mr. Ballou. Right 24, left 9, right 15," Little answered smartly, showing off a touch.

A rustling, then silence. The tension mounted. Royal paced.

"Nervous as a long-tailed cat under a rocking chair" had been his grandfather's favorite expression. Royal heard the ruslting again.

"What's clockwise, Mr. Ballou?" Little asked timidly.

"Aw, shit," Royal cursed under his breath. "As you face the safe, turn it toward your right hand."

Royal saw a white, toothy grin crease the boy's face. "You mean this hand?" He held up his left hand.

"No, damn it!" he snapped. "The other, right hand," Royal hissed.

"I understand." Little Smith smiled and disappeared.

Royal heard footsteps in the alley. That damned deputy! Royal knew he couldn't reach the ditch in time, so he pressed against the wall. The man strolled around the corner as casually as before. He nearly walked past Royal but tripped on his foot. As the man stumbled forward, Royal clubbed him at the base of his skull. The deputy fell like a side of beef and greeted the ground face-first.

Royal heard another man walk down the alley. He sprinted to the ditch as the deputy cleared the corner. "Hey, Dusty, what you doin' there?"

Royal spoke away from the man to shield his voice. "I'm checking something here." He squatted on his haunches. "Be back in a minute!"

"Well, spur it." The deputy was impatient. "Curly wants to make the rounds."

"Go ahead," Royal told him. "I'll catch up."

"All right, but hurry."

Royal glanced back as the man disappeared in the alley. Several seconds later, a dove coo called him to the jail window.

"It won't open, Mr. Ballou," Little Smith whispered softly.

Thoughts raced through Royal's head. What to do? How can I help? In desperation Royal offered, "Go the other direction."

"I'll do it," Little Smith replied, and ducked inside.

Little Smith had moved four steps into the office when the door opened. Caught! Curly's big hand came through the door, set the coffeepot on the shelf, and pulled the door closed. Little Smith wiped his brow. Indians aren't supposed to sweat, he thought. At least, that's what Father keeps telling me. He scampered to the safe, lined up the dial, and went "the other way": 24 left, 9 right, 15 left. He twisted the handle.

Click! It opened. Little Smith pulled on the heavy door. Inside was a small strongbox, two leather bags, and a ledger. "I want everything in the safe" had been Mr. Ballou's instructions. The boy cradled the ledger and box against his chest and hooked a finger through the leather ties of the bags. As he left the office, he realized the safe door was open. With arms loaded, he pushed the door shut with the heel of his foot and stepped on the handle. Using his toes, he spun the knob. His arms were getting tired from the contents of the safe as he walked toward the cell.

"Mr. Ballou!" Excitement was thick in his voice. "I got it!"

"Good work, lad." Royal was delighted and waited beneath the window. "Drop it to me."

"Here's the strongbox. It's heavy," Little Smith warned. He turned the box on edge and dropped it. Royal partially caught the box, letting it slip to the ground.

"Here's the rest. Two bags and a book," Little Smith forewarned. Royal caught all three. He stood below and waited as Little Smith squeezed through the frame. Royal raised his hands, cupped the boy's heels, then slowly lowered him to the ground.

"Nice work, my friend." Royal patted him on the head. He fought to contain his glee. "Let's get out of here. We've pushed our luck."

When they were back in Doc Shu's store, Royal and the doc sorted through the loot.

"Will you look at that cash!" Doc Shu whistled as he stacked the gold coins. "Must be well-nigh a thousand dollars here."

"One thousand four hundred and seventy-five, to be precise." Royal read from the ledger. "Want to know where your Improvement Commission money goes, Doc?" Royal tapped the ledger. "Business trips, expenses, horses, jewelry, cards." Royal ran his finger down columns of numbers and figures. "It's split six ways between the council, the mayor, the sheriff, and Colburn."

"You know something, Royal?" Doc Shu looked at him. "I'll bet Elliot would love to print this in the *Gazette*." He tried to keep a smile off his face but couldn't.

"It would make good reading, that's for sure." Royal was beaming. "I'll stop and ask him. I'd be surprised if he didn't. Look at this, Doc." He underscored an entry with his finger.

The notation was "for services rendered" and was paid to George Petts and Dolph Stickney—one hundred dollars each.

"I'll venture all my wages that this entry is the date Clem's reservoir was blasted and Lucas's barns were fired," Royal said with conviction. "Not a doubt in my mind."

"I've got the date noted on my calendar. Won't take but a second to check." Doc Shu moved to his desk and returned in a flash. "That all took place on a Tuesday night, correct?"

"Right you are. They were paid that day." Royal had the proof in his hand. "Not very smart of those two—but when you consider who we're dealing with, it's what you'd expect."

"I assume you're talking about George and Dolph," Doc Shu suggested. "This is Curly's only slip-up."

They were quiet as they reflected on the doc's words.

CHAPTER
11

Saturday proved to be an exciting day for the citizenry of Jacob's Well. The Ladies Auxiliary of the church was holding its annual fund-raising social. Ladies only. *La grande affaire* was *the* social event of the year, attended by invitation only. Millicent Tilden served as the matron, with support from Eulalia Albee and Maude Hemmingway. Preacher Smith had blessed the occasion and gratefully departed.

Millie, talking the hind leg off a mule, spied a young delivery boy stalled in mortal fear at the front entrance. The lad was terrified at the prospect of entering the room. Millie touched her nose with her handkerchief and to spare the lad further embarrassment bustled to the door. "How may I help you, young man?" she inquired.

"Ma'am, I have a special post package for Mrs. Tilden." The boy spoke well and repeated everything just as Sophie had coached him.

"My land!" Millie was suddenly aglow with anticipation. "A special post for me? Whatever in the world could it be? And from whom?" She snatched the package, startling the boy in her eagerness. "Stay by your horse in case I want to send a reply," she instructed him, and went inside the church.

Lay Albee watched this exchange and cruised over. Curiosity had bested her. "What's this, Millie? A present from a secret admirer?"

"I don't know what to do." Millie dabbed again with her hanky. She was flustered yet secretly delighted. "Who would send me something all the way from *Kansas City*?"

"Open it, Millie. Don't keep us guessing any longer." Maude had joined the ladies, her interest piqued. They gathered around as Millie unwrapped the package. She destroyed the heavy paper and disemboweled the box in her haste to reach

the contents. As she shredded the tissue paper, the beauty of
the dress became readily apparent. Exclamations gushed forth
as she held the dress against her slender frame.

"Who sent it, Millie? A friend?" Gales of laughter escaped
from the ladies present.

"Mercy me!" she breathed excitedly. "Here's a card." She
fumbled nervously to open the envelope. "To Millie, my sweet,
from a dear friend. Love as always."

"Tell us who your admirer is, Millie," an inquisitive voice
called.

"It isn't signed, but it is my husband's hand. Isn't he a dear
to think of me." She shook her head, flushed with tender feelings. "After he scolded me for spending too much money, he
surprises me with this dress. Where's that delivery boy?"

Millie spotted him in front of the church throwing rocks.
"Yoo-hoo! Up here!" she called, and waved her handkerchief.
With dread on his face, the boy returned to the church. Millie
met him at the bottom of the steps. Spared again, thought the
lad.

"Find Mr. Tilden." Her look softened when she mentioned
Lem. She clutched the boy's arm, preventing his escape. "Tell
him thank you for the precious dress and that I love him. Will
you do that? Please."

The boy blushed bright red around the neck. "Yes, ma'am,
I'll tell him."

"Exactly as I told you," she admonished and fluttered her
handkerchief. But she had wasted those words on the boy—he
was in full flight and out of earshot.

The boy found Lem Tilden dining with the other council
members at the hotel. He was reluctant to interrupt their lunch,
but Millie's admonition was fresh in his mind. He wormed his
way through the crowded room and edged close to Lem. He
spoke softly, wanting to avoid attention. " 'Scuse me, Mr.
Tilden . . ."

Lem cupped his hand to his ear. "What did you say, son? I'm
stone deaf." He laughed as he toyed with the boy. His mouth
was tight as he struggled to control the tic.

"Your wife thanks you for the new dress!" the boy boomed.
The entire room heard this proclamation. "And she loves—"
Lem hushed the boy with a sweep of his hand and dismissed
him.

As the dining room settled into the din of small talk, Ellery Albee broke the silence. "New dress for the missus?" he asked Lem pointedly. "Didn't you mention several days ago how tight money was?" He forked another portion of mashed potatoes into his mouth. "Fall into some sudden wealth, Lem?"

"You can talk straight with us," Asa butted in. "We're in this together. Right, old friend?" The dig was unnecessary, but he saw Lem's weakness and exploited it.

" 'Scuse me, gentlemen. I'm feeling poorly." Lem stood, his mouth quivering, and left the table.

"He does look unwell," Hervey commented as he puffed on his cigar. "Where do you suppose he got the money? His business doin' well?" Hervey glanced at Asa, but Asa wouldn't hold his gaze.

Asa was still bitter over the incident with the colt and was pleased to see Lem fall under suspicion.

The council members were beginning to lose trust in each other.

While Mayor Albee and the remaining council members lunched, a telegraph delivery boy approached the H bar C. The night clerk, Elihu Jones, had sent him on this errand. His instructions were to deliver the telegram personally to Ham Colburn. The boy rode hard—the telegram must be delivered.

He slowed his horse to a trot and crossed the trestle that spanned the river. He rode past countless stock pens plum full of cattle, ready for a trail drive. As he angled for the house, he saw a tight group of men on the loading platform. Colburn was talking to his foreman. The boy yanked his horse around, spurted toward the group, and reined to a dusty stop. His feet barely kissin' terra firma, he covered the considerable distance quickly and ran to Colburn.

"What in the world have we here? A dust devil, a stampede, and a gully washer all thrown into one." Colburn directed everyone's attention to the boy as a smile creased his face. "Calm down, lad. We aren't goin' anyplace."

"I have . . . a special . . . telegram . . . for you." The boy got the words out between gulps of air.

"Well, give it to me, son. I'm standing right in front of you." Colburn grinned as he looked around at his men. They enjoyed watching the little dude deliver his telegram.

The boy fumbled with his pocket button and harassed it open. He handed the telegram to Colburn, his face shining with pride.

"Thanks, son. Fine job." He gave the lad four bits. "Buy something next time you're in the store." The boy clenched the coins in his hand, leaped off the dock, and sprinted to his horse. In one smooth step, he was mounted and on his way.

"Keep an eye on that lad, Stoney," Colburn told his foreman as he watched the boy ride away. "In two years time, he'll make one hell of a good hand."

Colburn unfolded the telegram and read it. His face, still smiling after the boy, now turned hard, and his mood became black. "Saddle my horse, Stoney," he ordered. "I'm going to town." He near-stampeded toward the main house.

Livid, he punished his horse impatient to get to Jacob's Well, wondering how Ellery Albee had had the gall to go against him. He would come down hard on the man, teach him a lesson that would not be lost on the council. When Colburn's horse stumbled and nearly went down, he realized he had to slow his pace. He eased the horse into trot, then a slow walk, and came to a stop on the trail. The horse was a scant touch away from being wind broke—his neck and chest were lathered, and he was dripping wet between his hind legs.

Colburn rubbed down the horse and wiped him dry as best he could. They had walked well-nigh a half mile before Colburn mounted again. A slow trot would suffice to Jacob's Well. Colburn forced his anger into control. When they arrived, he hitched the horse to the rail and stepped inside the land office. He climbed the stairs and barged into the mayor's outer office, startling the receptionist. "Don't bother. I know my way." The woman had no time to move.

Mayor Albee and the council were in "executive session." Albee was dealing cards when Colburn stormed through the door. The council watched in silence as he approached. Colburn dug into his pocket and pulled out the telegram. He threw it on the table in front of Ellery. "What in the hell is the meaning of this, Your Honor?" he demanded sarcastically.

Ellery fought with the folded paper, his pudgy fingers all afumble. He carefully mouthed every word. Then he chortled and threw the telegram onto the table. "No, sir, I had nothing to do with that." As he shook his head, his chin disappeared into his collar.

"You tellin' me you don't know who Charlie Wiggins is?"

"That's common knowledge," retorted the mayor with a cagey look on his face.

"Who's Charlie Wiggins?" Lem asked, not aware of the power-brokering going on. The corner of his mouth moved uncontrollably.

"Read the damned telegram yourself." Colburn snatched the paper off the table and threw it at Lem.

fm.
C.W. Wiggins
El Paso del Norte, Texas
to
Ellery Albee
Jacob's Well
N.M. Territory

Beef prices down. rcmd u buy 500 head. No latr mid Aug. Sell to Col. H. Hawkins, U.S. Army, Fort Bell. Del date Sep. 27. Rply rqusted. Charlie.

"So who is Charlie?" Lem asked again.

"Mr. Charles Wiggins," Colburn said, straining to control his temper, while looking at Ellery, "is the biggest cattle buyer this side of the Pecos River. That's who. Why, shit, he could buy and sell me twice over and still have money to spend." A touch of awe and fear cut his voice.

"You dealin' on the sly, Ellery?" Hervey Brown bluntly asked, blowing a thick cloud of cigar smoke toward the ceiling.

"No!" Ellery shot back and slammed his fist on the table. His entire body shook. "And don't you think I am! I know nothing about this telegram."

Loud pounding footsteps caught the attention of the men. The receptionist opened the door, and a deputy, Chip Shelton, rushed inside.

"Mr. Mayor," he gasped between breaths, "you'd better come quick. We have big trouble. Curly's on a binge." Chip's features were deeply creased with stress.

The mayor strained to get his bulk out of the chair and struggled into his coat. He steamed toward the door on the heels of the deputy. "I'll get back with you, Ham," he called. The council members folded their cards, tidied up the mess, and followed Ellery.

Ellery and the deputy walked briskly along the boardwalk toward The Dusty Rose. Ellery worked hard to keep pace with the long-stridin' lawman. As they approached the saloon, Ellery saw an angry crowd gathered out front. Two armed deputies were keeping them out of The Rose. When one of the deputies saw the mayor plowing through the crowd, he cleared a pathway and let Ellery pass.

Once inside the saloon, Ellery spotted Curly bellied up to the bar. He was drinking with a purpose. The mayor approached, unsure of what awaited him. The deputy had not informed him of the problem.

"Curly," the mayor said cautiously as he signaled for a drink from the bartender, "why don't we go into the back room and talk. Curly?" Drink in hand, the mayor motioned him to follow.

"Good idea, Mr. Mayor," the sheriff said pleasantly. "You go in there, and I'll stay here and get drunk."

Ellery persisted, forceful yet afraid to push too hard. "Come on. Let's talk."

Curly read the mayor's thoughts and addressed him with a cold look. "Our problem, Ellery, is that the safe in my office is empty. No money and no records." Curly looked the man in the eye, watching for a response.

Ellery's face failed to conceal his shock. He took on a sudden pallor and stood dumbstruck.

"Empty, Mr. Fancy Mayor. How do you like that?" Curly dumped the responsibility squarely on the mayor.

The councilmen trooped into the saloon. Ellery snapped out of his trance and moved toward the back room. The men ordered drinks and followed him. He turned back to the bar. "Curly, join us."

The sheriff plucked his bottle from the bar and slowly made his way to the mayor.

Once seated, Ellery poured drinks with a shaking hand. "Gentlemen, we have a damned serious problem," Ellery lamented. "The ledger and all our money has been stolen from the safe in Curly's office."

Panic ran rampant around the table.

"What! Stolen? How can it be?" asked Asa. He pointedly accused Ellery. "You told us the safe was secure."

"What can I say? It was secure. Otherwise I wouldn't have put my money there," the mayor answered forcefully, his jowls firmly set.

"It's your fault," whined Hervey. He pointed his cigar at Ellery. "You're the one who wanted to keep records of our transactions."

"How are you going to explain this to the mob out front?" Lem asked in a condescending tone, the corner of his mouth quivering. He gloated in pressuring the mayor.

"My, aren't we righteous," Ellery hissed. "Now it's *my* problem. What am I going to do? If you have anything of importance to say, do so. Otherwise bite your tongues." The mayor's face turned beet red.

In the heated exchange, Ham Colburn had entered the room. He stood aside and witnessed the backbiting until he could tolerate it no longer. Then he stepped forward and took command of the deteriorating situation.

"Gentlemen, please. Take a look at yourselves." He paused, glancing around the table. "Name-calling, mudslinging. That won't solve anything, will it?"

An embarrassed quiet stilled the room. No one was strong enough to speak.

"Curly, would you care to join us?" Colburn asked the sheriff, who was sitting away from the table. Curly gave it thought, then reluctantly pulled his chair forward. "We have to make the best of a nasty situation, right?"

"Answers. We need answers, Ham," Lem interrupted, then the tic interrupted Lem. "No fancy claptrap."

"Lem," Colburn said with a withering glare, "if you don't have anything of value to add, then *shut up!*" Colburn slammed his fist down on the table, knocking the glasses askew. Then he stood, viciously kicked his chair away, and slowly circled the table. With deliberate ceremony, he lit a cigar. Not a word had been spoken since his outburst. "Let's try to make the best of this crisis. We'll take the heat off us and direct it toward someone else."

"Who'd you have in mind, Ham?" Hervey asked as he chewed his cigar.

Colburn smiled, acknowledging his handling of the situation. "Point the finger at the only person with the combination—Royal Ballou. He would know it. After all, the safe used to be his." He took a deep drag on his cigar and slowly exhaled a trail of smoke.

"Good idea!" exclaimed the mayor, shaking with delight. "Why didn't I think of that?"

"You didn't think of it, Mr. Mayor, because you aren't smart enough," Asa acidly cut. He sat back, pleased with the put-down. "Until we get that ledger back, we've taken a lease on time."

"You have a better plan, Asa? Let's hear it," Colburn challenged. The men in the room stared at Asa and waited for a response. "Just as I thought—smoke talk. Since you offer no hope, stifle the smart-ass remarks. If you don't like what we're doing, there's the door." The councilman sat in silence, a meaty aroma surrounding him. Colburn glanced at Curly. "What do you think, Sheriff?"

The whiskey had temporarily calmed Curly, but a look told Colburn the man was on the edge. His reputation had been smeared—honor among thieves. His solution was to kill Royal.

"What do you think, Curley?" Colburn repeated to the silent lawman.

"Go for it, Ham" was Curly's vacant reply. "Do whatever is best."

"Mr. Mayor," Colburn volunteered, "it's your obligation to address the problem. Talk to the folks out front and explain the situation." He had neatly sidestepped the crisis. "A drink to our continued success." The men went through the motions, but not one believed the partnership had much of a future.

The clamor outside faded as Mayor Albee parted the batwing doors with his bulk. He conveniently positioned himself between the deputies, although they had to step apart to accommodate his mass.

Before the mayor had a chance to open his mouth, someone shouted, "Any truth to the rumor 'bout our money being stolt?"

Not waiting for a reply, another voice boomed, "Seen any

owntown improvements, Mr. Mayor? I ain't." Laughter from
ne crowd.

"Let me explain, please." Mayor Albee held up his beefy
white hands to quiet the rowdies. He laid it on the line. "The
afe in Sheriff Hall's office was broken into last night. All the
unds targeted for business improvements were taken. We know
ho did it. All we have to do is apprehend him."

"He's right inside the saloon" came a shout. "Put the chains
n Curly!"

"No! It wasn't Curly," someone contested. "It was the
ayor." A wave of laughter rippled through the people.

"Listen up!" the mayor shouted above the din, hoping for
rowd approval. "There is only one other person who knows
ne combination to the safe: Royal Ballou."

"Horseshit, Mr. Mayor" came the angry response, "and you
now it."

"Here's what we think of your fibbin', Mayor." No sooner
ad the words died than Ellery was pelted with a half-dozen
orse muffins. A cheer from the crowd followed as Ellery
ucked inside the saloon. He had failed. The crowd broke into
chant.

"We want our money! We want our money."

The mayor hustled his massive body around the tables to-
vard the back-room door. His council awaited his return with
xpectations of a resolved crisis. The mayor walked past them
vithout breaking stride. "Boys, I'm getting out of here. You
an join me if you feel inclined." A small-scale stampede fol-
owed the mayor as the men fell in line.

Deputy Chip Shelton escorted the government of Jacob's
Well away from The Rose and danger. Then he went back
nside the saloon and sought Curly. He found the sheriff seated
ipping whiskey. "Boss, we gotta leave. Those folks out front
re getting riled."

"Screw 'em all," Curly snapped. He was stewing and getting
nadder by the minute. "If they want me outta office, they'll
ave to drag me out feet first."

Chip offered an alternative. "We'll get them another day. We
an't lick 'em now. Come on."

The sheriff slowly stood and walked beside the deputy. As
ney neared the front of the saloon, Curly walked straight to

the batwings. Chip grabbed his arm, but the sheriff brushed
him off.

Curly plowed through the doors, slamming both against the
wall. They clattered back and forth until they were still. He
stepped between his deputies and stood defiantly on the board
walk, challenging the crowd. No one met his eye. The lawman
turned his back in disdain and walked away.

"Hey, Sheriff Hall!" a voice confronted. "Where's our
money?"

Curly spun around in a blur, strode angrily to the edge of the
boardwalk, and searched for the dissenting voice. "Who said
that?" he threatened as he quick-glanced the crowd.

The town's menfolk parted without a word, singling out Abner Walker. The drover looked around for support. He got
none.

"Aw, if it ain't Mr. Trail Rider himself," Curly ridiculed
Abner. The maleficent lawman prodded the cowboy. "Pretty
big talk coming from a cowpuncher. Would you care to repeat
your last question?"

Abner fully realized the gravity of his offhand comment.
Death stood fifteen feet away, insulting him, destroying his
pride and self-respect. He was afraid to move. He tried to speak
but croaked hoarsely.

"Got a frog in your throat, boy?" Curly goaded.

"No" came the falsetto reply. Abner cleared his throat.
"No."

"Ain't choked up?" Curly persisted, not letting him off the
hook.

If I want to die in front of all these people, I can draw my
gun. Abner gave the thought serious consideration. No! I want
to live. His knees started to shake. He tightened his thigh muscles, but that only made it worse. His entire lower half shook
like a leaf in a breeze.

"Got the shakes, Abner? Scared a little?" Curly smiled as he
relentlessly pushed the cowboy. "Don't want to die just yet?"

Abner was looking at a fiend incarnate. The man would kill
him in an instant and not have the slightest compunction about
it.

"Your move, boy. Make it good, or it'll be your last." Having
delivered the ultimatum, Curly stood on the boardwalk and

aited. He had been in this situation before and was not flus-
red.

Abner slowly raised both hands waist high. Curly lifted his
ght hand above the butt of his Colt. Abner continued to raise
is hands and with considerable effort folded them across his
est.

Curly laughed with contempt, turned away, and headed for
is office. The crowd started to break up.

"Drinks are on me!" Deputy Shelton shouted from the
oardwalk. "And I'm gonna be the first in line." He had ex-
ected to witness an excution in the street. Relief swept over
e lawman as the crowd followed him into the saloon.

Abner Walker stood rooted to the spot. He was breathing
eeply, trying to bring his body under control. A friend ap-
roached and slapped him on the back. "Abner, that was by far
e dumbest thing I ever heard you say. Ever!" The man left
bner and bounded up the steps. A split second before he dis-
ppeared into The Rose, he turned and addressed the cowboy.
But it was the smartest move you've ever made."

The next morning, Curly barged into the stable with bottle in
and. He was tight, but not drunk. "The hair of the dog," he
xplained to Joe Mex. "A nasty day you cooked up." Curly
ook the rain off his slicker and kicked his boots together in a
tile attempt to knock off caked mud. The day was dreary,
ith low-hanging clouds and a steady drizzle. "I need my
orse, Joe. Right away."

Joe Mex had not finished shoeing the horse, but he knew the
eriff. He set the horse's hoof down and straightened. "Don't
o gettin' muleheaded on me again," he playfully threatened
e animal, "or I'll tie your damned hoof to the rafter." The
orse snorted at him, then dipped its head in anticipation of an
ar-scratching.

Curly was short with him. "Come on, Joe. I'm on to some-
ing."

Never once did Curly offer to help get his gear. Joe brought
urly's horse out of the stall. He slipped the bridle over its
ead, fit the bit tenderly into the mouth, then snugged and
uckled the latch. Tying the horse to the railing, Joe grabbed a
ool blanket and threw it onto the horse's back. He adjusted
is hat and accidentally buried the goat's-head burr deep into

his thumb. He remembered placing it there on his painful walk back from the swimming hole. "Ouch!" he hissed as he spotted the burr. Hello sweet thing, he mused. Revenge is mine, sayeth Joe Mex.

Joe plucked the burr out of his thumb and held it daintly between his fingers. He swung Curly's saddle onto the wool pad. As he fussed with the saddle, he slipped the burr beneath the pad. "Sorry, my friend. I must do it," he said softly to the horse.

"Say what, you want me?" Curly looked at Joe.

"No, I was talking to your critter," Joe answered calmly.

"Step on it, man," Curly directed, pacing. "I'm losing valuable time."

Joe grabbed the cinch, ducked underneath, fastened it through the latigo, and delicately tightened it. He avoided pulling it tight, and hoped Curly would not notice the slack. Then dropping the stirrup, Joe stepped back. "There you go, ready to ride." He patted the horse lightly on the rump.

"I'll be back after dark. Grain him when I return." Another set of orders, and not a word of thanks.

Joe touched his hat and opened the stable door.

"He's a little skittish, ain't he, Joe?" Curly held the reins tightly.

"Naw," Joe passed it off. "Must be the weather. Rain'll do that to a horse."

Curly waited inside the door as Joe slopped through the muck to unfasten the corral gate. As Joe stepped out of the rain, the sheriff mounted with the casual nonchalance of an experienced rider. The instant Curly's beefy buttocks touched the saddle, the horse let fly with an explosive forward leap. Curly's feet never retouched the stirrups as he hurtled ahead on the tameless horse. When the animal touched ground far into the slop, Curly's butt hit the saddle with a wet smack. The horse came undone trying to escape from the pain. The animal lunged violently sideways, then leaped heavenward. Curly, never firmly in the saddle, exited in a slow roll, fork end up. He landed flat on his back in the ooze with a muffled *sploop,* followed quickly by a *whoosh* as his breath was knocked out.

The horse, startled by the unusual noises, shied away. The reins were wrapped tightly around Curly's wrist. The horse would have done a roping pony proud. He backed and pulled tightly against the reins and dragged Curly through the mud. The sheriff dredged a foot-deep trough in the muck as the horse skidded him. The majority of the mud went inside the neck of his slicker.

Joe moved to the animal, circled away from his hooves, and grabbed the reins. He held the horse and managed to calm him. Curly relaxed and released the reins as his arm plopped into the muck. Joe wiggled his hand underneath the blanket and felt for the burr. He found it right in the end of his finger. He used his teeth to pluck the burr from his finger and spat it over the railing. The horse quieted and allowed Joe to lead him into the stable.

Curly, encased in the mire, moaned but did not move. The rain steadily pelted his face. Joe trudged toward the sheriff and reluctantly offered a hand. He struggled and used his leg strength to move Curly. The sheriff gradually came upright, breaking free with a loud pop. He sat for a moment and searched for his horse. "I oughta shoot that son of a bitch," he swore as he turned onto his knees. The more thought Curly gave to the brief ride, the madder he became at his horse. He yanked his slicker open and went for his gun. His hands were muddy, and as he drew his pistol, he dropped it. He groped to find it. With the movements of a hundred-year-old man, he slowly and painfully stood. "What in the damned hell is wrong with that animal?" He pointed his mud-clogged pistol at the horse.

"You want me to give it a try?" Joe volunteered.

"Be my guest, but watch out." Curly placed a cautioning hand on Joe's arms as mud and slop dripped out of his slicker.

Joe walked inside the stable and untied the horse. He smacked his hand dry on the saddle. The horse did not flinch. Joe wiggled the saddle before he mounted. Nothing. He stepped into the stirrup and swung up. The horse waited for Joe's lead. Joe heeled him gently and worked through several tight figure-eights inside the stable. "Looks fine to me, Curly."

"Damned animal," Curly cursed. "I wouldn't waste a good bullet on his thick head." He regarded the horse with loathing. Muddy water pooled beneath himself. "Hell with it, Joe. I'm going to get cleaned up. I'll probably have to take a bath to get this shit off." He turned and sloshed away, his boots squishing with every footstep.

Joe Mex slipped out of the saddle, flipped up the stirrup, and loosened the latigo. He unfastened the cinch, threw the saddle onto the railing, and led the horse into his stall. The head rigging came off as Joe said to the animal, "Here you go, my friend. A nice big handful of oats and the freshest hay in the barn. Anything else you want, just let me know." He patted the horse on the neck and laughed out loud. He felt better now. He laughed as he recalled the sheriff's short-lived ride. Curly's riding demonstration made the memory of Joe's swim bearable.

Royal looked with apprehension at Elliot Lightshield, the proprietor of the *Gazette*. Concern for him prompted Royal to ask again, "The last time you printed something like this, you were damned near ruined. You sure you want to go through with this?"

"I do, Royal." Elliot was adamant. "This time I'll have the people behind me. If I don't, then I'll leave with no regret. This town won't be worth my time."

"Good man, Elliot." Royal liked what he heard. "We're in this together."

At that moment, Lucas Boothe came into the print shop. He proudly carried a new shotgun from his store. He winked at Royal and faced Elliot. "Where do you want me?"

Elliot wasn't expecting help. He quickly scanned the room and pointed Lucas toward the ink barrels beside the press. "Right by those barrels. That way you can watch both the back door and the front office."

"You don't mind a little security now, do you, Elliot?" the gunsmith asked.

Elliot beamed. "Thank you, gentlemen. Now, if you'll permit me, I have work to do." He returned to his typesetting table and put the finishing touches on the plate. "This special edition will hit the streets in two hours."

Royal stood beside Elliot. The *Gazette* headlines bannered the news.

YOUR MONEY
WHERE IT WENT

The expense accounts of Ellery Albee, Asa Hemmingway, Lemuel Tilden, Hervey Brown, Rutherford Hall

Business Expenses: Trips, Horses, Land, Stock. $525.00
Social Expenses: Gifts, Whiskey, Gaming Tables. $350.00
Misc. Expenses: Judge Williams, Elihu Jones, George Petts, Dolph Stickney. $400.00
Charities: Cattleman's Association, Stockman's Benevolence Fund, $300.00

Royal laughed. "I especially like the charities. Want to venture a guess who profited from those?"

Elliot was pleased with the layout. "I think the funds for Judge Williams and Elihu might raise a few eyebrows in the territory. Time will tell." Elliot moved the printing plate to his press. "I'll put copies on the afternoon stage headed for the governor, legislators, and a few select judges." He remembered the night George Petts and Dolph Stickney had bashed him about and nearly destroyed his business.

"I think we might be looking at a complete change of government in Jacob's Well, don't you, Elliot?" Royal sought confirmation from the printer.

"I do. Be the best thing that happened around here in months."

CHAPTER
12

Royal rode away from Doc Shu's before sunup. Reviewing his efforts of the past days gave him a feeling of accomplishment. The town council had been thrown into turmoil. The councilmen's wives were arguing with their husbands about money spent by other husbands. Royal's only regret was not staying in town to witness the consequences of the *Gazette* special edition.

On two occasions Royal had searched for Abbie. Both had nearly resulted in his capture. The first search had ended with Royal camouflaged in thick underbrush of the Little Colorado as the posse scoured the river bottom in the rapidly fading daylight.

His second attempt was no more successful. He dodged posse riders and backtracked to such an extent that he was forced from the area he wanted to search.

As Royal rode the perimeter of Clem's lower ranch, he smelled smoke. Not from the cabin, he thought. His curiosity was aroused. Mindful of Curly's "visits," he cut into the thick cottonwoods as the first rays of sun probed the gloomy depths. The sheltered river bottom, with water and wood, was a logical spot to camp.

The mare picked her way through the willows with scarcely a sound. The smell grew stronger. Royal looked downstream and saw a wisp of smoke highlighted by the sun. He off-horsed and pulled his rifle from the scabbard. A quick check showed the cap still firmly in place. With renewed caution, he headed toward the smoke.

Fifty yards farther along, Royal eased around a fallen log and spotted a dappled mare picketed in a tight clearing. As he stepped in front of the log, the mare's ears perked forward, and she turned toward him. He spotted movement and dropped to his knee, rifle shouldered. "Don't move," Royal called to the figure. "I've got a bead on you."

The man froze. "Royal, that you?" the man probingly asked.

"Ya, who are you? Step forward into the sunlight," Royal ordered keeping his rifle on the man.

"Luther Fenbow. I used to be the hashburner at the H bar C. I'll tell you straight out that I quit." He made no move toward his pistol. Royal looked at him and realized he probably couldn't reach his pistol anyway. His belly dropped over his belt and partially obstructed his movements. The stranger was scruffy looking with several days' growth on his face and neck. His clothes were filthy, greasy, and badly in need of repair. A dip in a stock tank wouldn't have hurt the man.

Luther wiped his nose on the sleeve of his shirt and slouch-walked to the fire. He poured a cup of coffee, sat to warm himself, and made no effort to get away from the smoke. Royal eased into the small campsite and leaned against a stump. His rifle never left his hands.

"You're a little out of your territory on this side, pardner," Royal queried.

"I know. I left yesterday afternoon. I'm plum fed up with that tired fart." He sipped his coffee and looked at Royal. "Ham is crazy—bossin' everyone around and goin' off half cocked. He don't have no crew at the ranch. All of a sudden, the crews show up. Twenty-five or thirty of them, and Ham's screamin' at me to feed them. I got wore out and told the old coot to stuff it." He laughed sadly. "You lookin' at his answer. I don't need that job anyways. I'll pick me up some trail herd and survive." He sipped his coffee, then spat it out. "Damn, tastes like sheep dip."

"So where you headed?"

"I'm gonna head south. El Paso. Plenty of work there for a good cook." He poured his coffee over the fire and kicked dirt on the coals. Then he broke camp and packed his gear within minutes.

Royal never relaxed his distrust of the man. He laughed when Luther mentioned being a good cook. The man's eyes even looked dirty. "I'll ride with you to the property line. Make sure you get headed in the right direction." Royal's offer left no room for discussion.

"Appreciate that. I ain't been in these parts often." Luther finished his chores and saddled his horse quickly. Royal walked with Luther to get the mare. He didn't leave the man alone for a second. As the two rode toward the fence line, Luther said, "There's another reason I'm leavin' that spread. Ham is possessed. Now he's into tradin' people. Holdin' them for ransom. Royal, I mean, like a week past, he got a girl. Says he's holding her at his ranch wantin' to make a deal."

Royal's heart stopped. He caught his breath and stayed calm. "What's he doin' with her?" He tried to sound casual.

"Can't say, but it sure rubs against my grain. She's an innocent bystander. Sure is a pretty thing, though." He leered. "Dark brown hair and green eyes. Uh-huh, a real beauty. Maybe he'll marry her." He laughed.

Royal flashed a toothy grin. "He should be so lucky." His guts were churning at the suggestion. "Well, here we are. You ride through the cut yonder, and you'll be on the trial to El Paso." Royal pointed with his rifle. "Best of luck."

Luther tipped his greasy hat and urged his horse into motion. Royal waited until the man was a distant speck before he turned the mare around and rode hell-bent for Clem's cabin.

Royal rousted Clem out of bed. Clem had come off the range after another fruitless search for Abbie and could have slept for a week.

"What in the hell! You mean you know where she is?" Clem asked in sleepy disbelief.

Royal detailed his encounter with Luther Fenbow. He was champing at the bit to follow the lead. Clem fumbled around the kitchen, made coffee, and tolerated Royal.

"You gonna go on that cock 'n' bull? You don't know that jasper from Adam," Clem challenged.

"You have anything better?" Royal shot back.

Clem had no answer. "I still think you should be mindful of that man and his story."

"What do I have to lose? It's worth a try, isn't it?" Royal pressured Clem. "No offense, but you've been searching all over this country and still don't have a thing to show for it, right?" Clem nodded and rubbed his head with his bandaged hand. "Well, let me take a crack at the H bar C."

Clem frowned. "I'll tell you this. I don't like it. It's too neat. The man sets up camp where you're sure to spot him. It stinks." Clem eyeballed Royal and saw his mule stubbornness surface. "So what can I do to help?" he asked with resignation.

Royal left Clem's ranch after midnight. He sought to be through the high country and into the grasslands before sunrise. He knew the posse would be searching for him and planned to beat them to the day.

Leaving the mesa, Royal dropped into cattle country. The gently sloping hills were dotted with gray-green cedars. He loved the sweet smell, which was sharper than the high-country pine. The rolling open country was thick with prairie grass, golden yellow and belly deep to his mare. As the sun rose, he stayed close to the trees, seeking as much cover as possible.

Royal left the mare in the trees and bellied down behind a fallen cedar. With Clem's binoculars, he searched the vast grasslands for signs of riders. No one was around. He forced himself to recheck the fields. Not a rider in sight. To look afar was wasted effort. The shimmering early-morning heat waves distorted his vision. The horizon was a moving mirage. These half-dozen sections were deserted. Royal was satisfied that this would work to his advantage.

Cautiously trotting down the grassy slope, he carefully straddle-stepped a bob-wire fence and knelt at the boundary of the field. A rich yellow carpet of grass spread as far as he could see. A slight breeze from the mountains cooled his back. Good, he thought, it will spread the fire. He knew midday temperatures would rise up against the mountains. He squatted, gathered a handful of dried weeds, and nested them in the grass. With reluctance, he thumbnail-struck a match, knowing full well what he was about to unleash.

Poof! The weeds burst into flames. A small wisp of white smoke rose into the air. In seconds the grass was burning, stalks popping and whistling from the heat. He stepped away from the fire as the heat touched his face. He hopped the fence, ran to the mare, and mounted. He pushed the mare hard, covered considerable ground and started half a dozen fires. Then he rested the mare who was breathing heavily and looked over his shoulder at the growing conflagration. He was stunned. The grasslands were engulfed in a huge, whirlwind firestorm. He could hear the thunderous roar as the fire fed on itself. The sky was pewter gray in color and obscured the sun behind the thick cloud. The fire skipped roads and ditch lines and burned out of control.

Royal knew he would have to ride through the smoke bank to hit the road that connected with the H bar C. He paralleled the line of smoke. A second before plunging into the darkness, he pulled his neckerchief over his nose. The smoke was blinding. He leaned forward and hugged the mare's neck. Hot sparks from the fire swirled, and several burned his hands and neck. He gagged on the acrid smoke. He breathed shallow breaths and knew he could not survive long in that deadly atmosphere. He dug into the mare, sending her blindly down the road.

The light grew brighter, and suddenly they were out of the smoke. Jerking the bandanna from his face, Royal gulped deep breaths of fresh air. The mare snorted and breathed easier also. She settled into her pace and rode away from the fire. Royal glanced back. The mountains were completely blotted out. The wall of gray-white smoked stretched along the horizon and climbed several thousand feet into the sky.

Ahead, Royal saw a rider charging toward him along the same road. He kicked the mare into a hard gallop, pulled his bandanna over his face, and rode to meet the man. They converged rapidly. Royal spoke first. "We got one hell of a fire here!" he shouted through the cloth. "Find the section crew," he instructed. "I'll go for help." Royal was in motion as the man shouted his answer.

"Right, and hurry!" the man pleaded. "From here, it don't look like I can do much good." He waved to Royal and spurred his horse toward the massive fire. Royal rode for a spell, then slowed the mare. He pulled his bandanna off and smiled.

"Hurry?" He laughed out loud. "You bet I'll hurry. Here's to you, Ham." Royal turned and spread his arms wide as he faced the fire.

For the next hour, Royal sweltered as he rode toward the H bar C. He had lost elevation and was in scrub grassland. The pungent smell of sage stung his nose. Colburn raised several types of cattle on the H bar C spread. This scrub grass and semiarid terrain was Longhorn country—they thrived here. Now the cattle sought shade beneath the scraggly cedars that dotted the land. The Longhorns were half wild and skittish. They watched Royal with suspicion as he rode past.

Royal left the road and sought shade and water in the river

bottom. The vegetation was lush, multihued green, and dense. He could not see twenty yards ahead. After watering the mare, he poured a Stetson full of water over his head. He would have gladly fallen into the water, but he didn't want to ride wet. A half-hour ride south, and he would see the barrancas. These red sandstone cliffs separated the grasslands from the desert. Any vegetation on the other side of these wind-sculptured cliffs was either prickly or spiny. The wildlife, sparse as it was, either poisoned or stung the hell out of you.

Staying in the cover of the river bottom, Royal rode toward the H bar C. It was late afternoon, and the day's heat was past. He noticed four huge holding pens on the other side of the river filled with several thousand head of cattle. It looked as if Colburn was rounding up for a drive. The profits from beef sales to the government had made him a wealthy man. Royal could not help but notice the lack of men around the stockyards and ranch. He smiled with satisfaction. They're looking for me, and I'm in their backyard, he thought.

The main house of the H bar C and the stock pens were nestled against the barrancas. The house was isolated from the surrounding ranchland by the steep riverbed. The banks were water cut and twenty feet high. Colburn had built a connecting trestle. Access into and out of the house and pens was over this wooden structure. It was approximately eighty feet long and twenty feet wide, with high side walls. The trestle was supported in the middle by two massive rough-sawn timbers. The river at this time of year pooled deep around the supports and was slow flowing. Royal studied the trestle and marked the timbers as the weak links of the bridge.

He unbuckled his saddlebag and tenderly removed a bundle of dynamite. It was the same unexploded bundle that George Petts and Dolph Stickney had planted in Clem Dowden's reservoir. Royal sat and separated the dynamite into two equal bundles. Clem had helped him with the blasting caps and fuses. He clustered four sticks around the fused one and tied them together. Clem had given him two minute fuses for each charge. Royal took lengths of leather strap and tied them around his waist.

Leaving the mare back in the willows, Royal worked his way downstream until he was beside the earthen retaining wall at the end of the trestle. He shucked his boots and shirt and cautiously approached the water. He had four matches clenched between his teeth. He left one bundle and the matches on the bank and slipped into the water. He crouched and kept the dynamite high and dry. Then he pushed off from the bank. The distance wasn't great, but he dog-paddled awkwardly, using one hand. He struggled to the timber and reached for a handhold, and slipped off. The submerged portion of the timber was moss covered. He fought to gain purchase but failed. Frantically, he swam for the crossed support braces between the timbers and painfully struck one of the submerged planks. As his legs weakened, he kicked strongly and draped an arm over the wood.

After a moment of rest, Royal slipped down the cross member to touch the timber. On tiptoe, he reached around the timber with one of the leather straps and held himself in place. He lashed the bundle of dynamite to the timber and swam back to the bank to retrieve the other charge. Repeating the procedure, he strapped the other bundle to the opposite timber. On the third trip, he returned with the matches clenched in his teeth.

Royal fanned his right hand in the air to dry it, then plucked a match from his teeth, thumbnail-struck it, and lit the fuse. It sputtered, then sparked into life. He kicked away from the timber and swam to the other one. He wedged his foot between the cross brace and the timber and struck the second match. The sulphur head dissolved and fell into the water. "Shit!" he hissed between clenched teeth. The third match flared and died before he could reach the fuse. Panic crawled up his spine. He had to get the fuse lit.

"Make it good, you little bugger!" he scolded the last match. He spotted an embedded nail in the timber and struck the match against it. The head popped off. The biting stink of the burning fuse gave him an idea. He quickly swam to it and held the match against the sputtering tip. The remaining sulphur on the match head burst into flame. Cupping both hands around the match, Royal pushed away from the timber and floated downstream. He rolled onto his stomach, churned the water with his legs, and reached to light the fuse. It caught with a flare. Royal then swam underwater toward the bank. When his fingertips grounded, he erupted from the water in a headlong lunge. Sprinting through the sand, he stumbled and fell. Fear of the blasts pushed him to his feet at a run.

Royal raced past the retaining wall when the first charge detonated. Boom . . . *Boom* . . . BOOM . . . ! A sharp, ear-splitting crack followed by rebounding echoes from the cliff face rumbled throughout the ranch. The cattle in the holding pens were on their feet, startled by the blast.

Boom . . . *Boom* . . . BOOM . . . ! The second explosion cascaded off the barrancas.

Twenty-five hundred head of cattle stampeded. The wooden corrals and pens were splintered. Bob-wire fences were snapped apart behind the mass of running cattle. The few hands left on the ranch scrambled for their lives. The main body of cattle ran away from the trestle, past the barrancas, into the desert. Royal stuck his head around the retaining wall, expecting to see the trestle lying in the river. He was awestruck. The trestle stood, both timbers in place. Shouts from the stock pens sent him running for his mare, boots in hand and shirt jammed into his mouth.

Royal splashed unseen through the water in the riverbed and reached the mare. He muscled his boots on and rode into the deep underbrush. The mare needed no encouragement. Upstream, Royal turned and looked at that damned trestle. With dismay, he watched a handful of men gather on the bridge. Colburn was shouting, giving orders. "What in sweet Jesus' name were those explosions?" his voice carried to Royal.

"Don't know, Mr. Colburn," the foreman defended. "All I heard was two loud bangs."

"Damn it, man!" Colburn hollered with frustration. "Don't just stand there. Do something!"

Before the man could move, the two were nearly run over by a small stampede of cattle running over the trestle. Both men dived for cover off the end of the trestle. Colburn came up onto the embankment, hopping mad. "Stoney, where in the hell did those cattle come from?"

The foreman, harried by the cattle and badgered by his boss, lost his temper. "Son of a bitch, boss! We got cattle spread from Old Mexico to the White Mountains. I'm doing the damned best I can! I don't have enough hands for a poker game, let alone to control a stampede!"

Colburn agreed with his foreman. "Calm down. Do what you can." He spoke with precision. "Take the ranch crew, cookie, house help—whoever you need. Use the herding crew.

If you can stop them critters from getting far into the desert, we'll be in pretty good shape."

"We don't have no herdin' crews," Stoney pleaded. "You sent them looking for whoever the hell he is," he snapped.

"Just do it, damn it! I don't care how." Colburn's anger was on the rise again. "I'll check this bridge myself." He had taken a step off the embankment when a shout held him in place. A rider galloped hard toward them. The winded horse slowed, then trotted to Stoney. The rider, singed and soot covered, leaned forward to dismount and fell out of the saddle. Stoney caught him before he hit the ground. Both men tumbled in a heap. The foreman struggled to his knees and gently turned the man over.

"What the hell? It's Darcy. I didn't recognize you, lad. Talk to me. What happened to you?"

The man tried to speak but could not. Stoney leaped to his feet to get water for him. He looked at Colburn, snatched the boss's fancy Stetson off his head, and slid down to the river. Stoney scooped a hatful of water and climbed the bank. Colburn stood rooted, running his hand through his sparse hair. The foreman knelt beside the rider, cupped the hat brim, and poured water onto the man's face. The rider came around and reached for the hat. Stoney tipped it, and the exhausted man gulped mouthfuls of water. The horse smelled the water and crowded in. Stoney let the animal drink too. Then the foreman dumped the remainder over the rider's head.

The man had recovered enough to speak. "Mr. Colburn. Two, maybe three sections of the northwest sector are on fire. We have the damnedest fire going there you ever seen."

Colburn slowly sat down on the embankment next to the rider. His face was masked with defeat. He knew what a range fire meant. "Will it spread to other sections?" He was reluctant to ask, fearing the worst.

"I don't think so." Colburn perked at the reply. "The afternoon winds have picked up pretty good. It seems to be confined to those three sections. I think it'll burn itself out."

"And we don't have men to fight it?" Colburn asked an unnecessary question. The rider nodded. "Get cleaned up, son. That horse doctor will give you what you need. Then get some grub."

The rider struggled to his feet. Colburn felt like an old man toney handed him his waterlogged Stetson. "Sorry, boss. line's straw." Colburn took the hat, jammed it on his head, nd started toward the ranch house. He spryly dodged several ray head on his march.

Stoney offered his friend a hand. "That bad out there, arcy?" He wanted to hear all he could. Chances were pretty ood he would be out there fighting it soon.

"Stoney," the rider said seriously to the foreman, "that's hat hell must look like. I ain't never seen nothin' like it. Fire. solid wall as far as I could see." He spread his arms wide. Smoke so thick you can't see your horse. Nothin' gonna stop . It'll have to burn itself out."

"There goes our winter grazing," Stoney reflected. "Well, ne thing sure. We'll have good grass next year."

"Stoney," the cowboy emphatically stressed, "there ain't a ing out there that ain't scorched black. Nothin'."

Royal overheard the discussion, but he felt little consolation. he trestle still stood.

CHAPTER
13

As the sun set behind the low hills, Royal lay in the sandston(e)
barrancas and looked down over the H bar C. The cliffs were
soft red in color, reflecting the fiery sunset. He would wait unt(il)
dark to come off the cliffs. The sprawling adobe ranch hous(e)
blended into the desert. The low rectangular building was cen(-)
tered around an open courtyard that was filled with a colorf(ul)
splash of flowers. A high adobe wall surrounded the hous(e.)
Access to the structure was through a wide wooden gate. Off t(o)
the side was a large root cellar, dug into the hillside. Produc(e,)
staples, canned goods, and ranch supplies were stored in th(is)
underground building. A small corral and shed for Colburn('s)
horses flanked the cellar. Behind the corral and bermed into th(e)
hillside was a small powder locker. The ranch hands occasion(-)
ally needed dynamite, and Colburn kept a supply.

Fronting the house and corral was a hard-packed dirt yar(d)
with hitching posts, and water troughs. Across the open spac(e)
six small cabins, staggered in rows of three each. This semici(r-)
cle of cabins enclosed the perimeter of the yard. The first ro(w)
consisted of the supply, feed, and blacksmith sheds. The secon(d)
row was made up of the tack shed, the cookshed, and th(e)
bunkhouse.

Royal waited until near dark before he made his move. Usin(g)
a narrow game trial, he worked across the smooth slopin(g)
rocks. He stepped too quickly, lost his footing, and slid off th(e)
trail. Frantically grasping for a handhold, he broke his skid b(y)
grabbing a small sagebush. Numerous rocks tumbled over th(e)
edge of the cliff face and hit the ground seconds later. Roy(al)
muscled his way back to the trail. When his knees stoppe(d)
shaking, he continued but with a renewed sense of caution.

Once on level ground, he skirted the cabins to avoid acciden(-)
tal discovery. The ranch house would be a good place to sta(rt)

is search for Abbie. Darting around the far side of the yard, he
opped next to the corral and listened. All was quiet. The
orses in the corral sidled over to him and sniffed his offered
and. He patted them before he continued on his circuitous trip
the house. A shaft of light sliced from the cellar door. A
uckboard and team were standing out front. With guarded
ovements, Royal tiptoed past the horses and hugged the side
the buckboard. He took a step away from the wagon and
umped into Luther Fenbow.

"Get him, boys!" Luther shouted as he dove for Royal's legs.
Royal nearly made it out of the cowpuncher's grasp, but
uther clung to his leg. Royal pummeled the man with hard,
lling blows and felt the grip lessen. Royal jerked his foot free
d turned to run. J. P. caught him midstride and knocked him
to the root cellar with a flying tackle. Royal struggled to his
ees just as Luther landed on top of him. The three men
iled and battered each other with wild fury. Royal lashed out
d hit everything he could but was overpowered.

With a final burst of strength, Royal twisted and fought to
s feet. Luther was on his hands and knees gasping for breath.
P. was flat on his back. Royal stumbled toward the darkness
tside the cellar and was leveled by a pounding blow. He
nded on his side, pushed the sack of potatoes off his chest,
d looked around at the third cowboy. This was the respite
uther and J. P. needed. They piled on quick as thought. Lu-
er had a chokehold on Royal's throat, and J. P. was trying to
eak Royal's fingers. Howard "Mom" Rummy, the real H bar
cook, looped a rope around Royal's feet.

"Got him, boys," Mom called, and began to pull Royal off
e dirt floor. Seconds later, Royal was hanging upside down
om the rafters. Mom tied the rope off, and the three H bar C
nds stood and watched Royal spin around. Royal could not
uch the ground—his fingertips three inches shy of Mother
arth. He gradually stopped spinning clockwise, only to un-
ind and spin counterclockwise. While Royal twirled like a
p, the three hands went outside to the trough to clean up.
hey rinsed their cuts and bruises and drank the cool refresh-
g water from the pump. The three laughed and joked as they
oked at Royal.

"Looks like a side of beef, don't he, boys?" Luther laughed.
And about as smart as one too." Royal knew what he meant.

"Ya, maybe we oughta leave him till he cures," J. P. volunteered with a wide smile.

Royal had stopped spinning. His head hurt from the punches, and his eyes felt slightly puffy. The throbbing beat of his heart was magnified in his head—it pounded every time his heart did. His hearing was acute due to the pressure in his head. He was flushed, his head laden with blood. A high piercing whine gradually built in his ears. He wanted to scream, to beg to be let down. A grinding pain spread from the base of his skull. Luther strolled casually to Royal and gave him a hard spin. Royal gnashed his teeth to keep from screaming out. Luther and the others stood back and watched the spectacle.

On the ragged edge of consciousness, Royal felt the sweet firmness of the dirt floor greet his bloated fingertips. He was being lowered to the ground. When his shoulders touched the damp earth, he was turned over roughly, hands tied behind his back. Mom let go of the rope, and Royal's feet thudded to the ground. Relishing the escape from hanging, Royal lay on the dirt floor without moving. He had no feeling in his toes and tried to wiggle them. Thousands of tiny pinpricks tingled as the circulation returned. Royal was manhandled to his feet but could not stand. He fell forward, and Luther caught him.

Luther toyed with Royal. He stood him up, then let him fall. "He looks like old Henry did last week drunk, don't he?" Luther was amused with the game.

"Who we got, Luther?" J. P. wanted to know. "Is he a horse thief?"

Mom cut in, "If'n you was a horse thief, mister"—he poked Royal in the chest—"you'd be swingin' from the rafters by the other end. We don't cotton to horse thievin'. He's a sneak thief, I'm guessin'."

"Naw, you're both wrong," Luther said with a mean laugh. "This here is none other than Mr. Royal Ballou, the not-so-smart ex-lawman of Jacob's Well." Luther shook his head. "I've seen setups work in my time, but you, mister, you take the prize." Luther leisurely circled behind Royal. The ranch hand suddenly hit him in the back, a wicked kidney punch Royal buckled and fell against Mom. Together they went down on the dirt floor. Luther stood over Royal. "Remember me Mr. Fancy Lawman? You threw me in your jail last year. Said I was a drunk. You remember that?"

Mom got to his feet and helped Royal up. Royal glared at Luther. "I remember it. And I'd do it again. You're still a drunk."

"Why, you—" Luther lunged forward and took a swing at Royal. Royal anticipated the move and ducked. The blow gazed his head and sent him sprawling. He hit shoulder-first in a stack of wooden crates and knocked them over in his fall.

Royal twisted onto his back and baited, "What I said still holds, Luther. You're well heeled to a bottle. A liquid hero." Royal doubled up as best he could, knowing the consequences of his remarks.

Luther came undone and plunged into the scattered stack of crates. He raised one over his head and threatened Royal with it.

"Stop!" Mom confronted Luther, a pick handle in hand. "I'm not going to stand by and watch you beat a helpless man to death, Luther! Now drop it, or I'll knock the stuffin's out of you."

Luther seethed and held the crate. Mom lambasted the crate with the pick handle and sent it spinning out of Luther's hands. "He's mine, Mom. You stay out of it."

Mom threw the pick into the shadows and braced himself. "I've got two hands free, Luther. You'll have to go through me first."

Luther knew he was beat. He wiped a trickle of blood from his nose, snatched his hat off the dirt floor, and stormed out of the spud cellar. With J. P. on one side and Mom on the other, Royal was escorted to the main house.

The living room was immense, the walls decorated with tanned cowhides. The room was dominated by a massive fireplace. Several pictures of Colburn's prize breeding steers adorned the mantel. Facing the fireplace was a long oak table, complete with tablecloth and fresh flowers. A dozen straight-backed chairs surrounded it. Colburn and Stoney were seated at the well-stocked bar talking about the pending cattle drive when Mom entered the room.

"What's the meaning of this intrusion?" Colburn slipped off his stool. "You aren't to be in this house."

"Found a friend snooping around, Mr. Colburn." Mom motioned to J. P. "We had a talk with him first." They led Royal into the room and stopped in front of Colburn. "What you want us to do with him?"

Colburn's eyes measured Royal as he drew closer. He carefully chose his words. "Mr. Ballou—I use that term because I am a gentleman," he said with confidence. "You have caused me considerable grief, not to mention a fair sum of money." He appraised Royal like he would a good steer. "It goes without saying that I'm glad—no!—relieved that my troubles are over. Finished."

Royal looked at the man with no outward emotion. He tried to gauge the heartbreak and ruin Colburn had caused. With money and a warped sense of justice, he controlled the greater part of the New Mexico Territory. He bought people off, intimidated others, and killed those who stood in his way.

"I won't list your achievements, Mr. Ballou," Colburn continued in his patronizing tone, "but they are considerable. It's a shame such talent is wasted. You could have fit nicely into my organization. I need good men like you."

Deep inside, Royal raged. He hated this corrupt, dishonest demigod with a loathing that bordered on the maniacal. Royal was proud of his upbringing, and Colburn disgusted him. Royal watched him with indolence. This worked under Colburn's skin. He was beginning to get hot.

Eliciting no response from Royal, Colburn terminated the one-sided conversation. "Howard, take him to the cellar and chain him in the storage room. I want a twenty-four-hour guard on him. Understand?"

"Yes, sir. We'll keep a real close eye on him." Mom puffed up like a bullfrog knowing Colburn trusted him. With Royal sandwiched between them, Mom and J. P. exited the house.

Stoney had held his tongue throughout the lopsided discussion. Colburn returned to the bar, poured a shot, and proposed an unashamed toast. "To my continued success. I couldn't do it without men like you, Stoney." He raised his glass and downed his whiskey.

Stoney nursed his drink. "Ham. you'll get your pound of flesh from Ballou. But what will you do with Abbie?" Stoney queried his boss. "You said you'd let her go as soon as you had that lawman."

"Yes, I did say that." Colburn paused and schemed. "I've

changed my mind. She might come in handy the next couple of weeks. I'm going to hang on to her."

Colburn had reneged on his word, and Stoney didn't like it. Something about Abbie unsettled him. She was a nestling and didn't belong in the corrupt, sometimes fatal world of Ham Colburn. Stoney would not let him destroy her.

After an often-heated discussion with Colburn concerning the lack of manpower on the ranch and the devastating range fire, Stoney excused himself to turn in. He went into the kitchen, sticky-fingered a piece of apple pie, and let himself out the back door. As he rounded the corner, he heard voices coming from the dining room. Strange, he thought. I left Ham alone. He eased between the bushy lilacs and stood beneath the partially open window.

". . . you understand?" Colburn grilled. "I don't want a trace of him found."

"You bet, Mr. Colburn," Luther Fenbow assured the H bar C boss. "I'll handle it personal. Besides, I got me a score to settle with that man."

"One more thing, Luther," Colburn alerted him. "I want you to keep an eye on Stoney. He's taken a shine to Abbie. I don't trust him. She's my ace."

Stoney stepped away from the window. "Damn it all to hell —I've got to act fast!" he cursed under his breath. "I've 'bout fifteen minutes before Luther checks on Royal." He sprinted across the yard, and his lanky frame covered the ground rapidly. He slowed, then walked through the double barn doors of the cellar. A faint yellow glow came from the far end of the underground structure. Stoney moved purposefully to the storage shed. J. P. was sitting guard, his chair tipped against the wall, his feet propped on a nail keg. He heard Stoney step into the ring of light and lazily raised the shotgun off his lap.

"J. P.," Stoney forced himself to ask calmly, " 'bout ready for a break?"

The young man was surprised. "I've been here short of an hour. I'm fine." J. P. was as lazy as a hound dog in the noonday sun. In his grandfather's words, "The boy burned daylight."

"Why don't you catch some shut-eye?" Stoney suggested. "We're going to fight range fires tomorrow. You'll need to be rested."

"Luther was to relieve me." J. P. dawdled. "I'll wait for him."

"Suit yourself," Stoney declared. "This is straight from the boss's mouth, Mr. Colburn. You have doubts, I'll gladly fetch him here. We'll get this settled in a hurry." Stoney turned on his heel and headed for the door, hoping his bluff would work.

"No, no. I'll go." J. P. leaned forward, dropping the chair on all fours. He stood and handed the shotgun to Stoney. "No need to get the boss riled."

"Our prisoner doing fine?"

"Yep, been asleep since I got here." J. P. gave an uninterested answer. "I'm turnin' in."

The young ranch hand stepped around Stoney on his way out of the cellar. It took several seconds for his eyes to adjust to the darkness outside. As he paused, Stoney clipped him at the base of the skull with the butt plate of the scattergun. J. P. was out for the full count.

Stoney dragged the ranch hand to the storage-room door and dropped him. He unhooked the latch and started in. Royal was watching him.

"Royal, get outta here," Stoney firmly instructed as he pulled J. P. into the cramped space.

"Can't go far, Stoney," Royal answered, and held out his manacled hands. The connecting chain circled his waist and was locked to a set of ankle bracelets.

"Damn," Stoney berated Mom's thoroughness, and quickly gave J. P. a pat-down. Keys jangled in his shirt pocket. The foreman ripped the shirt in his haste to get them. He fumbled with the key ring, then dropped it to the floor.

"Calm down, Stoney. We have time."

"Like hell we do! Luther's on his way over. If he shows up before you've made your escape, you're a dead man. Get my drift?"

Royal removed the manacles from his hands, pulled the chain from around his waist, and sat on the floor to unlock his ankles. He handed Stoney the wrist manacles. "Here. Put them on J. P."

"Good idea, lad. We'll dump him in the corner out of the light." He finished locking J. P.'s wrists. With Royal's help, he deposited the hand behind the grain sacks.

"Why you doin' this for me, Stoney? You're an H bar C man through and through," Royal asked suspiciously.

"Was," Stoney bitterly replied. "I'm done as of ten minutes ago. Ham's plottin' agin' me. And that young lady, Abbie. I'm done—"

"Abbie!" Royal cut him off. "Where is she? Is she all right? She's special to me, Stoney," he blurted to his new friend. "I've got to get her back."

"Hold your water, boy." The foreman put a hand on Royal's shoulder. "She's fine. I'll get her out soon as I can."

Royal stared at him, uncertainty clouding his eyes.

"I've never gone back on my word," Stoney reassured. "I give it to you now."

A voice called out in the darkness, from the front of the cellar. "J. P., you in there?" Luther asked in a near-childlike voice.

Panic touched the men. Royal bolted for the doors, but Stoney grabbed him by the scruff of the neck. "No, go up the air vent," he whispered, and pointed to the ventilation shaft above them. "It goes to the sod roof. Just push the grate to one side."

Royal climbed the storage shelves. He was crouched on the top shelf when Stoney stopped him. "Royal, here. Take this." He handed him a Colt .44.

"I've got my horse in the barrancas. I'll ride from there."

"No, wait," Stoney instructed. "Meet me by the tack shed in fifteen minutes."

"I'll be there." His feet disappeared up the shaft.

Luther called once more. "J. P., I'm coming in!" His voice was closer.

Stoney glanced at J. P.'s partially obscured body. He appeared to be sleeping. Stoney unbuckled his gunbelt, cast it behind the grain sacks, and quietly stepped into the light. He closed the door without a sound and plopped into the chair.

The foreman heard Luther's clumsy approach through the long interior of the cellar. He was drunk, stumbled over a sack of potatoes, and fell face-first onto the dusty floor. Stoney helped Luther into the circle of light. Luther sat heavily on a nail keg.

"Whew, am I drunk." Luther steadied himself with both hands on the keg. "I had a few drinks with Mr. Colburn. He's

one hell of a nice man." A stuporous smile washed over
Luther's unshaved face. He was mellow and quiet.

"That he is, Luther," Stoney lied. "You won't find any better."

"Where in the deuce is J. P.? He's to be guarding our prisoner."

"I happened by and found the boy nearly asleep," Stoney
replied. "I told him to hit the sack."

"That damned Royal in there?" Luther lurched to his feet
and squinted into the storage room.

"Sure as hell is. Want to see him?" Stoney steadied Luther as
he raised the lantern. The yellow light filtered between the
planks and illuminated J. P.'s lower trunk. The chains glittered
in the light. Stoney grinned. "He's locked up tighter than a
schoolmarm's bedroom at night."

"I'm gonna kill him tomorrow," Luther stated with no emotion. "I want him to be good and rested for it."

Stoney declined comment on Luther's compassion.

A trickle of dirt sprinkled down the airshaft. Luther looked
up, and nearly keeled over backward as he raised his head.
"What's that?"

"Rats" was Stoney's snap answer. "I near shot one awhile
back. Big as a damned bobcat."

"Let me take over," Luther offered. "I want to guard my
man."

"Now you're cookin'. That way you can be first at him tomorrow." Stoney knew Luther would fall asleep as soon as he
took the watch.

"Ya." Luther chuckled. "Keep a condemned man company."

"Let me make sure he stays in there." Stoney glanced at the
hardware bin and spotted a lock. He clicked it in place on the
door and pocketed the key. "There. He won't be goin' any
place. I'm gonna turn in, Luther."

Luther waved him off as he slumped into the chair. The
foreman was out of the light before Luther hailed him. "Stoney,
how am I gonna get him out if'n you got the key?"

"It slipped my mind, Luther. Here it is." Stoney reached into
his pocket and handed him the key to J. P.'s manacles. He was
counting on Luther to overlook the fact that he needed two
keys. Luther tucked the key into his vest pocket and patted it
safe.

As Stoney turned to leave, Luther caught his arm. "Stoney, I can't bridle my tongue. I'm tellin' you this 'cause you being a foreman and all. Ham told me to keep a sharp eye on you." Luther sneered at his next suggestion. "Says you got the hots for that gal he took."

"Can't blame a man for tryin'." Stoney forced a laugh and slapped Luther on the shoulder. His impulse to waylay Luther was overridden by his sense of urgency to help Royal and Abbie.

Stoney exited the cellar and paused in the fresh night air. He checked the corral and yard—not a thing stirred. He ducked between the rails of the corral and hooked two halters off the post. The horses smelled him and approached their friend. He stroked them, found two he wanted, and bridled them. With horses in tow, he left the corral and walked away from the sheds. There was a small open area downstream, and Stoney tied both animals there. "I'll be back shortly," he whispered. The horses rubbed against him. "You're my ride out of here."

Stoney gave wide berth to the bunkhouse and approached the tack shed. He looked closely for Royal and saw his dark shape blended against the weathered wood.

"Royal, it's me, Stoney," he whispered. "Come to the tack shed."

Stoney knew the shed by heart. Many a morning he had been up before dawn, grabbing gear to ready the crews. He stationed Royal in the deep shadows and slipped inside. He passed seven saddle benches, took three steps to the right, and reached waist high for a doorknob. He felt along the frame and found the key. The lock opened with a muffled snap. He stuck his head in the small room. "Abbie, you awake?" No response. "Abbie, it's Stoney," he called louder.

"What do you want?" came the frightened reply.

"Listen carefully. I'm getting you out of here."

"You can't do that, Stoney. What will happen to you when Ham finds out?"

"Let me rephrase that: I'm getting *us* out of here. You dressed?" He wanted to ride as soon as possible.

"Let me slip my boots on." He heard rustling as she moved, then stifled plops as her boots were yanked on.

"Remember that spot where we lunched the other day? The place with the rusty red jack oak you liked so much?"

"I sure do," she answered.

"If we're separated, meet there. I left two horses."

Stoney heard her move toward him. She bumped into th
wall. "Here, Miss Abbie—take my hand."

Stoney reached out, found her, and assisted her through th
inner door. "I'm ready to ride away from the H bar C," sh
whispered.

"Shush up," he warned. "Some of the boys are playing cards
so we'll have to be quiet. Hold on to me—I know my wa
around this shed." They moved without a sound. "Stay by th
door. I want to check outside." Stoney eased around the corne
and bumped into Royal. He lost his train of thought an
reached for his gun.

"What in the hell you grabbin' for, Stoney?" Royal kidded

"I've got your pistol."

"You've made your point," Stoney conceded sheepishly
"I'm going crazy on this spread. Grab that gal beside the door
She's missed you somethin' fierce."

Royal called with a hushed voice, "Abbie, come here." H
rapped his knuckles lightly on the side of the shed. She felt fo
his hand and found it. He gave her a strong pull.

"You don't have to yank my danged arm off, Stoney," sh
cheerfully complained.

As she stumbled, Stoney said, "Weren't me, ma'am. He don
it," and pointed toward Royal.

Abbie did a double take and started to speak. Royal clampe
his hand over her mouth. "Not a word," he cautioned. "G
with Stoney and ride like hell away from this place. I'll explai
later."

Abbie's eyes were the size of two bit pieces. She started t
mumble something, but Royal kissed her heartily before sh
could talk. He gently held her away and whispered, "Now g
with him. Stoney, I'll fetch my horse in a minute."

"Where you headed?" The foreman sensed that Royal wa
up to no good.

"I'm going to stir things up a bit for Ham." The dee
shadow did not hide the toothy white grin that creased his face
"See you two at Doc Shu's place." With that he disappeare
into the night and ran between the row of sheds. He had n
particular plan in mind.

Meanwhile, Luther decided to check on Royal. Unable t

open the lock, he smashed in the door. When he realized the prisoner was gone, he fled the cellar with J. P. on his heels. They shouted that the prisoner had escaped. J. P. tripped and fell forward, and accidentally touched off his rifle. Luther, still drunk, thought they were being fired upon. He didn't hesitate to fire both barrels of his shotgun. Fortunately, J. P. was lying on the ground when Luther shot. The racket shattered the night and reverberated off the cliffs. The ranch hands who were playing poker ran out of the bunkhouse. Royal crouched and dropped behind the water trough.

"Over here, men! By the cellar," Royal shouted as he shot in the direction of the cellar. He crawled to the end of the trough, then shot at the bunkhouse. He bellied to the ground as the fight heated up.

Luther and J. P. had taken shelter inside the cellar and returned fire. Royal stuck the .44 in the back of his pants and wormed away from the trough. He followed a shallow depression to get clear of the raging battle. He rose to his feet and ran behind the sheds. He laughed at the thought of Colburn's reaction to the gunfight.

Luther was on a roll. He winged two hands with a single blast from the shotgun. He discarded the empty scattergun and drew his Colt. While trading shots with the hands, he accidently hit the kerosene lantern in the bunkhouse. The first traces of flames reflected in the windows. Luther, convinced he needed more firepower, sprinted to the powder magazine. With no key for the lock, he stuck the muzzle of his pistol against the lock, partially shielded his body against the wall, and shot. The lock snapped open. He bolted inside to the stash of readied charges. With four sticks of dynamite in hand, he returned to the cellar, still exchanging shots with the bunkhouse crew.

Taking a headlong dive, Luther cleared the doors of the cellar and rolled into the safety of the interior. Aided by alcohol and adrenaline, Luther was a man possessed.

"I don't know who they are, Luther, but they're readyin' to rush us," J. P. warned. He had seen the hands outlined against the burning bunkhouse. In truth, they were at the trough to get water to salvage their sleeping quarters and gear.

"I'll handle it." Luther boldly accepted the challenge.

He struck a match, lighted two fuses, and headed for the twin doors. With his whiskey-impaired skills, he threw the dynamite. The first stick grazed a corral pole and fell to the ground next to the trough. It exploded with a loud crack, sending a geyser of water and debris twenty feet into the air. The second stick landed in the hard-packed yard, bounced end over end, and came to rest under the supply shed. It detonated with a muffled *whomp!* The kerosene in storage exploded with a blinding flash. Colburn's prize horses panicked at the spectacle and destroyed the corral in their flight away from the madness.

The gun battle ceased. The hands froze in awe as the world around them exploded and burned. They watched in silence as a single can of kerosene, trailing a streamer of flames, rocketed through the smoke and landed on the dry cedar shakes of the tack shed. In no time, the shed was engulfed in flames.

Luther and J. P. watched the ranch burn, the result of their private war. Neither man spoke. Flames from the bunkhouse and tack shed spread quickly to the adjoining sheds, and soon they too were ablaze.

Half dressed, Colburn came running over to the men. "Did you do that?" he screamed at Luther as he pointed to the burning sheds. A look of disbelief twisted his features.

"We was being attacked, Mr. Colburn. I run 'em off," Luther stated proudly.

"I'm going to kill you! You dumb bastard!" Colburn yelled as he raised his pistol. Before he could pull the trigger, other hands restrained him, and his pistol discharged into the night.

"Get him out of my sight before I shoot him!" Colburn raved as he struggled against his men. J. P. took Luther in hand and walked him away from Colburn.

With Luther gone, Colburn ceased struggling. "Did anyone see the young lady escape?" he asked softly.

Not a word was spoken. The hands were sickened by the thought that Abbie was trapped inside. They held no malice toward her. As a matter of fact, they appreciated having her around. She had improved Mom's cookin'.

Colburn was inwardly relieved to have Abbie out of the way. No loose ends. He wasn't pleased with how she had died, but it had been beyond his control. Any long-range repercussions could be passed off as a tragic accident caused by a drunken hand. Colburn, under control, turned to one of his men.

"Draw Luther's pay," he calmly stated. "Tell him to collect

his gear if it isn't burned up. Then run him off. Mention that if I ever set eyes on him again, I'll shoot him on the spot."

"Yes, sir. I'm on my way." The man knew Colburn was to be taken seriously.

CHAPTER
14

Ham Colburn, J. P., and Howard "Mom" Rummy, the new H bar C foreman, rode into Jacob's Well. Colburn did not know what to expect from the citizenry. The *Gazette* article had doomed Ellery Albee and his three puppets, and they had tendered their resignations. Colburn had anticipated this and was already plotting the formation of a new council and mayor for Jacob's Well. He hoped that within a month this affair would blow over. Judge Williams was expendable. If he collected on favors owed, Colburn could have a new judge in a matter of months. J. P., elevated to a new position, now regarded himself as a bad-assed enforcer. He bought a new pistol and worked diligently to hone his marginal skills. Howard Rummy wasn't much of a thinker, but he was dependable. Ham felt comfortable with his choice of hands. He wasn't expecting trouble, and besides, Curly was available in case he needed help.

Colburn and Howard headed for The Rose, while J. P. went for Curly. Seated at a table in the corner, Colburn discussed H bar C business with his new foreman until J. P. and Curly joined them. J. P.'s head was singing from the praise Curly had heaped upon him, the new bodyguard. A tough job for a good man.

"You're looking relaxed today, Curly," Colburn observed with pleasure. He watched his lawman closely and saw no cracks. "Not feeling any heat yet?"

Curly eased around the table, patted Ham on the back, and pulled up a chair. "Nothing, Ham. I told the interim council that if they wanted me out of office, they would have to drag me out." He laughed heavily. "End of conversation. Why aren't we using the back room?" Curly felt uncomfortable in the saloon.

"Something about varnish on the floor," Colburn briefed

im. "We're stuck out here. No matter—business as usual."
The old confidence welled. Curly was still his ace in Jacob's
Well. "We've got some loose ends to tidy up. I'll work on a new
council and judge. We'll give Judge Williams a gift or two. He'll
ake care of us."

Curly sensed the H bar C boss did not fully appreciate the
udge's predicament. "Ham, we might oughta send the judge on
n extended fishin' trip. His tenure could get real dicey. Only a
hort blurb about him in the *Gazette* article. I don't like it. I'm
vaiting for the other shoe to drop." Curly looked at Ham with
aised eyebrows.

"Maybe not a bad idea, Curly," Colburn agreed. "Let me
hink on it." He broached a tender subject. "How much we into
im for?"

"Damned near nine hundred dollars over the last two years."

"Worth every penny of it. He helped with profitable land
eals, boundary disputes, and grazing permits. Do you think a
isit to the *Gazette* and Mr. Lightshield might be in order?"

"Excellent idea." Curly smiled slightly, anticipation quicken-
g his pulse. "Seems our local printer needs a refresher on
olitics in this town. I'll see to it."

The batwing doors clattered open as Doc Shu and two men
ntered the saloon. The doc scanned the room, then walked to
he corner table. "May we join you, Ham?"

"No," Colburn rudely told the old man. "We don't have
nything to talk about."

"Thanks. Nice of you to offer." The doc motioned to his
ompanions to sit, and the three men found chairs. "Allow me
o introduce my friends, Ham. This is Judge Augustus Black."
Ie placed his hand on the judge's shoulder. "Chief Justice,
'irst Judicial District, Santa Fe."

The judge, in his midsixties, was dressed in a black jacket, a
ark shirt, and black trousers. He was tall and burly, and a
hick moustache and long sideburns etched his face. He merely
odded in acknowledgment. His piercing eyes circled the table
aking each man's measure.

Colburn concealed his despair. He felt poor-spirited, so timo-
ous that he even reached for his coffee with an unsteady hand.
Ie knew Judge Black by reputation. Known as "Black Jack"
lack, he was tougher than a hog's nose. His sentences were
arsh—most of the men who had faced him were still doing

time. Colburn began to have misgivings about his questionable business transactions.

"His companion"—Doc Shu pointed to the other man—"is Deputy U.S. Marshal Thad Buford, First District, Santa Fe. These men are here to investigate alleged irregularities in the election process and misappropriation of town funds. I might add that possible tampering with telegraph service will also come under close scrutiny."

"Why, you tired old man!" Colburn blurted out. He hoped bluster would hide his fear. "I resent your insinuations."

"Mr. Colburn, be quiet," Judge Black said sharply. His voice was smooth, his tone direct. "I'm going to tell you something that you'd better hear. I have every intention of looking into this town's politics for the past several years. If you're clean, then you have nothing to fear. Don't threaten me with your cheap theatrics." He leaned forward and looked at Colburn's drawn face.

"Do you realize who I am?" Colburn fought back. "I'm one of the wealthiest and most influential men in the territory. I buy and sell men like you every day." He was on the attack, going for the kill.

"Is that an offer, Mr. Colburn?" the judge quietly confronted him.

Colburn recovered quickly. "You're damned right it is. I'll pay you one thousand dollars to ride away from here and never look back." He waited for a response, confident he had bested the man.

The judge turned to his companion. "Deputy Buford, arrest that man for attempting to bribe a federal official."

The U.S. Marshal stood. Colburn leaped to his feet, stepped back from the table, and bumped into the wall.

"Boys," the judge called.

Out of the back room stepped another marshal, a shotgun cradled in his arm. The door to the storage room near Colburn burst open, and a shotgun barrel prodded him in the back. A third marshal stepped from the staircase. "Sit down and don't say a word." Colburn was pushed to his seat.

The judged looked at Curly. "Mr. Hall, I know you by reputation. I won't mince words. My advice to you is stay the hell out of this." He met and held Curly's burning glare.

Before anyone moved or spoke, Royal and a Texas Ranger

walked through the batwings and approached the table. Curly
cast a steely glance at Royal. Judge Black sensed tension and
cautioned the marshals to be ready.

"Judge Black"—the Ranger offered his hand—"I'm Wallace
Kenlaw, Texas Ranger from San Antone. Deputy Ballou wired
for assistance." The Ranger noticed a few frowns. The Texan,
in his midforties, was curt to the point of rudeness. "As far as
I'm concerned, he *is* a deputy. I come here to have a talk with
Rutherford Hallahan, alias Curly Hall."

"Concerning what, Mr. Kenlaw?" Judge Black asked.

"I'm gonna dig into two shootings that took place right here
in Jacob's Well. I want to close the books on them. Then I want
Mr. Hall to ride to Texas and answer charges there." Kenlaw
glanced at Curly, who was fiddling with his coffee cup.

"Your man is right there, Mr. Kenlaw." Judge Black pointed
to the sheriff.

Curly glanced at the Texan. A flicker of recognition came
into his eyes, but he kept silent.

"Mr. Hall, I would appreciate time to talk with you. Your
office will do fine." The Ranger's statement was not up for
discussion.

Curly was edgy. His deputies should have shown by now—
he had briefed them on the meeting and had told them to be
present. "Suits me," Curly answered easily, flashing a deceitful
smile.

Doc Shu had planned this encounter. He had been boarding
Judge Black and Deputy Marshal Buford in his back room
while awaiting the arrival of Ranger Kenlaw. He had met with
his friend Hank Reardon, the shotgun rider, and explained his
part in the morning's happenings. Hank had ambled into the
jail, disarmed and locked up Curly's deputies. He was comfort-
bly settled there now with both feet propped on the desk.
Larry, the barkeep at The Rose, had closed the back meeting
room to Colburn and his cronies.

Sheriff Hall placed both hands on the table. He slowly rose
and gently pushing his chair back with his foot. Once upright,
he violently shoved the table forward. The unexpected move
caught everyone off guard. Judge Black was clipped by the
table. As he fell, he grabbed Deputy Buford and dragged him
down. Howard Rummy and J. P., sitting slightly back from the
table, were untouched. Doc Shu had been resting both elbows

on the table and fell forward out of the line of fire. The marshals dove for cover. There were too many people for a shoot-out.

Wallace Kenlaw was bowled over as he took the full force of the table. Colburn leaned away and fell against the wall. Curly, with unexpected quickness, bolted for the staircase. In blurred motion, he drew his Colt and shot at his greatest threat, the Texas Ranger. Ranger Kenlaw scrambled behind the overturned table. The slug punched a hole through the oak top and flattened Kenlaw, his forearm shattered.

J. P. sprang to his feet to help Colburn. The young man fanned a hip shot at a marshal crouched by the door. J. P. watched his shot splinter the door above the marshal's head. Another quick shot—J. P. saw this one gouge a fist-size hole in the doorframe. He did not hear the shot that hit him in the chest. As he involuntarily back-pedaled, he was hit with another pile-driving blow. The room dimmed as he drifted toward the floor.

Howard would have lived if he had not drawn on the lawman. The marshal, on one knee with the 10-gauge shouldered, yelled, "Drop the gun!" Howard disregarded the order and raised his cocked .44. The deep-throated roar of the shotgun added to the din in The Rose. Howard was clubbed back into an adjoining table by 00 buck pellets. The marshal touched off the second barrel at Curly as he ran for the stairs. The frame and door disintegrated in a shower of wood splinters. Curly popped around the corner and snapped off a shot at the still-kneeling marshal. The marshal slammed into the wall as the bullet knocked his leg from beneath him.

Royal drew a steady bead on Curly, but Doc Shu inadvertently stepped between Royal and Curly. Royal, at the last possible second, jerked the pistol barrel up and slipped his finger off the trigger. Curly charged up the stairs.

Colburn scrambled to his feet and searched for Judge Black with an ungovernable feeling of vengeance. The judge, a threat to his empire, crouched beneath a table. Blood dripped from a deep cut over his eye. Deputy Marshal Buford shielded the judge from the gunfight, but Colburn had a clear shot at him. He carefully raised his Colt and steadied it on Judge Black.

"Don't do it, Ham!" Doc Shu yelled. Colburn, momentarily distracted, quickly re-aimed at the judge. The doc gripped John

Tibbetts's Remington derringer and aimed at the bulk of
Colburn's body. He shot. The .41-caliber pistol bit his hand
with an uncontrollable recoil. The doc peered through the
smoke to see Colburn holding his smashed and useless right
arm against his chest. His Colt was poorly held and pointed
toward the floor. Doc Shu hustled over and took the pistol.

Royal sprinted to the enclosed stairwell. He knelt down, removed his Stetson, and held it at arm's length above his head.
He eased the hat into the stairwell and peeked quickly around
the frame. Curly, crouched at the top of the stairs, shot at the
hat, which flew out of Royal's hand. Royal jerked his head back
as a bullet splintered the baseboard.

"Royal!" one of the marshals called. Royal looked at the
marshal holding a shotgun and took the 10-gauge. The marshal
held up two fingers—both barrels were loaded. Royal hugged
the wall. With a fluid motion, he poked the shotgun around the
corner and touched off both barrels, one on the heel of the
other. The blatant racket shook the narrow stairwell. Dust and
pieces of plaster fell from the ceiling.

The sound of running told Royal that Curly was headed
down the hallway toward the outside staircase. Royal ran for
the rear of The Rose. He handed the shotgun to the startled
marshal as he bolted past. The footrace was on. If Curly
reached the staircase first, he would escape. If Royal beat him
there, Curly would have to stand and fight. Royal ran headlong
through the storage room, dodging beer kegs and stacked furni-
ture. At the door he paused, breathing rapidly. He palmed the
door with a featherlight touch. *Click!* It sprang open and
squeaked as it swung with the warp of the loading dock. No
sound came from outside. Royal cautiously exited, keeping his
eyes on the second-floor landing.

"Hey, Doc!" Royal yelled into the saloon as he hugged the
wall.

"What ya need, boy?" came the distant reply.

"Cover the stairwell," Royal instructed. "Curly's somewhere
upstairs."

"Will do. Need any help?"

"No, I'll take my time."

Royal hopped off the dock. Not once did he take his eyes off
the landing. He had a clear view of the alley—it was safe. Cir-
cling the stairs, Royal tested each tread before weighting it. The

second step from the top moaned as he stepped off it. He pressed against the siding and opened the door with his pistol barrel. The door creaked noisily and hit the railing with a loud *thunk*. He peered into the dark interior of the hallway. It was impossible to see the length of it, as his eyes had not adjusted to the dim light. A small smoking foyer was inside the door. With a quick wish-me-luck prayer, Royal lunged through the door. Surprise washed over him—he had expected a .36 ball to greet him.

As his eyes grew acustomed to the darkness, Royal glanced down the hallway. There were ten rooms in the corridor. He would need all his skill to get out of this alive. He stuck close to the wall as he worked his way along the left-hand side. The door to room number three was ajar. He saw a figure sprawled across the bed asleep. As he approached room number one, he heard a rustling from within. He raised his pistol and stepped across the corridor. Debating on whether to kick the door, he heard a woman giggle inside the room. An excellent way to get myself killed, he thought. Barge in on some cowboy and his girl. He holstered his pistol.

Royal heard a door open at the end of the hall. He turned to face room number two and pretended to dig for his room key. A young woman with an infant on her hip and a small child clutched to her side exited the room. She moved against the far side of the hall and waited. Her husband stepped from the room, his back toward Royal. He had a toddler perched on his arm. Big man, Royal thought as he watched the family walk to the landing. Another glance at the woman's face revealed a terrified look. As the family squeezed together at the exit, the woman handed the baby to the four-year-old. With a mother's protective instinct, she snatched the toddler out of the man's arms. The move was so bold, he didn't realize what had happened until the woman and children were safe in the foyer and out of the line of fire.

"Curly!" Royal yelled.

Royal waited for Curly to draw his pistol. As the sheriff turned, Royal knew he had miscalculated. Curly, gun in hand, took aim at Royal. The moment Curly shot, the woman hurled a small throw pillow. It hit him on the arm and knocked the shot off target. The bullet shattered one of the small lanterns that lighted the corridor. Before Royal could react, Curly had ducked out the door and bounded down the stairs.

Royal ran the length of the hall to the foyer. The young woman calmed her children, who were crying. "Are you all right, ma'am?"

"I am—but would you check my husband? That animal beat him badly," she said bitterly. "He's in our room."

Striding quickly to the door, Royal saw the young man struggling to his knees. He had a broken nose. "Take it slow, cowboy," Royal cautioned. "I'll help you to your feet."

"How's my wife? My family?" he asked anxiously.

His wife appeared. "We're fine. Let's get you to the bed," she said tenderly.

"Oh, my head," he moaned. He felt for the knot that proudly bulged at the base of his skull. Royal stepped into the hallway and shouted, "Doc, get up here!" In a few seconds he could hear the old man fussing as he climbed the stairs. "Check on this hard-headed lad, would you? Curly got away down the backstairs." Royal stepped around the old man. "I'm going after him."

Royal hustled down the corridor. "Thanks, mister!" the woman called to him.

"I owe you the thanks for saving my life," Royal offered, and stepped out the door.

Royal anticipated Curly's moves as he bounded down the stairs. Curly would need his guns and a horse. He probably wanted to stay out of sight and would use the back alley on his flight to the jail and stable. Royal made good time and headed for Main Street and the boardwalk. He could cover the distance more quickly this way, and he might catch Curly off guard. The street was deserted with no folks to worry about. As he reached the alley, he hesitated momentarily. This was where he had been bushwacked a half-year before. The hairs on his neck stood up as he leaped off the boardwalk.

The instant Royal's boot touched ground, his left leg collapsed beneath him. He fell heavily, rolled onto his back, and clutched at his knee. A stabbing pain raced through it, burning like molten lead. Within seconds the fierce pain fled, to be replaced by a soothing warmth. I've twisted my knee, he thought as he pushed himself erect and took a step. He fell face forward, and he caught himself with his hands. His left leg had given out again. Royal glanced at the boot and saw that the heel was missing. He spotted it in the dirt, bullet-shattered on one side. He struggled to understand what he saw. A shot hit the heel and sent it flying into the street.

"How you doin', Deputy Ballou? Hurtin' a little?" Curly's voice boomed out of the alley. "I'll say one thing for you. You are the hardest-headed lawman I ever seen." He laughed deeply. "Not very bright, but you hang in there."

Royal crawled to the adjacent boardwalk and ducked under it. A third shot kicked up dirt by his foot. Royal fired blindly down the alley.

"Nice shot, Ballou. Try aiming next time."

Royal fired in the direction of Curly's voice.

In a blast of splinters, Curly drove Royal deeper under the boardwalk. Royal knew he couldn't stay there—Curly would trap him like a rat. Cross the street, he told himself, desperate to outwit Curly. He holstered his pistol and scooted out from beneath the boardwalk. He fought off the stabbing pain in his knee and pushed to his feet. Royal hobbled into the street, expecting Curly to walk out of the alley by The Rose.

He was angling across the street when a shot between his feet stopped him in midstride. It had come from the side, not the alley. As he struggled for balance, Curly stepped away from the building next to The Rose. He had circled the building hoping to sneak up on Royal. But Royal had made it much easier for him. He was caught in the open.

Curly holstered his pistol as he stepped into the street. He had another pistol stuck in the waistband of his pants. The sheriff wanted to make this gunfight as straight as possible. His self-confidence surfaced; he was in control again. Curly had waited a long time for this opportunity. "I got a score to settle, Ballou," Curly spat. "You've been real tough on my family and kinfolk." His manner was cold and emotionless.

"Who in the hell you talkin' about?" Royal questioned.

"Remember that shoot-out in Salina?" he asked. "The one that killed your brother Grady?" Curly paused to let the impact hit Royal. "I lost an in-law there, Peter Hoose. And Dallas Detweiller? You gunned him down in Hobbs." Curly spoke softly. "He was a cousin."

"Trash like them don't deserve to stay alive," Royal baited as he struggled to remain standing.

"My twin brother Lefty and me ambushed you several months ago. Right in that very spot." Curly nodded toward the alley beside The Rose. He was slow burning. "That damned Tibbetts gunned him down. Then Perley got drunk, and Tibbetts murdered him too."

Royal's anger flared. "Our only mistake there was not getting both of you. Thanks for telling me you were in on that ambush. John Tibbetts suspected you all along." He felt a strange satisfaction.

"Shows what nosin' around in other people's business gets you—dead." Curly smiled.

"You're pretty good at bushwacking people," Royal needled, "and at taking on old-timers like Tibbetts. I'm not going to let you off that easy."

"You're dead either way, lawman." Curly was businesslike as he looked forward to the killing.

Royal made a move. He casually removed his Stetson with his left hand. As he lowered the hat in front of his body, he drew his pistol. Curly anticipated the move and drew his Colt. The sheriff got off the first shot. His bullet nicked Royal's hand and gouged a deep groove across it. Royal's pistol thudded to the ground in front of him.

"I'm gonna make you suffer long and painful." Curly laughed with loathing on his voice. He stepped forward with his pistol at his side. Ten feet separated the men.

"No, you don't!" A woman's voice froze Curly.

Both men looked at the boardwalk. Abbie stood in front of the Mercantile. She held John Tibbetts's 10-gauge steady. Royal knew the look on her face—he had seen it once before. She would not be dissuaded from her task.

"Now, don't do anything rash, young lady," Curly cautioned with his hand held up. Fear cut through his voice.

"You know who Sheriff Tibbetts was?" she asked firmly.

"A tired old lawman that's been retired permanentlike." Curly forced a laugh, but he was scared.

"Wrong, Curly. Doc Shu knew the truth, and he hid it for almost twenty years." Abbie lost her concentration and relaxed a little.

"Well, enlighten me. I can hardly wait." Curly teased her as he played for time and waited for the moment when she dropped her guard.

"John Tibbetts was my father," she painfully sobbed as her eyes filled with tears.

"No," Curly begged. Dread distorted his shocked face. He spun toward Abbie, his pistol on the upswing.

Both barrels of the 10-gauge exploded a heartbeat apart. Curly was riddled. The first barrel cut his legs out from beneath him. The second barrel blasted his upper body. He slammed backward to the ground. Abbie stood stock-still. The shotgun rested on the boardwalk.

Curly twitched, then slowly rolled to his stomach. Because of his bulk, he survived the twin blasts. He struggled slowly to his knees, painfully dragging his shattered legs. Ashen-faced and shaking, he looked at Abbie, his eyes riveted on her. Curly mustered a dying effort and raised his Colt. At waist level he palmed back the hammer and continued to bring the pistol up. With both hands wrapped around the grip, he sighted down the barrel.

Abbie was mesmerized by the sight. She was stone struck since she had shot Curly. Royal dove for his pistol.

Curly took a deep breath; blood seeped from the corner of his mouth. He pulled the trigger.

Boom! The two shots startled Abbie. She stumbled back against the storefront window, then slumped to the boardwalk as the pane beside her shattered. Royal, in a crouch, jerked his head around. He fully expected to see Abbie dead on the sidewalk.

Curly had been lifted partially off his knees by Royal's shot. He tumbled onto his back in the dusty street. Tiny moils of dust spurted from around his body, lazed momentarily in the slight breeze, and fell back to the ground.

Royal limped onto the boardwalk, reached for Abbie, and gently pulled her to her feet. Tears welled in her eyes as he softly kissed her. She fell into his arms and hugged him tightly. Then Doc Shu walked up behind and put his arms around them both. "It's over, child. We've settled the debt."

"He was an awful man," Abbie sobbed. She looked at the body in the street with a feeling of relief.

"Not 'nuff payment for the loss of John Tibbetts," Royal added bitterly.

As they walked toward the drugstore, Doc Shu broke the solemn silence. "Why don't you two ride out to the Dowde read. Clem and Libby will be pleased to know you're well, bbie. And I'll wager she has baked a fresh apple pie." He inked at Royal.

Doc Shu stood framed in the door of his store, and with a owing sense of satisfaction watched Royal and Abbie walk way side by side.